Tips Up

Tips Up

A Fake Dating Romantic Comedy

Christina Hill

To my Mom, a true breast cancer survivor.

And to the French fries at my favorite ski resort for being the best. Ever.

Chapter One

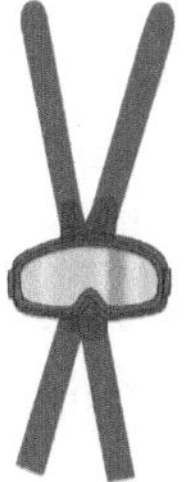

Myra

"This wine is soooo good. What kind did you say it is?" I ask my older brother.

The red liquid sloshes over the rim as I belch loud enough for the partridge in the pear tree to hear outside. I immediately press my pointer finger to my lips while keeping my pinky raised for maximum fanciness. "Be quiet, Frankie, or they'll find us!"

Home for the holidays is the last place I want to be, but it's the only place I have to go.

Frankie, always the voice of reason, shoves a hand in my face. "Okay, ew," he says louder than my burp. "Myra, Mom and Dad went to sleep hours ago. You know how much pretending to be a happy family wears them out. And the wine is Merlot, for the thousandth time."

I shift to lean closer to him on the twin bed with two turtle doves carved into the headboard my parents keep made up in the basement like I'm Cinder-freaking-ella. It's three floors and a shit ton of expensive paintings and ceramic dishes away from their bedroom suite.

I twirl a finger in his face. "Don't roll your eyes at me. I'm tired, too. I got divorced a few days ago."

He scrunches his nose and flops to his back on the end of the bed—*my* bed—and undoes the top few buttons of his dress shirt. "You don't have to remind me," he groans. "I was there, remember? Or maybe you don't since you went from Margaritas to Merlot in the span of twenty-four hours."

"Watch out for those margaritas, by the way. The ones in the can…they're so strooooong!" I give him the infamous finger guns I've been throwing up all night without a permit to do so. Mom and Dad didn't think it was very funny when I interrupted their lavish Christmas dinner to finger-gun the three stuffed French hens like they were other people at the table.

Frankie thought it was hilarious.

So did the four calling birds, but that could have been the ridiculous music they had on.

I did, too, and laughed well into the moment the hired angels (or servers) brought the dessert of chocolate Soufflé out. It's what Mom has someone else make every year for Christmas dinner so she doesn't have to remove her five golden rings. Add the six enormous swan ice sculptures in the middle of the table— or was it seven?—plates with tiny hand-painted wreaths with six geese around the edges, and predictably canned conversation to round out an evening with my parents.

My velvet black dress starts to feel stifling as I stretch my feet out on the bed and fan myself. I nudge Frankie's shoulder with my stockinged foot. "You know what we should do?"

"I have zero idea what could be going through that addled mind of yours while under the influence, but it better not have anything to do with filling Wade's Tesla with glitter like you've already suggested."

"Hey," I say with a slur, pulling the strap of my dress up—the same one I left the tags on so I could return it tomorrow. "Putting glitter in my ex-husband's car, which he stole from me in the divorce, was a great idea!" I defend. "I wasn't going to suggest that, though."

Frankie looks from the ceiling to me. "Enlighten me then. What should we do?"

I grab the bottle of Merlot from my nightstand with fumbling hands—not worrying about a little red wine on the carpet since the eight maids my parents have will take care of it —and pour a little more into the large glass that probably cost Mom a thousand dollars and was kissed by a prince in the made-up country of Genovia. "We should get tattoos. I know a guy."

Frankie slaps his forehead. "We already got tattoos last month, remember? And if you force me to go again, I will scream. One green Care Bear on my bicep was enough. God, I should've gotten blue. It looks like I have a weird fungus now." He rolls to his side and props his head in his hand. "Look, I've been trying to be supportive since I know you've been going through a rough patch—"

"Six months is not a *patch*." My voice echoes as I speak directly into the Genovian wine glass resting on my bottom lip.

He sighs. "This divorce has been tough on you, but you have to start looking ahead, Myra. Go get a hobby. Learn a new skill, like cooking or cleaning. Your apartment needs it. And then, in a couple of months, you'll remember this Christmas as a turning point. And for the love of Merlot, no more tattoos!"

I hold my glass out wide. "A tattoo is better than falling in love and moving to Genovia to marry Prince Albert the Third and sit through an hour of nine ladies dancing before every meal. I won't do it!"

The strap of my dress falls again, but I don't bother lifting it this time. I'm passionate about not ending up in any of those feel-good romantic movies. I don't feel good. Periodt.

Frankie pushes off my bed and stands. "What are you even talking about?" He waves his hand. "You know what, you're drunk, and I'm going to bed because breakfast is coming, and I cannot face another meal with Mom and Dad without a full twelve hours of sleep. You should try to rest, too, before Prince Albert the Third comes to fetch you."

"He will never fetch me!"

I don't want nine dancing ladies to serenade me, but I might take ten leaping men.

I swirl the remaining wine in my glass as he glides out of my bedroom to cross the hall toward his. Turning my lips inward, I bite them as tears show up out of nowhere. I'm alone again. It's been like this for the last year and probably even longer. My marriage might have had an end date, but all of the reasons he left started well before.

I sniffle and stare up at the ceiling and trace the plastic stars with adhesive backs stuck in random places with my finger in the air. I put them there when we first moved into this big, fancy house when I was twelve. Frankie, being only slightly older at thirteen, thought it was childish, but not me.

They reminded me how big the world is.

Galaxies that span millions of miles and stars that still don't have names because they haven't been discovered yet. It made me feel like I had a place somewhere in the vast universe. Even if I felt smaller in the world my parents inhabited.

High-class living isn't for the weak. You have to be physically strong to swipe a credit card so many times in a day. We didn't always have money and clout. My parents came into it later on, after a few solid investments took off. It's the same universe where I met Wade.

And also the same one he left me in.

I drop my hand, tear my gaze from the ceiling, and look to my nightstand for the bottle of wine. Instead, I spy my laptop underneath it. I brought it here with me in case Christmas with my parents turned out to be more unbearable than eleven pipers piping away on their bagpipes, and I needed to escape to my basement lair to grade papers for my students. It's not exactly how I wanted to spend my whole winter break, but my life has become dull since Wade left. At least when we were still living together, we fought. It wasn't necessarily fun, but it made me feel like I wasn't a robot.

Now, I'm not so sure.

Setting the wine bottle off to the side with very little grace, I grab my laptop and open it up, typing in my code four times before finally getting it right and navigate to an open search bar. I tap my finger on the smooth space beside the keys. Maybe Frankie is right. I should find a hobby, something that I can do to get my mind off Wade, the divorce, and this damn loneliness.

Learning to cook is probably at the bottom of my list, and cleaning is a close second. Maybe I should try ice skating, though I'm not sure ice exists in Arizona. It may be winter, but Phoenix didn't get the memo.

I could go somewhere, find a small inn or bed and breakfast I could hide out in, and take up baking. It would beat staying with my parents for the expected next couple of days or returning to my empty apartment with oak-colored everything and crap water pressure.

However, I'd be setting myself up for a prime-time, heartwarming Christmas movie special where I meet the single, windowed dad who is lost and looking for love and offers to teach me how to make his family's cinnamon roll recipe for his daughter's school bake sale. He sounds better than Prince Albert the Third but…

No inns, I tell myself.

I type in the name of the airline I've been earning frequent flier miles for every time I buy gas and groceries—I do a lot more of this since I don't have a rich husband anymore—and see what specials they have. New York, Los Angeles, and Seattle are all listed with discounted rates, but I can't tell since they are all still too expensive for me. I keep scrolling to find somewhere cheaper until I reach a flight to Bozeman, Montana that is more in line with my teacher's salary budget of good thoughts and cheap vibes.

I click it. What's there to do in Montana?

My friend Liv is in Bozeman, so at least I'd know someone. She left Phoenix a year ago for snowier pastures (a.k.a. a principal gig). I could probably ask to stay with her.

I pull up another search window and type *what is there to do in Montana*? Immediately, pictures and articles of different ski resorts fill the screen. The snow, beautiful views of mountains, and the promise of spending time in a place where I don't risk bumping into Wade has me seeing Montana as my hero in spandex and a cape.

I reach for the bottle of wine, faltering enough to knock off a self-help book I've been reading for the last six months. So much help it's been. Pouring a hearty glass for me, myself, and I now that Frankie is gone, I set my laptop on the bed and hike up my dress to find the tattoo.

My sheer black nylons have a rip near my cooch that would cause my mother to faint. I run the pad of my thumb over the tiny pink bear on my inner thigh. I didn't even know what a Care Bear was until I got to the tattoo shop with Frankie. It's mostly healed up now and no longer forces me to walk like I'm carrying a ball between my knees. It was my small act of defiance against my parents, something entirely out of their control. It only took thirty-five years for me to do it.

Wade didn't like tattoos, either.

I guess I got it in spite of him, too.

Wade also hated Merlot. But I can't see why. Taking a sip and then tipping the glass as far as it will go without any wine spilling, I think of all the other things my ex hated.

He hated animal fur, dirt, dirt on animals, and Schitt's Creek. I should have seen the red flags then, but I was in love—almost as much as my parents loved him.

Wade also hated skiing.

I stand my glass upright and grab my laptop again. I've never tried skiing before. It could be the thing that takes me from lost to found. I would stop moping around here and could see another part of the country—one that's the complete opposite of here. I need that right now. Something different enough to shake me out of this slump and find something that makes me feel like me again.

Plus, skiing probably isn't that hard to learn as an adult.

Twelve drums start drumming out of nowhere—or somewhere in my head—as I add the trip to my cart.

I pour more wine and lift the glass in the air. "To Genovia."

I mean Montana.

Chapter Two

Myra

I'm never drinking wine again," I say under my breath.

The mountain doesn't respond.

I'm on top of the world with fiberglass boards strapped to my feet and fire-poking poles—minus the fire—gripped tightly in my sweaty palms. It doesn't matter that I'm wearing winter gloves; fear has made me sweat through them.

If it weren't for Merlot, I wouldn't be here.

We are no longer friends.

I'm looking down instead of up, but neither view would make the Bridger mountains in Montana appear any smaller. They're massive, jutting up like a wall, slicing the endless expanse of sky in half. I'm boxed in by these snow-covered knuckles at all angles.

Somehow, I made it to the top of the lift on a moving walkway I'd heard someone call the *magic carpet*. If it can teach me to ski, then I'll believe in the magic, but all it's done so far is deposit me at the top of this hill. By *deposit*, I really mean that it spit me out, and I stumbled forward, flinging the poles I rented in different directions and falling epically on the side of my ass. I took out two kids in the process, and while both of them bounced back like they were hiding springs in their snow pants, it took three adults to get me up. *Three.*

I'm already setting records.

"Okay," I assure myself through a shaky breath. "I made it. The hardest part is over. At least, I think it's the hardest part."

I've never been skiing, so I can't say which part is the hardest. So far, parking in the crowded lot and hitchhiking to the lodge was tricky. It was tough to buy my pass for the day when my driver's license still had my ex-husband's last name on it. And getting fitted for the one thousand pieces of gear required for this hobby was next level. I live in Arizona and have no need for clothing worn for weather below seventy degrees. I had a pair of ski pants stashed in my closet by some miracle, but apparently, as a fully grown woman who has been surviving off cheap wine and chocolate for the last six months, you can grow out of them. Breakups are hard, but divorces take the cake—or chocolate in this case.

A young teen in the rental shop with a name tag reading *Jeff* informed me one base layer, snow pants, gloves, a helmet, and something he called a *baklava* would keep my head, neck, and chin warm in the below-thirty temps. Or maybe it was a *balaclava*? He then fitted me for ski boots and had to hold one of them between his knees while I tried shoving my foot in. I'm sure he has never heard the f-word so many times. More like he's never heard a thirty-five-year-old woman scream *fudgsicle* with as much vitriol as the actual f-word.

"I can do anything," I say to myself, then gag. I sound like an uplifting quote plastered on a bathroom mirror. I haven't sunk that low yet. Closing my eyes, I release a long breath, then open them again. "I survived a divorce, flew here on my own, purchased thermal underwear from a teen the same age as some of my students, and made it to—*mostly*—the top of this ginormous mountain. I'm totally fine and not having a mid-life crisis at all."

Okay…crisis, yes. Mid-life? I will deny it if asked.

Being here is way better than sitting at home in different kind of underwear with practical width and stretch, my apartment door locked to the outside world, and *Runaway Bride* playing on repeat while I eat chips and queso in my bed. Yes, there were crumbs, and no, I didn't care. Signing divorce papers after six months of separation is just as bad as they say. Though, I'm not sure who's saying it since no one I know has gotten divorced like me. My parents have been married for over forty years, and all my friends had stepped into motherhood and were too busy to get divorced. I'm the only one I know who kissed goodbye a life—and a man—I'd lived with for five years.

"You are a strong, independent, and spectacular woman." Mirror quote be damned. "You will get down this mountain and buy yourself the fucking cocoa you deserve. Extra large, naturally. Maybe spiked."

"Are you talking to yourself?"

I startle at the voice and flail my hands. I'm holding two s'mores sticks and fast becoming a hazard to everyone else around me. Also, I definitely just said *fuck* out loud in front of this child. Where is *fudgsicle* when I need it?

"I wasn't talking to myself."

"Yes, you were," the young girl with a honey-sweet smile says.

My laugh is weak and unconvincing. "No."

"You were."

I need to get better at talking to myself in my head. "Even if I were—"

Oh no.

My skis are moving without me but also with me. I'm not ready. I need at least three more pep talks, five business days, and maybe a license before I can do this. Skiing feels like a sport you should have a permit for. One foot slides and then the other, and it's like I'm going backward on an elliptical, just trying to stay up here and not…down there.

A small, pink gloved hand flies out in front of my chest, stopping my forward momentum with…what? Sheer will and determination? Is this young child who barely reaches my tits actually the Hulk? My feet still try to slide out from under me, but with my upper body more balanced, I'm able to steady myself.

I look down at the girl. She has two dark braids, to my one, though hers are shorter, falling just below her shoulders. Mine would reach to my elbows if I hadn't shoved it inside this baklava —*damn it*—balaclava. "Who are you?"

She lifts her goggles and rests them on her forehead. "Sadie."

I check my head to see if Jeff gave me goggles. Yup. "Thanks for uh…you know—"

"Saving you?"

I laugh. "I don't know if *saving* is the right word here."

She blinks several times, and I don't think it's because of how bright it is out here.

"Mhm, well, okay." I clear my throat. "Thank you for *helping* —"

"Saving," she corrects.

Good thing five years with my ex-husband qualified me to fight with a child. I've learned to pick my battles. "Thank you for *saving* me." There's a bitter taste in my mouth.

"You're welcome." Her smile is ten times brighter than mine. "What's your name?"

"Myra."

"I'm eight."

"I'm not eight."

She tilts her head. "So, you're like…fifty?"

"Fifty?" My mouth falls open with a gasp.

She shrugs. "Forty?"

Maybe my mid-life crisis vibes are screaming too loudly. "I'm thirty-five."

"My mom's younger than you."

I open my mouth to say something but think better of it. She keeps smiling as I put the straps of my poles around my wrists. I expect her to ski off to whatever portal she came from, but she doesn't make a move to leave. She also doesn't stop staring.

I check my helmet strap, pretending like I'm getting ready to ski down this slope any second. I got up here because I have just the right amount of delusional confidence. There's no turning back now, mostly because I can't unless I want to crawl. *No thanks.* And getting down any other way besides skis would be admitting defeat. I'd rather lose my big toe than admit to my brother, Frankie, that Merlot was the one who booked this last-minute trip to Montana to avoid being home alone during winter break.

Merlot wanted to learn new things.

Merlot wanted to see the sights.

Merlot wanted to forget she signed divorce papers a little over a week ago.

When I saw the confirmation email for this trip the morning after Christmas, I convinced myself taking this solo vacay would help heal my broken heart. *Maybe Merlot was onto something.* My good friend, Liv, who lives here, doesn't ski but confirmed I could stay in her guest cabin when I told her about the trip. She was on

Merlot's side. But the way my calves shudder and threaten to disown me convinces me that skiing for the first time ever might also break my spirit.

I peer over at Sadie, and she's still staring.

I point downhill. "Go ahead."

"Nope. My dad always says to let the new skiers go first so they don't crash into you."

Some version of a snort laugh comes out of me. "I'm not going to crash."

She looks me up and down. When I do the same, noting what I'm wearing, I see her point. I'm Ski Trip Barbie with all the fancy gear—canary yellow jacket and pink boots included—and none of the skill.

"Like I said, you can go first." Not because I think I possess any skill not to avoid her, but because I need to watch a few people do this first.

I also need to adjust my wedgie.

I bought myself new just-for-me underwear. Not the thermal type or the no-one-will-ever-see-these kind, but the ones you buy yourself to remember you are a desirable human being with a body that isn't tainted by the ex-whoever—*that* kind of underwear.

But they aren't cut out for strenuous activity.

"You go," she says in a stern voice that somehow belongs to a kid and not my mother, even though it sounds eerily similar.

I shake my head just as a toddler maneuvers down in front of us. *Oh, great.* Toddlers are better at this than I am.

Sadie shrugs. "It's just a hill."

"It's a mountain!"

She huffs loudly. "Just go already!"

"You go!" I spit back.

"No, you go."

"You."

She glowers up at me. "You."

I glare down at her. "No."

"It's just the bunny hill. What are you afraid of?"

Lots of things. *This.* Skiing, being alone for the rest of my life, spiders, or getting trapped in an elevator. I don't say any of that out loud, though. "I'm not afraid." My shaky emphasis on the last word is not very convincing. "And if the bunny hill is so easy, why are you up here?"

She huffs. "I mouthed off to my mom, so now I have to go down this hill five times before I can go anywhere else."

I wish I could say I'm surprised. "Then you should go first."

"You go."

I will not give in. This is the hill—I mean, *mountain*—I will die on. "I'm not going, and it's a mountain."

She puts her hands on her puffy hips. "Hill."

I try to cross my arms, but the skewers I'm holding prevent me. "Mountain."

"If you're not afraid, then just go." She throws her hands up.

"Why don't you go?"

"Because…because you're old."

My mouth falls open. "And you're—"

I don't get a chance to finish as the same arm Sadie used to stop me is now pushing at my back. I'm sliding again, my feet lifting to try and backpedal but making it look as if I'm performing the Kazotsky kick dance.

Sadie is smiling just as my balance fails me and sends me careening down the mountainside at a speed I won't even do in my car. My arms flail with the pitchforks still clutched tightly in my hands, becoming a danger to everyone just trying to have a good time.

I can't stop myself. The further I go, the faster these skis are.

So, I scream.

And then scream louder.

But that isn't helping me slow down. Leaning backward and staying upright isn't working how I thought it would, so I lean forward. Except now I'm positive I'll land on my face. The white ground is rushing past me, making me dizzy, and I can't get it to slow down. These skis are slick and set on one direction—down. I watched Jeff wax them for crying out loud. I should have ripped the silver container out of his hand and thrown it across the room.

"I hate you, Jeff!" I scream between my screams.

The people that were once small bugs dotting the ground are getting closer. But the closer they get, the more I realize how little space there is. I won't fit. Even this science teacher knows the probability of making it through this sea of people without taking a few out is low.

I start to wave my windshield wipers in front of me. "Out of the way! Can't stop!"

The bottom of the mountain comes and quickly flattens out. I can't tell if I'm going faster or slower. What I do know is that a man in a red jacket, who I am set on destroying like a homing device, isn't moving.

"Move!"

Other people are scattering, I'm making sounds with my mouth I've never heard before, and time has slowed. Red Jacket's mouth opens as wide as his eyes, matching mine. My arms are two pinwheels moving, and I swear grass grows faster than this moment is playing out.

Physics confirms my fears. The momentum of the skis, the mass of my body, and the velocity at which I'm moving toward Red Jacket equals destruction. There isn't time for him to move or for me to YouTube how to stop these things on my feet. I lean farther back, hoping it will slow me down. Instead, my knees bend to accommodate said lean until my back hits the ground with a thud. The skis keep going because they don't have an off-switch and, you know, *science*. One moment, I'm staring at the bluest blue skies I've ever seen, waiting to enter the great beyond. Next, I'm between Red Jacket's legs, staring up at his crotch as he holds my sides with his ankles after finally coming to a full stop.

I'm heaving, my chest rising and falling erratically. I never thought I'd consider being sandwiched between a man's legs a safe place, but here I am. I've traded what was supposed to be a fun adventure for *this*.

"That was definitely a mountain," I say to his crotch.

He releases me and braces his hands on his knees. "Are you okay?"

"I'm…alive."

"You are," he confirms. "Is anything hurt?"

Everything, I think to myself. "Yes and no," I supply instead.

There's a clicking sound, a tug on my feet, and then a sweet release when my knees aren't pointing to the sky but rather stretched out in front of me. I close my eyes so the falling snow doesn't freeze my eyeballs since I never had time to deploy the goggles Jeff sold me for the low cost of half my monthly rent.

The man's calm voice fills my ears. "What's your name?" I think I say *Myra* since he replies with, "I'm Lincoln. Do you think you're okay to sit up?"

Absolutely not. "Sure." I shoot one gloved hand straight into the air for him to do something with.

He crouches beside me, grabs me behind my elbow with one hand, and behind my shoulder with the other. "Up you go," he says with a strain as he lifts my dead weight. "How do you feel now?"

Sitting on my sore ass with my feet kicked out in front of me and still panting as if I've just been through battle, I notice who I'm talking to…a dog.

He was wrong. *I have to be dead.*

So, all dogs *do* go to Heaven…

Without warning, the dog's tongue makes contact with my shocked face.

"Otto! Give her some space, bud," Red Jacket—*Lincoln*—says, pulling his dog back by the collar. "Sorry. He's just worried about you."

Of course, he is. I'm worried about me, too. My entire ass is probably covered in bruises, my underwear is doing unholy things inside my snow pants, and I'm pretty sure my face is frozen stiff.

Lincoln is squatting beside me now, brows knit together. *Those eyebrows.* They're perfect. Then I note the rest of his face is pretty perfect, too. Deep green eyes, stubbled jawline, and hair that just barely flips up around the edges of his helmet like he tried and failed to shove it all underneath.

"How's your head?"

"My head?" I touch the side of my face to confirm it's still attached to the rest of me.

"That was a pretty spectacular fall," he says with a growing smile.

So glad to know his smile is flawless, too. "I was thinking about going down the mountain and then got shoved—"

"Shoved?" he asks, lifting those perfect brows in unison.

Otto barks from beside him, and I startle. He wags his tail as if nothing is amiss. The dark gray areas of his coat appear as if they could be blue and separated by lighter brown and black patches. I don't know that I've seen a more beautiful animal. The fact we both aren't in Heaven right now makes me want to cry with relief.

I really did hit my head.

"Quit," he says to the dog, then turns his attention back on me. *Yay.* "Who pushed you?"

Just as I open my mouth to explain that an Amazonian woman with braids and muscles the size of my head did it, and not a small child, a waterfall of snow kicks up over my legs.

Here's the menace now.

Sadie.

I would challenge her to a ski-off if I weren't still questioning whether my legs work and my head is attached. That would require knowing how to ski, though.

"Seems you made it down the hill just fine," Sadie says, brushing bits of snow from the front of her jacket. "Hi, Otto."

I'm in complete shock, either from the fall or how this eight-year-old bested me.

"Hey, Sadie." Lincoln tips his chin in her direction.

She waves her small hand of destruction and then skis off toward a different lift.

"You know her?"

He brushes the excess snow off my pants—thanks, but also no thanks, to Sadie—and stands, offering me his hand. "I know all of the regulars around here. It's the blessing and curse of being a local."

I take his hand and let him pull me up. The way my limp body is no issue for him to lift has me thinking he's hiding muscles under that snow jacket.

"Sadie's a regular then," I state as I hold my head that's currently swimming laps.

He pets the top of Otto's head. "Yeah, I see her here often, especially during break. It's a small enough resort; you get used to seeing the same people all winter."

I wouldn't know what that's like since this is my first time at a ski resort. I'm used to the resorts with pools and palm trees, not wood and more wood. I peer down at Otto, who is the picture of cool, calm, and collected. He's wearing a red vest reading

Avalanche Dog. Opening my mouth to ask about it, Lincoln starts talking first.

"Are you sure you're alright?" He tips my chin up to stare into each of my eyes.

I stare back, and then the realization hits.

Oh my God. He's going to kiss me.

I'm fully aware of the bare skin of his hands touching the underside of my chin. He must have removed his gloves to help me. Peering down, I note there's no ring on any of his fingers, which isn't something I've ever thought of until I took mine off. I now take inventory of every piece of jewelry on people's hands or lack thereof.

He smiles again, and I can't help but notice his perfect, plump lips stretching across those straight teeth. His nose is slightly crooked, and the rough skin of his cheeks is inviting me to run my hand across them and have a whole sensory experience right here, right now. Fortunately, my lowered inhibitions—aka *Merlot*—aren't here today to convince me to indulge.

He leans closer, and I lift my gaze back to his. I'm pretty sure I lean in, too. My lips part as I stare at his, waiting for our mouths to collide. This is how it happens. Those rare scenarios only acted out in movies and books. But it's going to happen to me—any second. I keep staring at his lips and lick mine.

His gaze tracks the movement of my tongue then quickly drops his hand away. "I'm a medic." He clears his throat. "You don't appear to have any visible injuries, but we could go inside the lodge, and I can check you over?"

Ice flows through my veins, and I force my gaze up to his. So, no kiss then. Clearly, I need that extra large cocoa. "I'm good, promise. It just took me by surprise."

I must have hit my head hard enough to think we shared some kind of moment. There's a white cross stitched over his bicep with the words *ski patrol* beneath it that I must have missed.

"Well, if you need anything, be sure to ask," he says.

"I will. And thank you…Lincoln."

"I'll catch you around." He nods once and then clicks into his skis to skate over to one of the lifts with Otto.

I exhale long and slow, peering between the lodge, promising a hot cup with floating marshmallows, and the mountain I just catapulted down. I paid enough for the skis to give it another shot, minus any eight-year-olds, but I have zero desire to try again today. Maybe later.

Maybe later.

I've said that enough times while lying flat on my couch like a human surfboard. Maybe later I'll get up. Maybe later I'll stop feeling so sad. Maybe later I won't need to cry on Frankie's shoulder. It took several *laters* before I was ready, but I eventually got off my couch—or bed—and came here.

But this time, I'm serious; I'll get back on my skis…later.

Chapter Three

Lincoln

L oad up." Otto trots over to jump on the chair lift as I ski forward, glancing over my shoulder so the lift doesn't hit me where it hurts as it rounds the corner.

He's already seated on the bench when it picks me up, and guests snap pictures, take videos, and gawk in amazement. They love seeing our avy dogs do their thing. The dogs are local celebrities who get more catcalls than miniskirts do. Good thing they're trained to ignore all of it. Otto's been riding lifts since he opened his eyes, learning to be held the whole ride up, and then get on and off without my help all while smiling for the cameras.

Once settled, I allow myself one more look over my shoulder. *One. More.*

But this time, I'm not noting Otto's adoring fans or the chair ready to scoop me up. I'm looking for a particular shade of yellow. It's facing away from me as she walks toward the lodge and disappears inside.

I stare forward and scrub my jaw. What happened back there? I could've sworn she leaned closer, her lower lip jutting further than her top. Did she think I was going to kiss her? Hell, maybe I should've. My younger brother, Jake, would have.

But I'm not Jake.

I'm the older, more responsible brother who treats flirting like a national emergency. *Call in the calvary!* Kissing would cause me to overthink so hard, my brain would get tired, and I'd be in bed for the next week.

But now I'm overthinking *not* kissing her.

Shaking my head, I put it out of my mind and rest my arm on the bench behind Otto. He no longer barks in my ear to alert me every time a skier passes below us like he did in his younger years. Newsflash: it happens often. He got his certification two years ago when I worked in Whistler, and we've kept up with his training here in Montana, too.

His blue heeler cattle dog instincts have given him plenty of advantages even though no particular breed is used for avalanche rescue. Gone are the days of the St. Bernard, with the whiskey barrel hanging around his neck as the only search and rescue breed. Speed, stamina, and focus are a few of Otto's notable qualities. Too bad he couldn't save me from the whiplash that was moving back home. Nine months with my parents was long enough before moving in with my brother, Jake, and Ted— another ski patroller—forsaking Taco Tuesdays and Face Mask Fridays with my parents.

I'm not ready to talk about it.

Even though I came home with a new best friend with four paws and a hankering for digging holes in their backyard, my parents welcomed us. That's what family does. Or, at least, mine did. Mom's breast cancer news hit me hard, and I didn't see any other option than to be here for her. I still don't. But no one tells you just how hard it is to live with your parents as an adult after doing your own laundry for years.

We've always been close, but seeing Dad in a fluffy robe and green tea face mask did things to my mind I can't recover from. We do better with weekly family dinners and daily GIFs on the family text thread.

I mindlessly scratch behind Otto's ears—his favorite spot— as kids and adults, ski schools, and enthusiasts rush down the mountain in "S" patterns below. There's something soothing about being up here on the mountain I learned to ski on. It's familiar, like closing your eyes and walking from the bedroom to the bathroom without bumping into anything. And up here, everything's quiet. I like quiet.

My life has been full of *loud* the last few years. Not the rock music turned full blast in your headphones kind of loud, but the regular kind of loud that comes with a full life. Or at least it does with my family. I traveled from one place to the next. It was chaotic and free, two words I'd never used to describe myself, yet I wouldn't trade those experiences for the world.

Well, maybe the time I got stung by a jellyfish in the Philippines. Or the food poisoning in Mexico…okay, so maybe there are a few things I could have done without. But getting my Outdoor Emergency Care certification to become a ski patroller in Canada and then getting Otto gave me a purpose that felt right.

The lift starts to slow as we reach the top and Otto sits at attention, front paws tap dancing on the seat. He's ready to jump but won't do it until I release him. The brisk wind slapping against my face has lessened as the lift slows. Waving at the lifty operator, I scoot forward, grab my poles from under my thigh, raise my skis so the tips point up, and get ready to stand when we get closer. At the last second, I say, "Off," and Otto leaps down in front of me and descends the small hill of packed snow.

He shakes his ears and does a few celebratory rolls in the snow. Mornings like this one make me forget why I'm back in my hometown, working with my little brother during the day and helping Dad with whatever he needs evenings and weekends. Mom wouldn't have been okay with me moving home just because of her, so I made sure to get a job I could stand while also being available for my family.

Swiveling my heels out to cut my speed, I bend to praise Otto before skiing over to the small lift used only for patrollers and head up the steep slope to the patrol hut with Otto on my heels. Unclicking my boots from the bindings, I lean them on the rack outside. Otto is already up the flight of stairs before I've even put my foot on the first step. He circles at the top until I open the door and let him in. This hut is our posting station for the day, which means I'll get to see...

"Jake."

He darts his eyes up just as I pull off his knit beanie. "What the hell was that for?" he barks. I kick the door shut, and he stares blankly at me while I unzip my jacket. "A nice *hi good morning* isn't sufficient anymore?" He points at me. "I want my beanie back. I'm having a bad hair day."

"Nope. I hate this hat on you. Makes you look even more like a douche than your hair."

The mustache wasn't enough, so he got himself a mullet. High and tight on the sides with slightly longer brown locks on the very top and bottom and missing a considerable amount of length somewhere in the middle.

I throw the beanie, and it does a triple backflip before landing on his chest. "Hey, you got any Vaseline? Forgot to put some on Otto's feet this morning."

"Check back there by the crates," Jake says, waving behind his shoulder as he continues filling out paperwork at the wooden desk stretching from one side of the space to the other.

The small hut is akin to a basic cabin with few amenities. There's a desk to work from with some office supplies that need a good reorganizing, emergency radio, and plenty of gear for us and the dogs. Multiple hooks line the back wall above the few kennels we have in here for other avalanche dogs, holding backpacks with emergency supplies, leashes, snacks, and jackets.

"What are the conditions like today?" I ask, rifling through everything while knowing exactly what a fresh coat of powder means for the resort before I even ask: more guests on the mountain. It's been snowing since I woke up this morning.

Bernie, Jake's Golden Retriever, walks out of his kennel and wags his tail, eager to bump noses with Otto. All of his enthusiasm filters through his tail.

"Chance of another light snow later on, but all other conditions are perfect," he says, eyes down. "Today's the kind of day you want to be skiing, not stuck in here."

"Got it." I toss and catch the Vaseline in the air. "Otto, sit." He sits on command while Bernie continues to sniff his pal as if he doesn't live with him. "Paw." Otto puts his dark paw in my hand, and I rub the Vaseline between his toes to prevent irritating clumps of snow from getting in there.

"What took you so long to get here this morning?" Jake asks, swiveling around in his chair. It makes an annoying squeak like always. "Don't tell me you decided to play hooky and ski an extra run before coming up here."

I'd never. But my alter ego, Jake, would.

After suiting up in the locker room first thing this morning, we left the dogs in the large kennel and went out to assess avalanche conditions by checking the snowpack. When I went to get Otto to head up to our posting station, I got caught up by a few guests before the sun almost took me down. Looking at her was like staring at a bright ray of sunshine. Mostly because of the jacket but also because she was beautiful. The kind that made my pulse race and my mouth feel too dry.

I cap the Vaseline and toss it back on top of the kennel. "Had a run-in with a skier. Literally."

His eyes widen. "Someone mowed you down?"

"Sort of. She slid right through my legs." I lean on the desk beside him, crossing my arms.

I don't tell him this woman had a soft brush of freckles dotting her red-tipped nose. Or when I got close to see if her pupils were dilated, I noticed flecks of gold in her light brown eyes. Telling him that she leaned in as if I were going to kiss her wouldn't help matters, or the fact I didn't have the guts to do it. I don't say any of that because, with that kind of information, Jake is nosy and close to lethal.

I could have been way off. It's not like women are flocking to me, puckering up, and wanting me to kiss them. I've had a whopping total of zero girlfriends. All I've got going for me are a few hookups here, a sprinkle of high school experimentation there, with a dash of spin the bottle.

"Oh, damn. Was she alright?"

"I mean, from what I could tell. No concussion or obvious abrasions." A little embarrassment and shock, which don't leave visible cuts. "I gave her a once-over, though, and she seemed fine."

He waggles his brows. "Yeah, you did."

I roll my eyes.

"Was she hot?"

I shrug and cross my ankles. "I was late."

"You didn't answer the question."

Otto and Bernie find a toy to tug, filling the room with low, challenging growls. Their tails are wagging, and hints of smiles on both of their faces indicate they are all bark and no bite.

"I said all I'm going to say."

"So, she's hot and probably not in her sixties, based on your avoidant responses. Please tell me you at least got her number?" he asks, leaning further back in his chair and cradling his head with laced hands.

"She was in complete shock after falling, and the last thing I'm sure she'd want is someone asking for her number," I explain in a matter-of-fact tone. "Plus, she isn't a local."

"Even better."

I scoff. "Says who?"

"Says the guy who knows for a fact vacationers make better flings." He strokes his mustache like he's a freaking wizard with a staff and magical powers.

"I don't want a fling," I say, shaking my head.

I've never been good at them. Even while traveling the world after high school, meeting women abroad for the sole purpose of getting them in bed felt wrong. I like knowing the woman first. Favorite foods, family history, and how they like their eggs cooked in the morning when I make them breakfast—the basic stuff.

Jake waves me off. "Might be good for you since you've lived as an eighty-year-old man since you were fourteen."

"Have not," I retort, ruffling the squirrel tail on his head.

He smacks my hand away.

Despite all his prodding, he's my younger brother and also one of my best friends. As much as I don't want to admit it, he knows me better than most.

"Just because I don't like to bag a woman and prefer to get to know her doesn't mean I'm eighty years old," I say. "My hips are way better."

"Psh. You know how to keep your hips limber?" He smirks. "It would be good for you to ease up on the old-fashioned ways for a hot minute so you could actually enjoy the female species."

"The fact you just referred to women as a *species* makes me wonder how you got them to sleep with you in the first place." I cross my arms again more to deflect than anything.

"It's my charm." He flashes me a creepy smile.

"Charms, more like it. What are you casting spells on them or something?"

He laughs and kicks my boot. "Get outta my hut if you're gonna be a dick."

"Your hut?" I laugh and stand straighter. This is classic *Jake math*. "You must have forgotten the twenty other ski patrollers who work here every day. We have to go anyway. Ted wants me to help with some projects, and I'm late."

He gives a low whistle. "Ted's gonna have words with you."

Jake's right. Our other roommate, Ted, started working here around the same time Jake did three years ago and hates it when we're late. No one would ever be able to tell from his five-nine frame, flaming red hair, and lackadaisical attitude that he'd be so obsessed with the clock, but he is.

"What projects?" Jake asks.

"Repairing boundary fences, fixing signage to move around the resort, shutting down runs. You know, random stuff."

My phone vibrates in my chest pocket, and I carefully pull off my gloves again to check in case it's Ted.

Dad: Game night this weekend?

I'm sure it took him at least twenty minutes to write this message, but I shoot off my reply in seconds.

Me: I'll be there.

I pocket my phone and ask Jake, "Are you going to game night this week?"

Christmas was last weekend and New Year's Day was yesterday, but there's been a standing rhythm that Jake and I show up for family game nights on Fridays now. I don't mind it. I go with an empty stomach and leave with leftovers that'll last me a week, extra rolls of toilet paper, an alarm clock they don't need, and an old math binder from high school my mom saved for reasons I can't even understand. It's my favorite store.

"Every week." He starts scrolling through his phone.

"And Gemma?"

He shrugs a shoulder. "Probably."

He barely takes his attention away from his phone screen as I put my gloves back on. "Don't you guys talk every day?"

"Yeah, so? We haven't talked about Friday, but she's there every other week, so why wouldn't she be there?"

I raise my brows. There's a defensiveness in his tone, and I know it's because of the blonde bombshell, Gemma. She's always been the girl-next-door type with pouty lips and stern eyes— a.k.a. Jake's type. They've been friends since they were kids, having played on the same hockey team, and even if he won't say it out loud, I know how he feels about her.

He calls it protective, but I've been there with him when Gemma's gone on dates. Protective isn't the right word. More like bat shit crazy. However, he's vehemently opposed to dating locals, so he's never pursued her.

"Alright, we're leaving," I say, hitting the side of my leg to grab Otto's attention. "Time to go, boy. Say goodbye to your friend."

Bernie follows us to the door with a few more friendly nudges as I snatch my coat and backpack, trailing Otto down the steps outside. I click back into my ski bindings and tap my back with a low whistle, bending forward. Otto jumps onto my backpack, and I position him around my shoulders. On days when time is crucial, we ride just like this. He enjoys it as much as I do. We ski down and join the run, plowing the fresh powder on the mountain together.

Our day is just getting started. From moving rope lines and clearing runs for guests before the resort opens to performing sweeps at the end of the day to ensure everyone's safely off the mountain, I love what I do. Moving home would've been harder if I had to give up this work. But with a few connections and tests, here we are, doing exactly what we were trained for.

Regardless of the good news or bad, the hard days or the worst ones, I've found solace on this mountain. A home that doesn't have four walls or a door. It's drafty and windowless but still better than any place I've ever lived.

Chapter Four

Lincoln

Morning projects take a few hours to complete, and by the time I'm finished, Otto's ready to get out of the kennel and run. I take him all the way up the Cedar run and tell him *out front*. He runs in front of me with his ears up and tongue out before I have him heel when we get to a place with more skiers. He's in his element, which happens to attract a lot of attention. People pull their phones out to record him leading the way.

So do I.

We ski down to where we have an area marked off for drills, and everyone's already there. Ted and Jake are talking to our social media manager, Amanda, while Bernie and Milo sit at their feet. The way Ted's standing makes him look constipated, which checks out since he always gets all weird whenever

Amanda's around. He usually sounds like he's swallowed his tongue and is trying to speak Swahili. No one understands him.

"Still running late," Ted says, making a tsking sound with his mouth.

I click out of my bindings and lean them against the snowbank to the side of the main run with a long exhale. "It's been a busy day."

Jake elbows Ted. "He met someone. A *woman*."

I roll my eyes, whistle for Otto to come over, and ignore my roommates. "Hi, Amanda."

She looks up from her phone. "Lincoln, hey. I thought we'd start with some action shots during the drills and then get some photos in the snow cave."

"Great. I—"

The snickering beside me is getting out of hand. I shoot the two cacklers a glare.

Ted elbows Jake. "Did he make her an origami swan and ask her father's permission to talk to her yet?"

Jake slaps Ted's back while laughing so hard he's on his knees, and the dogs think it's time to start playing. He swats them away as he continues to laugh. There's barking, licking, and pawing happening, but it isn't enough to make Jake quit.

"Yeah, yeah." I'm used to their quips. "Just because I like to take things slow doesn't mean I won't make a move when the time's right."

I make it sound like I'd do something about that woman, Myra. I'm not a direct person. I'd prefer just to wait for my soulmate to drop out of the sky. It's how my parents met. I mean, sort of. Dad was on vacation with another woman when he met my mom. He broke it off with the other woman after a few days and even fewer conversations with Mom. This wouldn't have been so bad if they all weren't on a cruise ship together.

I'd happily take any trope the entertainment industry wants to throw at me if it meant meeting someone worth falling for.

Jake claws his way up to a standing position with heavy breaths. "Prove it."

"Here we go," Amanda mutters under her breath.

I furrow my brows and have the audacity to look surprised. I'm not. I know what he's thinking. This is Jake, the brother I spent most of my life with. There isn't a challenge he wouldn't take or one he wouldn't offer.

"Make a move then." He takes a wide stance and puffs out his chest

I shake my head and call Otto back. He's already running further up the slope on the side of the run. "I said I'd make a move when the time's right."

Jake sucks on his pointer finger and holds it in the air. "Seems like a perfect day to catch a woman to me."

"Alright." Amanda holds out her hands. "Can we just start shooting? Otherwise, I'm gonna film this whole thing and show all of our followers what you both really spend your time doing."

Ted sucks in air through his teeth, shaking his head.

Jake lifts his brows and tips his head toward me in a silent challenge.

I just shake my head because I have nothing to say. All my words will trap me, and by the end, I will have committed to whatever game Jake's playing like some multi-level marketing gig I can't say no to. "I'll take the dogs up and send them down when you give the call."

"I'll get buried this time," Ted says.

Jake crosses his arms. "You did it last time."

"Fine," Ted huffs. "Get in the hole."

"That's what she said." Jake laughs even harder, stumbling his way down to the snow cave we dug out.

It's on the side of the hill, big enough to fit a grown, six-foot-two man like Jake and roomy enough for someone of Ted's hobbit size to comfortably live in for a week. Jake has a tug toy with him and an over-exuberant dog voice ready to deploy when he's found. This drill is meant to simulate a real-life scenario of someone being trapped beneath the snow as much as it is to play. The more praise and reward the dogs get, the better they are at their jobs.

Ted tries to call his black lab, Milo, over through a laugh, failing at speaking both Swahili and English. Amanda bites her lips to keep from smiling, then holds her camera to her eye to do some test shots. The consistent shutter of her camera is still the loudest noise behind me, even with people passing on the ski run below us. Eventually, I tune out all the noise so I can focus and trudge up the slope with my skis, poles, and the dogs.

Once I'm high enough up where the dogs can't see Jake, and before I give any commands, I pull off one glove with my teeth and check my phone. Mom has another appointment with her doctor today. It's supposed to outline her next round of chemo and has us all ready to know where we can help. Knowing there's something I can do in an otherwise helpless situation has been my sanity. But there are no new messages.

I promise myself I'll check in with Dad for an update after drills if I don't hear from him. For now, I pocket my phone as Amanda switches to hers and starts taking a video. I give Bernie the command to *search*, and he wastes no time using his nose to find Jake. He sniffs him out easily, clinching first place by a matter of ten seconds after Milo's run. Next up, it's Otto's turn.

We run these drills often. Our dogs are one tool of many we'd deploy in the unlikely event of an avalanche. But spending years training to save one life is worth it, and that's exactly what Otto's been practicing for.

"Alright, boy." He's already patiently staring up at me. I'm positive I could mouth the word at this point, and he'd be able to read my lips. "Search!" I yell, and he's off, nose to the ground, shoulder blades pitched behind him.

I follow him at a distance, watching to see where and how he does what he does. The more I observe, the more I know what alerts him. When does he catch a scent? How does that affect his route? All of these things tell me more about him and how we can work best together.

I check the stopwatch, and so far, he's making great time. In a life or death situation, the dogs can cover miles in minutes compared to the hours it would take humans. And every minute matters in an emergency. Fifteen minutes is a lifetime when trapped under the snow.

We often use sweaters we've been wearing for days, hiding multiple beneath the snow and watching the dogs find them with ease. It's part of what they need to do for their certification test, but beyond that, finding those items isn't always easy. Wind, the density of the snow, temperature, the depth it's buried, and how strong the scent is at the surface matter. But proving his unmatched skill, Otto has found items layers down that have been lost for over a month, making the scent almost nonexistent at that point.

Otto's tail stands straight up behind him as he catches a scent and veers in the other direction down the mountain and straight for where Jake is hiding. I'm so proud to see the time on the stopwatch.

He's already started digging by the time I get there, so I quickly drop to my knees and use my shovel to help. "You got it, bud! Keep digging! Almost there!"

Jake starts to yell, acting as though he is stuck beneath the snow. He's great at putting on a show and making it believable—

a true damsel in distress. His arm shoots out of the small opening Otto has dug out, tug toy in hand.

Otto latches on and starts yanking. He's strong, but Jake works to crawl out, following Otto's backward momentum. He flops to his back with his face turned to the sky. "Otto, you saved me."

"What did you clock that at?" Ted asks me just as he and Amanda come closer.

"Ninety seconds."

"You're fucking joking," Jake deadpans.

My mouth curls up, and I can't hide it.

Amanda whistles and gives Otto a vigorous pet on his back. "Got some great footage. Good job, guys!"

Jake points at Otto. "What are you feeding him?"

"Raw meat," I answer with a shrug. And one of Jake's shoes every once in a while. He still hasn't figured that one out, though.

"Damn you." Jake puts his hands on his hips, shaking his head slowly.

Bernie and Milo join the celebration, cranking up the energy levels of all the dogs that have become our companions.

I rub Otto's back vigorously. Someone's getting an extra treat tonight.

Just like he does every night.

After we run a few more drills with the dogs, the crew disperses to do their various jobs. I hang back with Otto and sit in the snow for a short break. I like being able to pause throughout my day.

Otto gets cozy beside me as I pull out my phone again. This time, there's a new message in the family thread.

Dad: Got the plan we were expecting and some news we weren't. Let's talk soon.

It takes everything in me not to tap Dad's icon, call him immediately, and ask what his cryptic text is all about. But I don't. I can't even if I wanted to since service up here is spotty. I'd get him on the phone only to blink and lose him again. I'll have to talk to him later, preferably when I'm not trying to focus on work.

I like his message, hoping it goes through, and put my phone away. I don't even have any energy to watch a few cat videos on social media, something I'd never reveal to Otto. He'd likely disown me.

Instead, I pet my best friend who is lucky enough not to know the intricacies of how cancer affects a family. To him, he's there in the moment to lend a soft coat of fur when I need it, and right now, that's enough.

Mom always asked when putting us to bed each night what made us smile that day. Nine-year-old me would say something about playing with my Spiderman action figure, while eleven-year-old me might have said winning my chess tournament. As I got older and Mom stopped tucking me in, she still asked in the form of a piece of paper slipped into my jacket pocket or sticky note on my car windshield. When I graduated and left the country, and we were in completely different time zones, she'd text me at some point in the middle of the night. I'd wake up to her message the next morning and start my day off with a smile.

After all this time, it's always her question that makes me smile the most, not my answer. A part of her seeking a part of me. On days like this, when smiling feels like it might actually hurt, I hear her voice whispering *there is always something to smile about.*

Otto does a slow blink of appreciation while I think about anything that made me smile today. A bright yellow jacket comes to mind, and my lips slowly lift toward the sun.

Chapter Five

Myra

I can't do this!" I scream at the sky.

I'm flat on my back on the snow-packed slope when another person stops beside me. The second one since I fell. "Are you okay?"

Tears well in my eyes as I keep squinting upward, wanting nothing more than to break one of my poles over my knee. But I can't since I don't know where they went when I crashed.

I grit my teeth. "I'm fine."

Or I will be in a minute. That is if I can manage to get back up without sliding, falling, or both. The person skis off, but I stay where I'm at, tits up and perpendicular to the lodge—a position I've been in most of the day and probably won't be in any other time outside of crashing.

Later came faster than I wanted it to. After a short stint in the lodge, drinking my weight in hot chocolate and warming my chilled face by the fire, I clicked these beams back on my feet and tried to get down this mountain again. And again.

And *again*.

The magic carpet is delivering zero magic today. I'm channeling more of a genie still stuck in a bottle with the number of times I've ridden the conveyor belt up and tripped over myself getting off. It's like my feet are moving out of sync and fighting like two immature children. The left wants to go one way, and the right is over it, making a case for staying still. Neither are willing to compromise, and I'm about to tie them both together until they work it out.

I feel now would also be an excellent time to remind myself that I'm on my period.

Yeah.

I sigh heavily, listening to the skiers rushing past me and feeling the movement shake the ground under my body. I'm still sweating after picking myself up from the last fall since standing up is a high-intensity interval training workout. Maybe I should have added more squats to the nonexistent exercise regimen I was working with before I got here. I couldn't even be bothered to climb a ladder to take down the Halloween, Thanksgiving, *and* Christmas decorations my brother, Frankie, put up in my apartment during a blackout moment of seasonal cheer.

I'm happy with my quads. Just don't tell my hamstrings.

Now I have to pee, which means going back inside and stripping off all these layers. The seat will be cold, and I will probably scream another expletive some child has never heard.

I pull my balaclava off my chin so I can breathe better. I'm not good at this, and I hate that. Usually, I can run circles around my goals, but this requires a route similar to a geometric shape with too many points. If I can't do something like teach myself to ski, I sure as fuck won't be able to teach myself how to live a happy life without a husband. All alone. By myself.

I want so badly to figure out how to be happy again and find what makes me feel like *me*. Not me during or after Wade. Though, I would take the *me* from before. She liked the gym a lot more.

I want the woman who completed two years of community college in high school, competed in a few half-marathons even though she hated running, and turned the music up loud in her apartment and danced like the older woman across the balcony was watching. It made her smile. But I stopped smiling the second he left, and I've had a permanent frown since I signed those papers. If I can't have *that* woman, I'd settle for the one who can make it through an episode of Gilmore Girls without bawling her eyes out.

I thought I had found the Luke to my Lorelei.

If Luke had just wanted to be married to me, we'd be living happily ever after in Stars Hollow. Or maybe just Phoenix still.

To be the best wife, the best homemaker, the best in bed, and the best at making coffee, I gave up parts of myself, thinking that's what I had to do to be in a successful relationship. I'd never been in one of those before. All of them ended with an epic disaster spelling *revenge*. I mean, it did with Wade, too. I just don't think he ever knew I was the one to put a rotten fish in his gym bag.

I want to be selfish and focus on myself for a change. That's what this whole trip is supposed to be about. I'm due for some selfish *wanting*.

If only it didn't physically hurt.

I gasp for breath, holding back tears. I'd rather throw up than cry right now. I'm angry. So fucking angry that I gave so much and got so little. Yet it still hurts to crawl into bed every night. I don't miss Wade, but I miss knowing someone was there.

Coming here was a mistake. My bones are made of sunshine and humidity, after all. Snow is basically my kryptonite. I should have gotten my imaginary dog instead. I spent weeks hyper-focusing on said dog all hours of the day and night. The dog who has his own monogrammed blanket and heart-shaped name tag hanging from his leopard print collar in my mind and Pinterest board. Yeah, *that* dog.

I told myself I'd get that dog when the divorce was final. But signing my name at the bottom of those legal documents did something to me. I panicked. I locked myself in my apartment and sent Frankie photos of me for proof of life until Christmas.

Christmas.

Merlot had her way with me that night.

She whispered *you should learn how to ski,* and I whispered right back, *I should.*

"Can I help you up?" another person skis by and stops to ask.

"No." I've run out of nicer ways to say this.

I'm lamenting, okay!

I close my eyes tightly. If I had just gotten my dog, I could have avoided sucking balls at skiing. I would be taking him on walks and visiting the dog park where I'd spend hours throwing his ball and waiting for him to return it. We would have driven through the coffee shop in town that offered *Puppuccinos* for furry guests. He'd get whipped cream on his nose and then try to lick me while I laughed.

On weekends, when I'd be out of school, he'd curl up on the end of the couch, sitting right on my feet and falling asleep while I watched Rory and Jess fall in love in season three. We'd go on vacations together, grocery trips, training classes because he'd have a bad habit of jumping up and using his nose to push the ice maker, leaving me with a wet floor to come home to. He'd have his own space in the closet with all his gear and a spot beside me in bed.

He'd fill the empty spaces that Wade left.

But I don't have a dog, I suck at skiing, and finding myself again is a lot harder when my cheeks are starting to freeze. And not the ones on my face.

I have *nothing* to show for this so-called adventure.

Well, other than another week with my monthly bestie, Flo. She's a real bitch, though.

Sitting up with my feet kicked out in front of me, I search around for my gear. One pole is lying beside me, while the other managed to stick straight up in the snow a few feet back. My skis popped off again and are beside me now, too. Someone must have put them there. Probably not the person who yelled *pizza* twelve times as I was speeding past them. I didn't understand the code word—still don't.

I shake my head. This was a bad idea. Coming here, thinking I could be good at this, escaping my parents who are constantly questioning my decisions, asking if I'm paying my bills on time, or need another batch of tree-shaped cookies made by someone other than Mom.

So no, I'm not fucking *okay*.

A hot rage fills my chest, and I unbuckle my helmet and toss it down the hill. It rolls, taking my goggles with it, but eventually stops. I roughly unzip my yellow coat, angry that I'm hot and even more upset I had it on in the first place because I was cold. "It shouldn't be this hard to be warm!" I yell into the void.

Except it's not the void, and multiple people turn to stare. But I can't even muster a wave to assure them I'm not out of my mind because maybe I am.

Life was supposed to be different. I was promised forever with one person. We were supposed to have kids together, raise them, and take the obligatory family pictures every fucking fall with matching outfits and holiday foliage in the background. Everyone we knew would hang that picture on their fridge and note how happy we looked. *Wade and Myra love each other*, they'd think. And in that photo, we would've been happy, but only because we had to pay for those photos. Damn right I'll smile for six-hundred dollars.

But outside of that picture, there'd be no kids because someone forgot to mention they didn't want them. Hint: it wasn't me. Sex would be harder to want, and we'd wonder how many times we could fall asleep and wake up in the same bed without screaming into our pillows. He'd find every reason not to come home, and I'd find every reason to beg him to. Distance would grow, resentment would bloom, and pretty soon, the photo on someone else's wall would fade and crack and be tossed in the trash to make room for next year's picture.

Except next year, there wouldn't be a photo.

Or the year after that.

Rage melts into sadness. But not just any kind of sadness. The lonely kind. The I'm-all-by-myself-in-these-feelings brand of lonely. Tears are a constant in this place, and they *hurt*. Crying isn't cathartic. It's war and bloodshed against everything I lost. Two signatures were our swords, and one mountain was supposed to be my bandage.

With pinched lips, I double down and try harder to hold the tears back, but they break through with a gasp, filling my eyes and then my cheeks. I cover my face with my gloved hands and weep. For all I've lost, all I don't know how to fix, and the fear of waking up another day feeling like a failure.

God, I just want a win.

I want to be the best at things again.

I want a dog.

I *want* so badly that I think it might just be a need at this point.

I wish *wanting* was enough to fix me.

As I drop my gloved hands away from my face, the warm tears turn cold immediately, so I swipe them away before they become icicles. I breathe the snap of cool air into my lungs and let it out in a cloud. The sun is falling below the puffs of white, and the capped peaks make the mountains dark, shadowed by the threat of snow-heavy clouds offering another layer of powder. I'm not sure I've seen mountains so beautiful. Their width seems unreal, like a photo zoomed in to its furthest point. At least I chose a place like this to fall apart. If any setting could handle my temper tantrums, it's these mountains.

A woman who appears to be my age with a young toddler attached to some kind of backpack leash stops beside me on her skis. "Need help up?"

I look at her outstretched hand and the prominent lines around her mouth. She seems trustworthy, but I'm not the best judge of character. Regardless, I grab her gloved hand and let her pull me up, mustering every bit of energy I have left.

"Thanks," I say, brushing snow off my chest and back.

She nods and skates off with ease.

Picking up my skis and poles with a body void of energy, I walk further down to retrieve my helmet while sniffling. The wants I have could swallow me whole if I let them. Except for one. I can manage one.

I want more hot cocoa.

Chapter Six

Lincoln

I am a despicable person.

"I have to go eat, Otto. And you have to stay down here."

He doesn't let me off the hook easily. He stares up with sad, pleading eyes while humming a low whine. It makes me feel like I'm a wretched human being—a horrible person who can't look in the mirror again without remembering this moment.

Those eyes and the quirk of his head say he can't possibly fathom this kind of rejection. Sometimes I forget to leave him down here in the kennels below the cafeteria and get overloaded by requests to pet, snuggle, and pick him up like he's a freaking baby. He's not. He's *my* baby. And he's working when the vest is on.

I tilt my head, too, like the weight of my conscience is too heavy. "We'll get you something to eat when we get back home."

Are his eyes misty? "I swear."

He tilts his head the other way from inside the kennel.

"And I'll give you that antler we've been saving and let you sleep on my bed." I wave one hand. "Final offer."

He huffs his reluctant agreement and lays down on the plush dog bed.

"I promise I won't be long," I say to him before walking out the door and up the steps to the main lodge before I can change my mind.

The shift in volume is immediate. Downstairs, few people are filtering in and out, but it's busy and loud up here. Noise bounces off the peaked wood beam ceiling, and all of the stonework acting as wainscoting on the walls doesn't dull it. But the raised volume drowns out most of my guilty thoughts for leaving Otto.

The thin carpeted areas where rows of tables, chairs, and ski gear sit, along with the tiled walkways, are full of bodies pressed close together as they move from one spot to the next. The volume beats against my tired skull, and while I'd prefer to grab my dinner and eat somewhere—*anywhere*—else, I've already been spotted by Ted. He waves and then points at Jake across the room, who seems to be chatting up a woman near the window— his favorite pastime. But we're both off the clock, so I don't give a damn what he does. I'm eating.

I wave back at Ted, then quickly jump in line and pull a tray from the stack before moving behind other hungry visitors. After an entire morning of projects, training, and dog runs, I followed it up by helping close off a few runs to do sweeps for people, making sure everyone was off the mountain before the resort closed. A lot of people have gone home already except for all of these lodge rats still finishing their food and a brew.

Loading a burger, fries, and a bottle of water on my tray, I scan my pass to pay for my meal and meander through the packed tables toward Ted. I decide to take the long route and annoy Jake just to see him squirm in front of the girl he's likely trying to convince to come home with him. How he gets so much game with that stache is baffling.

There's a perpetual-sounding thud from other people's ski boots as I navigate through bodies, making me grateful I took mine off in the locker room. Everyone is squished tightly together in the dining hall, and there's little room to move, let alone allow for proper airflow. But no one else seems to care.It's a minefield of gear and bodies, but I manage, by some miracle, to get through without tripping on one guy's ski boots and another person's helmet.

As the back of Jake's head gets closer, I can't decide whether to tug his squirrel tail or pinch his rib cage. I'll need to make this quick because I'm starving and hate small talk. He has one hand on his hip, facing the woman and blocking her completely from my view, and the other leaning on the table. I slow my gait and decide to bump him with my shoulder as I pass.

I brace my tray for impact.

One…two…

My shoulder rams into his, but I'm so focused on his reaction that I don't notice the bright yellow jacket on the chair across from the woman until afterward. I've seen that jacket before. It resembles the sun and is nearly as blinding.

He stumbles forward and mumbles, "What the…"

My expression sobers immediately when I see her.

The owner of the jacket is sitting at a two-seater table, staring up at me with a pensive look. Her full lips are slightly parted, and she doesn't blink. No one blinks. But from this short distance, she's even more beautiful without all of her bulky gear and the layer of snow she had on earlier.

"Hi," I say, be it more breathlessly than I would like. I lower my voice and try again. "Hey."

She smirks at me while Jake loops an arm around my neck and rubs my head with his fist. "Sorry. My big brother's a total dick sometimes."

I don't make a case for why Jake is the bigger dick or even care that he just messed up my already messed up hair. I'm too focused on *her* hair. It's dark and woven together in a loose braid hanging long over her shoulder. The white, cable-knit sweater she has on looks inviting. Maybe that's why my mouth has run dry, and I've completely forgotten we aren't alone.

She seems…whole. No bruises or scrapes from our run-in or any other potential ones she had after the fact, and I make sure to thoroughly scan her neck and lips to confirm.

My memories didn't do her justice.

I swallow. "Hi."

"Dude, you already said that," Jake says out of the side of his mouth from beside me, then grabs my burger to take a bite.

Myra gives an exasperated sigh in response to Jake but gives me her pretty smile. "Hi back."

The cacophony of sound around us is louder than an orchestra made up of only tambourines clanging together. I don't know how to casually back out of this now without seeming like a jerk and not asking how she's doing. But if I do that, Jake will know who this woman is—the one who slid through my legs and quite literally stole the breath in my lungs. At the time, I wasn't so sure she wouldn't hit my junk.

I weigh both options and decide I have to ask. "How's your head?"

Our eyes lock, and the light brown shade of hers pierces me like a kebab through the heart. Her cheeks are rosy either from the cool temperatures outside or the borderline miserable heat inside. Either way, it gives a glowy sheen to her skin, making it ten times more tempting.

She sits up straighter and tucks a stray hair behind her ear. "I'm doing fine. How are *you* doing after running into me?"

A corner of my mouth lifts. I'm about to tell her that's not how I remember it when Jake finally puts things together. I almost forgot he was here.

"Wait," Jake says from beside me. "Is she..." He looks back at her and then at me again. "Is she the woman?"

I don't pay Jake any attention. I see his face often enough. "Myra, right?"

She nods, gaze darting between Jake and me.

I'm usually no good in conversations like this. Jake's always been better at talking to strangers and beautiful women. Myra just so happens to be both. My wool underlayer is trying to suffocate me, and I might just let it if it'll get me out of this situation.

"Well, this is interesting." Jake reviews me with a sly grin.

Oh God, please, no.

He steals a fry and focuses back on Myra. "Linc told me you were beautiful; I just didn't believe him." He waves his fry around. "He's usually more into women with walkers. But clearly, he does have some taste somewhere inside him."

Myra scans Jake from his hat to his black crocs. I'm sure he thinks she's checking him out, but when she crosses her legs and leans over them, it seems more like she's going to light into him. "I left my walker at home for this trip, but I always make sure to pack Depends."

I start to breathe again and laugh. She's *funny.*

Jake doesn't laugh. "Anyway..." He glares over at me and then clears his throat. "Myra, if you want a tour of the area, text me." He nods at the slip of paper on the table.

He already gave her his number? I hadn't even noticed. And by the looks of it, he handed her one of the business cards he had printed with his information. However, I've never seen him hand them out for business purposes. Only personal, and only women.

There's a strong desire to snatch the card, rip it into shreds, and shove it down Jake's shirt. But the intrusive thought passes as Myra says, "I won't be texting you."

Jake doesn't even miss a beat. "Call me then. Seeya."

She sounds uninterested. Is she uninterested? Why do I care? Of course Jake would have approached her. She's a gorgeous woman, sitting alone and not wearing a ring. Two out of three of those are Jake's type. Wedding rings are not something he seems to notice, which is part of the problem he found himself in recently. But if there is one thing that automatically makes a woman off limits, it's if she's from Bozeman. According to Jake, transplants are fair game, and vacationers are ideal, but locals are trouble. His best friend, Gemma, calls bullshit every time he gets on his soapbox about it. But Jake doesn't like being held back by other people's opinions. And there are a lot of those in a growing town that still acts small.

Once Jake is out of earshot, I inspect Myra to make sure she doesn't have any lasting effects from that encounter. She seems content enough. I'm already deeper than I thought, so I might as well find the bottom. "Can I sit here?"

She smiles with her eyes, then points at the chair and says, "It's yours," before she stands to lean over the table and quickly clears her gear off, shoving it between her seat and the wall.

I sit, sliding my tray in front of me. Now that I'm here, I don't know what comes next, but I have to say something, or this silence will shank me. I peer up at her, and she's studying me. I smile. She smiles. We all smile, until I finally say, "How was the rest of your day since..." I nod at her head. "The accident?"

"Shitty."

She's honest, too.

"Skiing and I don't agree with each other…yet." She mumbles the last word. "Sorry about running into you or under you, by the way." She bites the inside of her cheek before saying, "It's not like I was aiming for you. I don't possess that skill. Steering and stopping are a lot harder than they should be. I could have at least watched a video…or seven."

"It's better to do it than watch someone else." I twist a fry in the air like a light saber before I realize what I'm doing and stop. "You've really never skied before?"

"I thought that part was obvious." Her laugh is dry and humorless as she rests her crossed arms on the table and peers outside. "Arizona isn't exactly known for having an abundance of snow."

The corners of her mouth don't turn up all the way, even though her lips are wide enough to accommodate a fuller one. If there's one thing I've learned from all my travels, it's that everyone has a story behind the one they're telling.

"How convenient that you crashed into a ski patroller who's been skiing his whole life then." I lean my forearms on the table, scooting my tray and matching her posture. "Have you ever thought of taking lessons? You'll learn how to stop."

She snort laughs, which I didn't know was cute until just now, and runs her tongue along her top teeth. "You know, it wasn't until I was careening down a mountain with weapons of mass destruction in each of my hands that I thought about it. I tend to just do stuff and figure it out as I go. Know anyone who could help me out?"

I panic. This feels a lot like flirting. Is she flirting?

I'm instantly thinking WWJD—*What Would Jake Do?* Myra is the first woman I've met to tell my younger brother off and flirt with *me* within the span of ten minutes. I'm still trying to sort that out in my head, but I can't mess this up.

Would Jake go with seductive, mysterious, or full-on douche? Seductive feels way too forward, and douche isn't working for Myra.

I go with mysterious. "Maybe."

Good start. Keep going.

"So, you want to learn how to ski…I know how to ski…you have time…I also have time…" I wave a hand between us and pause for dramatic effect. *Very mysterious.* So mysterious I worry I haven't been clear enough. Is it possible to be too mysterious?

She leans in as if we're sharing a secret. "Tell me where you want to meet, and I'll be there."

A thrill runs through me, using my loins as a trampoline. *Are we still talking about skiing?*

I go with that and twist a fry between my thumb and pointer finger. "I'm pretty expensive."

She quirks a brow and grins. "Oh yeah?"

"Yup." *I am nailing this.* Twirling the fry between my fingers, I add, "But for you, I will accept payment in french fries and dog treats."

She peers down at my tray of food and then steals a fry, biting into it and closing her eyes for a brief moment. Who knew someone could look so sexy eating a fried potato? "I've never met anyone before who likes dog treats. Do you prefer peanut butter or legume-free?"

I can't help but laugh. Her humor is refreshing, and the way she said *legume* is oddly hot "Otto isn't picky."

"Good; it's a deal." She steals another fry. "I'll bring the goods."

"It's a deal," I repeat, then grab the paper boat of fries and slide them across the table for her to finish. "First lesson is to eat dinner and get a good night's sleep."

Her eyes drop to the fries and back up again before picking one up and pointing it straight at my heart. "I can't wait."

Neither can I.

My phone buzzes in my pocket, but I ignore it. Whoever it is can wait.

It buzzes again and another time almost immediately after. I'm doing my best to focus on her and pretend my pants aren't dancing to the beat of their own vibrations. Unable to ignore it any longer, I slip my hand in to grab it. Dad's name flashes across the screen, and before I can even read the message, I hold up a finger and say, "One sec."

Dad: Who's that?

Mom: She's pretty!

Huh? I scroll back up to the top of the group text thread, which doesn't exist since we've had it for multiple years, and send too many GIFS a day to know where the top really is. The most recent message was sent from Jake reading: *Lincoln's new girlfriend.*

Below it, there's a picture. Of us. Of Myra and me. Me and Myra. The two of us right now, together at this table. Two people smiling and staring at each other like they're enjoying the conversation.

I snap my head up and immediately start searching the room. When I find him, he's sitting with Ted, covering his mouth with his hand and laughing like a damn hyena.

Dad: *GIF of two pieces of sushi hugging and reading *You are My Soy Mate.**

This isn't good.

Jake: *GIF of a woman pretending to slap a man's ass reading *Get It**

Dad: Is that Joey from Friends? I just watched that episode.
Mom: No, honey. That's definitely Ross. He dated Rachel.
Dad: So did Joey.
Mom: How do you know this? Have you been Googling again?

Now I'm panicking.

They reply back and forth at light speed, bombarding my phone with their messages. I know exactly where this is headed. My parents will go bananas with this information. They already are. They'll call and text and request more photos and badger me about the wedding details. Baby names will be discussed. *Oh no.* They'll want to meet her.

The one time I start talking and maybe even flirting with a woman, and Jake puts me on blast. How am I supposed to get out of this one unscathed?

Mom: When are you bringing her to family game night? This Friday???

I swallow and put my phone back in my pocket.
It has begun.
"Everything alright?" Myra asks, concern hugging each of her words like bubble wrap.

My leg bounces uncontrollably under the table, and I grab a fistful of my pants. There's really nothing clsc to do here except give her a thumbs up and say, "Super."

Chapter Seven

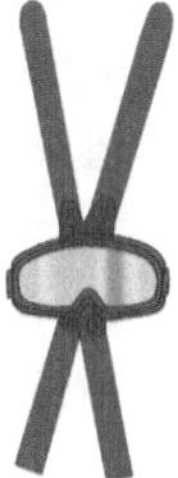

Myra

This is *not* a date.

He never called it that, and neither did I. But I woke up early this morning after some kind of fever dream and decided I needed to stress about what to wear for our *not* date. I can't do this. I haven't been on a date—*not* date—in forever. I barely went on dates with my husband—*ex-husband*.

Nothing in my suitcase is safe as I tear through it, tossing articles of clothing everywhere as nerves shoot up my spine, arms, and hands. It's a small enough space that I've managed to get clothes in every single room. A t-shirt on the kitchen counter, shoes I won't be able to wear in the snow on the bed, and underwear with tags still on them strewn over the couch. And I still have nothing to show for it.

Liv was kind enough to let me stay in the A-frame cabin behind her house for a whole ten days at the discounted rate of completely free. With a peaked roofline and windows covering the entire front side where the front door is, it doesn't feel as tiny as she described. There's plenty of room to pace when I can't sleep or cry in the shower if I need a change from the living room. Tiny and quaint are just fine for my needs.

Groaning, I sit back on my heels and stare at the ceiling. The layers Jeff sold me in the rental shop are the practical choice for skiing with Lincoln. I should just woman up and put those on. But then I get a visual of the small but mighty pile of just-for-me-underwear around the space and second-guess everything.

"No, Myra. You are not wearing those. Do not forget the last time you tried skiing in a thong." It also happened to be the first time I'd ever skied. "Wear your granny panties and send the message you want him to receive."

I don't have to wear the thong. There was a black lace pair…

"Stop it!" I cradle my head in my hands. This is *not* a date, and it's definitely *not* sex.

Lincoln has this alluring way about him that he seems totally oblivious to. He's gorgeous. All of those perfect features I noted the first time we met were the same last night when he stopped at my table, just closer, which is saying something since I thought he was going to kiss me the first time we met. On my way out, I tossed his brother's business card in the trash. Not that he wasn't attractive, too, but he seemed more than aware of that fact. I've already been with someone who was married to the mirror.

The way Lincoln's mouth gaped, and a bloom of red lit up his cheeks when he realized who I was made my stomach drop. At first, I thought it was because he remembered me as the girl who was going to let a stranger kiss her, but his eyes seemed to be committing me to memory one eyelash at a time.

My phone starts ringing somewhere under the piles I've created. I crawl on hands and knees, lifting shirts and tossing sweaters until I finally find it and answer.

"Frankie! Thank God you called." It's like my brother has a sixth sense anytime I have a fashion crisis.

He laughs. "Are you ready for me to come rescue you from your post-divorce-life crisis yet?"

I sit on the floor and lean against the bed, pushing aside my suitcase with my leg in the process. "I just got here two-ish days ago."

"So?" he says in a snappy tone.

I scoff. "I'm still finding myself."

"Lord help us all. And what are you discovering?"

Sighing deeply, I peer around the cabin. If I weren't in a post-divorce-life crisis, as my big brother coined it, then I wouldn't even be here. I need to start seeing the positive side of Merlot's sketchy and rash decision-making. One, I'll still have a few days of winter break left after I get home to stay in pajamas and prepare for school to start again. Two, I get to spend time with Liv. I've missed her since she fled Arizona to be an elementary school principal. And three, I get to learn how to ski from someone who actually knows how to stop. In seven days, I'll be teaching toddlers instead of the other way around.

I kick at a stray boot without its mate and stretch my legs out. "I'm discovering that skiing is hard."

It's his turn to scoff. "I could have told you that."

"And that I'm going to be the best damn skier by the time I get back," I counter, studying my horribly chipped nails that would make Mom recoil in disgust. They're only a little better than my skiing. "I decided to take lessons, and today is the first one."

"Well, don't die."

"I won't." Not when I have a hot ski patroller with me.

I immediately shut down the thought and then remember I don't have to. I'm not married anymore. Thinking another man is attractive, enjoying conversation with him, and going on a *not* date to learn how to ski isn't a bad thing. I'm a single woman, partaking in single-woman things.

Fiddling with the zipper on my suitcase, I say, "You know the ski patroller I ran into yesterday?"

"How could I forget? I'm still laughing about it," he says with a low chuckle.

"Shut up," I spit out. "He offered to teach me how to ski… and I accepted."

"What's the catch?"

I find a straggler hair tie in my suitcase and twirl it around my finger for something to do. "What do you mean *catch*? There's no catch…" I think back on our conversation. "I mean, he said he'd take french fries and dog treats as payment."

"Myra. There's *always* a catch. Did he ask you out?"

"No."

"Did he get your address?"

The hair tie loses momentum and slips down my finger. "Well, no. Not yet."

His voice gets louder. "What the hell do you mean *not yet*?"

My body instinctively goes rigid. "He's picking me up and driving me to the mountain for our ski lesson, so, yes, I'll have to give him my address. I can't use Liv's car every day."

The line is quiet for a heartbeat. It's as long as Frankie can handle between sentences. "Did you agree to sleep with him?"

"What? No! Frankie, I didn't pimp myself out for ski lessons." I start whipping the tie around my pointer finger even faster. "I agreed out of my own volition. And because I think he's kind of…cute."

"Stop right now," he gasps so hard he starts choking on the intake of air. "Are you referring to another male as *cute*? Has the entire male population been redeemed in your eyes because of a *cute* ski patroller? Has that ever happened before? I'm talking even before Mr. Self-Righteous-Prick broke your heart."

"Frankie," I say with an edge of warning as I slingshot the nylon tie across the room. It was no surprise that Wade was never Frankie's cup of anything. They are opposites in just about every way. But even the mention of Wade in this conversation feels like sawing through bone to get to my heart. "I'll have you know that I think lots of men are cute; I just don't say it out loud like you do."

"The world needs to know these things, and sometimes the men do, too," he says in a flat tone. "I need a picture of him ASAP."

That won't be happening. Frankie will only make this more of a *thing* than I want or need it to be. He'll somehow find Lincoln's number online, where he went to school, what he ate for breakfast on the fourth day in December a year ago, and then ask him if he likes me. He doesn't have social media, but his sleuthing skills are FBI-level good. I'm not taking the chance.

A laugh rumbles through my chest. "God, I miss you."

"I saw you three days ago, on Sunday, when I dropped you off at the airport for your flight. Remember?"

"Whatever." I cross my other arm over my stomach. It's Tuesday now, but Frankie lives in the same apartment building as me, so I'm used to seeing him at least once a week—usually all seven days. "Just admit you miss me, too, and tell me how Mom and Dad are."

"Mom and Dad are probably fine. I haven't seen them since last weekend when I was forced to endure New Year's Day brunch with them after taking you to the airport. But if it makes you feel better, I miss you like a clam misses its pearl. You really do suck at leaving home," Frankie says with a laugh.

He's mostly right. Working a full-time job for the past ten years since I graduated hasn't allowed for time to travel. I can't argue with him on this, but I still try. "Do not."

"Do too," he retorts.

We will always channel the six and five-year-old versions of ourselves in a disagreement. Since I'm younger, I like to think I always win. With only eighteen months separating us, Frankie and I are close. We had to fight for that closeness—quite literally —since he liked to karate chop the back of my knees like some Krav Maga maniac who also couldn't see over the kitchen counter.

Frankie lowers his voice and sighs into the phone. "*He* called Dad during brunch, ya know."

He needs no introduction since the acrid way Frankie says it is enough to know who we're talking about.

I grit my teeth before saying, "And?"

"It was right after we ate. Mom was on her second mimosa, and you know how champagne is basically her truth serum."

Of course I know this since it's the only redeeming quality of these brunch days.

Frankie barely takes a breath before continuing, "So, I was listening to her ramble on about how she didn't like their gardener—"

"Scandalous," I cut in.

"Tell me about it. Anyway, Wade called Dad's phone. He asked him to golf next weekend, which is actually the worst sport in the universe, BTW." An outraged finger is waving around right now. I'd put money on it. "Probably why that buffoon of a man likes it so much."

"It really is the worst. Trust me, I had to endure full Saturdays on the golf course, eating and drinking my weight in granola bars and mineral water," I say, rolling my eyes. "What did Dad say?"

He pauses. "Are you sure you want to know?"

He doesn't even need to tell me. Ken and Beth, my parents, love Wade…as in present tense. It broke them when I told them we were getting a divorce. Never mind that it was Wade's idea or that the five years we spent married—seven years we'd been together—he was still somehow the golden son-in-law who could do no wrong. I became the black sheep of my own family.

It's not like anything happened either. In fact, nothing did. Neither of us cheated; there were no nefarious findings or red flags except for the fact Wade disliked chocolate. He deserved the full milk chocolate bar I put in his suit jacket pocket before he moved out. We both just changed so much since the start of our relationship. Both of us liked talking late into the night until he stopped coming home after I was in bed. We both wanted kids and then he started dropping hints that he liked not having any. And both of us enjoyed spending time together on the weekends, until everyone else started to take precedence.

I exhale and switch the phone to my other ear. "So, Wade and Dad are going golfing next weekend?"

"Yup."

That bastard. Wade might have initiated the divorce, but he just can't seem to let go. He's spent more time with my dad than he ever did before, making it difficult for me to move on and forget his permanent smug expression and annoyingly high cheekbones.

Frankie's voice cuts off my downward spiral. "I don't understand why you don't just tell Mom and Dad to cut him off and quit inviting him to dinners and golfing like everything's fine. Everything is not fucking fine!"

"Wait." A cold sweat breaks out on my forehead as I sit ramrod straight. "They invited him to dinner?"

Frankie groans. "Mom did. And she wants me to be there. Can you believe that? I will murder my food with a butter knife just to avoid wringing his neck."

My parents have always been more akin to leeches than humans, as they latch on to any living thing with a pulse and never let go. Correction: anything with a pulse *and* money.

Wade's family came from wealth, so my parents made sure to befriend them at the country club. Normally, I ignore the small mentions of Wade and his family, and I've managed.

With Merlot.

I tilt over on my side and roll to my back with a pile of clothes beneath me. "I can't move on if Wade is pushing his perfectly coiffed blond hair into my life every chance he gets."

"You know he dyes it, right?"

"No, he doesn't!"

His laughter booms. "Yes, he absolutely does."

Resting my arm on the ground above my head, I say, "Does not. I was married to him! He never once went to a salon to dye his hair. I think I would know if he did."

"Have you ever heard of lying, sister? It's not that hard for someone like him, and I swear on my entire pocket square collection that he goes to the salon. You don't get that color blond naturally or from a box. You pay for it."

The confidence Frankie exudes is enough to have me second-guessing my stance. Pocket squares are his favorite article of clothing, and he would never have made such a flippant remark without being able to back it up. If Wade really did dye his hair, I would have known, or at least felt the difference. If he didn't tell me about his hair, there were likely other things he failed to mention.

If I find something out, I'm not above egging his house...or hair.

I rub my forehead. "You're making my head hurt, and I have a *not* date to get ready for."

He takes a sip of what I assume is his daily caramel macchiato he gets at the local coffee stand. "Okay, enough about Mr. Fake-Hair. Tell me about this *cute* ski patroller."

My face is hotter than a cast iron skillet. "He's delicious."

"Oh my God. You devoured him already!" he yells.

"Did not." I pull my legs up and hug my knees. I can tell Frankie about him as long as he doesn't find out who he is.

"But you want to."

Lies. Mostly…kind of. He's absolutely a ten, but I haven't said something like this out loud to anyone since Wade. There's no way I'm going to start now with a stranger who may or may not have cute eyebrows and even cuter disheveled hair. Sure, there were one-night stands in my early twenties, but I'm a thirty-five-year-old woman with a career and an indent on my ring finger I'm starting to think is a permanent part of me.

He aggressively starts shaking his cup, which seems to only have ice left. "I'm going to take your silence as confirmation."

I groan loudly. "I'm not good at *this*. Being single and constantly wondering if everyone can tell. I was a way better wife."

I hate being back in the singles club where I'm starting over from scratch. Life was comfortable, routine, and simple with Wade, even when he was equally married to his houseplants and watered them more than me.

"That's exactly the problem," he says. "You were a way better wife to Mr. Prick than he deserved. He took advantage of your faithfulness to him more times than—"

"Just…stop!" I cut in. The last thing I want is to talk about Wade. I've heard all of this from Frankie since I'm well-versed in his opinions. "I'm sorry I yelled, but I don't want to think about him right now," I add in a low voice.

In true Frankie fashion, he lets it go and changes the subject. "So, what are you going to wear?"

I tilt my head to either side, cataloguing the disaster I'm currently doing a backstroke in. "Good question. I was just trying to figure that out when you called. I decided to become a nudist and move to a colony—I mean community—that won't make me wear clothes or pick outfits."

"Liar."

"I swear. I'll call my sponsor right now and patch you through."

"Yeah, sure," he says through a forced laugh. "Your cream-colored sweater with the black skirt that hits you mid-thigh and black tights. Done. Give me a harder job next time."

"I can't wear that when I'm skiing," I say with a disbelieving laugh to the ceiling fan.

"Why not?"

"Because I have to wear my snow pants and jacket. The last thing I should be wearing is a skirt riding up my ass—"

"Thanks for the unnecessary visual," he says, not letting me finish. "Wear your black leggings and that cream, wide-neck sweater you just bought."

I don't even know why I try to choose an outfit myself. Frankie's ideas are always better. Sitting up, I push around the clothes until I find my leggings and the sweater he practically shoved into my hands when we went shopping for this trip. It was twice what I would have paid for a sweater, but Frankie wouldn't let me leave the store, let alone Phoenix, without it.

"You're too good at this. It's annoying."

He smacks his lips. "I know. It's a gift."

There's a knock on the cabin door that pulls my attention. "Frankie, I have to go. Liv's here."

"Tell her I say hi and to return you to me in one piece."

Every friend I've ever had has inherited my older brother as well. We're a package deal, and Liv was no exception.

"Will do. Talk later." On my way to the door, I trip on a stray heel and snag the underwear off the floor. I twist the handle, and my shoulders sag, sighing in relief when I see her. "Liv."

Her smile is as bright as her almost full head of gray hair. "Myra." She pulls me into one of her big hugs. "I saw your light on and thought I'd say hi before heading out for the day. Getting ready to hit the slopes?"

I pull back and open the door wider for her to enter. Her eyes widen when she sees the mess I've made of the cabin. "The good news is that I settled on an outfit thanks to Frankie."

She laughs and tucks her hands into her front jeans pockets. "He always did have an eye for putting together outfits."

"It's a blessing and curse." I move around the studio space, picking up shirts, pants, pajamas, and socks while she stands in the entryway. "What are you up to today?"

"I'm running into town to do some grocery shopping and wanted to see if you needed anything?" she asks.

I shove the stray items in my hands back into my open suitcase. "I could use a few things. I'll text them to you."

Liv is in her sixties and doesn't have a husband or kids but plenty of hobbies to keep her busy outside of work. I admire her for that.

She pushes one of her many ringlet curls away from her face. "Alright, I'm off. Text me your list, and maybe we can make dinner together tonight since I've got book club tomorrow."

I relax and clutch Frankie's outfit choice to my chest like it's my life ring in the treacherous sea of singledom. "I'd love that."

Liv leaves, and I finish cleaning the space before jumping in the shower. I stare at my razor and then down at my body. It's been a while since I shaved my legs. Seeing as it's winter, the friction around my ankles and calves helps keep my socks up. But if there were a day to shave them, this might be it. I'm not saying I have expectations, but I'd rather be prepared.

I pick up my razor and twist it between my fingers. Even these thoughts feel foreign to me, like someone entirely different has hijacked my body and is taking it for a joyride. But maybe that's a good thing. Maybe that means, in a small way, I'm moving on.

Nodding, I lather up my legs and start shaving, instantly regretting the razor in my hand.

I need a weed whacker for this job.

Chapter Eight

Lincoln

She can't stay standing, upright, anything close to vertical… I'd probably take squatting at this point. We're only an hour into the lesson, and she's spent the majority of the time on the ground, which I feel terrible about. Good thing we got a fresh dump of new snow last night, and the powder has cushioned her fall. Hopefully. At least she's falling with a smile on her face.

The first time she landed on the ground was getting off the chair lift. If you've never done it before, it can be intimidating. I told her what to do and yelled *tips up* as we got closer, but she might have thought I said something else. The look she cut me was a mix of shock and maybe curiosity.

Needless to say, she, in fact, did not point the tips of her skis up high enough, and she did a face plant that turned her into a pretzel and forced the lifty to stop everything. The pink coloring in her cheeks was more than from the cold, so I did everything in my power to mitigate the situation with ridiculous jokes I borrowed from my dad. My face was hotter than after eating an entire bag of flaming hot Cheetos, but it seemed to work, and eventually, she got up again. Her persistence is really something. She wants to learn despite the struggle.

I'm parallel to the slope a couple of feet down from where Myra is flat on her back, staring up at the sky sans skis since they popped off. Again.

"People do this for fun?"

I pull down my neck-gaiter that's been warming my chin. "It's more fun when you're able to stay standing."

"I disagree," she says, aggressively shaking her head. "Because you can't do this on skis." She moves her arms up and down while her legs go side to side.

"Nice snow angel." I unclick from my skis, making sure they stay put and don't slide down the mountain without me. Then I stab my poles into the snow and walk up to offer her my gloved hand. "Come on. Let's keep practicing. You'll get there."

She shakes her head more. "Not until you try this."

Her arms and legs move in sync, creating winged depressions in the snow. Her mouth is open, catching stray snowflakes, but her eyes aren't visible through her goggles, so I can't tell if she's serious.

"I'm not joking," she adds.

Alright, so she is serious.

"I haven't made a snow angel since I was about five or six."

She pauses her movements and lifts her head. I think she's staring at me. "That was probably the last time you fell on skis, too, huh?"

She's not wrong. Growing up in a skiing family meant weekends, and some weekdays, were dedicated to ski lessons and full days on the mountain. Dad would even stash candies in his pockets to give us after every run down just to keep us motivated.

I wonder what kind of candy Myra likes…

"Just try it," she says, resuming her rhythmic motions. "You might be a big-time skier now who never falls or has to pretend you stopped so people wouldn't ask if you needed help, but this is still fun. Promise."

I'm guessing she's sharing from experience.

Even though I've never made a snow angel on the ski slopes, watching her do it makes me incredibly curious. And at least we are in the middle of the run. So, I walk around the skirt and wings she's creating to give me enough space to make my own and fall back in what feels like slow motion. Being on my back in the snow isn't something I'm used to, but it doesn't stop my muscle memory from kicking into gear.

Pumping my arms and legs, I create an angel. If Ted and Jake saw me right now, they'd have a good laugh over how ridiculous I look. But hearing Myra's encouraging, *there you go*, and hearing her carefree laugh makes it feel like we're the only ones around.

I'd probably throw snowballs at Jake if he were here anyway. I lit into him last night about how he was playing with Mom's heart and almost didn't leave Otto under his supervision today. He knows better than to give Mom false hope. But Jake's under the impression that any hope is better than none at all. He had the nerve to say *you're welcome* for sending our picture to Mom and Dad, so I slammed his door and left.

I *never* slam doors.

I'm still moving my arms and legs, thinking about our conversation, when the light above me gets blocked, and Myra is leaning over me, hands on her knees. "I think your angel's done," she says with a quirk of her lips.

I stop moving and sit up carefully, glimpsing back at my creation but only seeing half of it.

"Here, grab my arm, and I'll pull you up so you don't mess it up." She grips behind my elbow as I grab hers.

"Thanks," I say, using my knees to stand as she hoists me to a more vertical position.

Her smile is radiant as we face each other, our mingling breath turning to a cold mist as it passes our lips. She tips her chin. "Check out your angel."

I turn to stare down at our angels, who are holding hands… or wings. My angel is at least a foot taller than hers, but hers is more prominent. I can't help smiling at them because she was right…that *was* fun.

"Now we can get back to skiing," she says beside me.

I'm so caught up in the nostalgia and enjoyment of this small moment I take a minute to think about what we were learning before this. Stopping, bent knees, staying upright…

I search the area for her skis and poles, bringing them back to rest parallel beside her. "This may seem unconventional, but why don't you ski with me? It will keep the tips of your skis pointing down the mountain, and you'll get a feel for going more than a few feet." My voice is hesitant, as if I'm proposing we move in together instead of skiing.

"I thought I was skiing with you…"

I lift my goggles so she can see my eyes. It's not that she hasn't made any progress, but making snow angels part way down the mountain isn't exactly indicative of someone actually *skiing*. If I can teach her anything today, it's how to feel more confident about her skis so she can trust them.

"We are skiing together, but I meant you should stand between my legs." I squint at her and shake my head, trying again. "If you stand between my skis, with your back to me, you can hold onto my poles. I'll steer, and you just…feel."

Despite having her balaclava curled around her neck, I still see her swallow as I say this, the smooth lines of her throat moving with the motion. She drops her chin. "Okay, if you think that will help."

"I do. It'll help you to feel your skis moving across the snow without falling." It's how I learned, standing between Mom's skis as she held onto the training backpack I always wore. However, I've never done this with another adult, and hope it'll work.

I lower my goggles and help her position her skis between mine. Then I offer her my hand as she steps into one binding and then the other. She wobbles slightly and grips my hand tighter.

On instinct, I steady her with my other hand at her waist. "Find your balance," I say into her ear, which is covered by the ear flap of her helmet. "We won't go too fast, but you'll need to focus on leaning forward still, okay?"

She nods. "I can do that."

I exhale slowly, reaching for both of our poles standing beside us in the snow. I tuck mine under one arm and hers under my other. "Loop your arms around the poles. But stay leaning forward."

She hooks her elbow around each set of poles. "We won't fall?"

"As long as you lean forward," I say with a pinched laugh. "Let yourself relax; your skis will take you down the mountain, and I'll steer."

She nods. "Lean forward. Relax. Trust you."

"And trust your skis." I lean in, touching my chest to her back. Her ass is pushed back, fitting flush against me in a way I'd like in any other circumstance. "Maybe don't lean forward that much," I say, for my own sake. I don't want a hard-on by the end of this.

She stands straighter, pitching forward but with much less of a lean. "Better?"

I let out a breathy "yeah" because I wasn't expecting her to feel this good. I've been with at least enough women to know I like how they feel, even if it was never for long. Traveling from place to place didn't cater to relationships. "There's a small lodge off this run. Make it there without falling, and the first round is on me."

There's worry in her tone when she asks, "What happens if I make us fall?"

"Then you buy."

She nods but says nothing more as I shuffle and point the tips of our skis downhill. She tenses as our view changes. We're now staring down where the bright white slope seems to go on forever. Jackets of all different colors are speckled across the neutral backdrop, and trees line the run with a few ski trails intertwining them. We'll save those for another day.

I skate with my skis until our momentum gets us started. Our speed is slow compared to what I'm used to. Even when I have Otto running alongside me and I'm forced to drop my speed. But this is still faster than she's allowed herself to go. Even if it feels counterintuitive, being too slow will trip a person up every time. Speed is a requirement.

The top of the main lodge becomes visible, and even on this less steep green run, it looks like we're taking a nosedive straight for it.

"Don't crash us!" she demands through a scream.

"I got this."

"It doesn't feel like you got this." Our speed increases even more, and her grip tightens around the poles.

I peer over her shoulder as I lean into the left side of my "S" curve. "I do. Promise."

Small snowflakes hit my goggles, melting into wet droplets that race down the slick surface. Whenever I face us downhill, gaining speed, Myra makes a noise. A squeak, squawk, or some other sound I can't describe. She probably doesn't even know she's doing it since it seems more like an instinctual response to the ride we're on.

The wind whips tendrils of her hair that have escaped her helmet in front of my face, but I'm not complaining when her hair smells like rosemary and mint. This is working out better than expected, and even though her body clenches as we ski across the slope, she still finds it in her to laugh, releasing some of that tension.

"This isn't so bad!" she yells back to me.

"You're doing great."

"I'm doing it. I'm skiing!" she says loud enough for me to hear over the rush of wind we're sailing on.

She starts to arch back, but I push my chest into her spine, reminding her with my body to stay forward. There's a reason I emphasized this so much. It's a natural bodily response to lean back to slow down. But ski boots are structured to pitch the body forward, offering better balance.

The outside of her skis bump against the insides of mine as I steer us. "See that lodge to the left?"

She lifts her head from our skis. "Yeah. The one with the green roof?"

"That's where we're going," I say, eyes locked on our destination. "I'll stop us when we get closer; you just keep doing exactly what you're doing."

She pushes herself farther into the crook my body creates for her. "I trust you."

Three words that feel lethal inside me. In order to have attempted this, she had to hand me her trust. I just didn't think it would feel this good to be holding it. Liquid fire courses through my veins, and I set my jaw, more determined to stick this landing.

One last turn, and we're facing the lodge. I run our skis horizontally to the slope, coasting closer to the outdoor racks for our gear. I dig my heels in, leaning on the edges of my skis to both guide us to our destination and slow us down.

This lodge is a lot smaller than the main one at the bottom of the hill, thankfully making it less crowded near the racks of skis and poles. I dig my heel in even more, and we finally slow to a stop.

I stand to my full height, but Myra doesn't move. The wind is no longer crashing in my ears, and the voices of those entering and exiting the lodge are muffled by the blanket of snow outside. And though her breaths are coming quickly now that we've stopped, she's frozen in place.

"How did that feel?" I ask, loosening my grip on the poles as she does too. I rest one set on the rack and use the other pole to click out of my skis.

"That…" she starts. "Was…"

I unclick her skis for her, waiting for her to finish her thought, but she doesn't. So, I fill in the blank. "There's nothing like it."

Stepping off her skis onto the snow, she turns to face me, pushing her goggles to her forehead. They're crooked, but she doesn't seem to care. "It felt like I was flying. That was so…" She stares around us, searching for the right word while waving her hand. "Freeing."

How many times have I thought the same thing? Skiing is like flying, minus the real wings but giving you invisible ones, like our angels.

"You did great. It takes a lot to trust your skis—"

She wraps her arms around my neck before I can finish, coiling tighter and with enough strength to strangle a bear. But

I'm sure that isn't her intention, especially when she whispers *thank you* loud enough for me to hear.

"You're welcome," I say back, just as quietly.

She's incredibly soft and plush with all her gear on, but the shape of her is still distinguishable under it all. My arms can circle all the way around her with room to spare. She's tall enough that her chin fits just above my shoulder without needing to stand on her toes, and she's firm, like a peach that has the right amount of softness to eat but isn't rotten.

She's just right.

Myra pulls away fast, sniffling against the cold that has reddened the tip of her nose. Bending for her skis, she stands them beside mine in a rush, bypassing what just happened before I can take my next breath.

"We should get that drink," she says over her shoulder, already heading for the lodge, pumping her arms as she hits the top speed her clunky ski boots will allow.

I pull my gloves off in a daze. "Yeah, we should."

I'm not sure what that was all about. There was some skiing, thanking, hugging, and now… speed-walking? Did I say something wrong? Do something worse? I slow my stride as I follow behind her. I think the moisture in her eyes might have been good, but I slow my pace down even more to give her a little time to process.

Since I haven't checked my phone in a couple of hours, I pull it out of my pocket to see if I have any messages.

Of course I do.

The fake news Jake sent in our family text thread is still going strong. I've been asked a dozen times *who she is, how we met, when this happened,* in every way possible. If I continue to ignore them, it'll only get worse. I'm going to start getting phone calls and random drop-ins to perform well-checks if I don't say something soon. But if I respond, what am I supposed to say?

Mom and Dad seem genuinely excited, and making Mom sad right now is the last thing I want to do. It doesn't bode well for the fight she needs to focus on. Everything could affect her healing, even something as simple as a *fake* girlfriend.

There's no way Mom wasn't going to go absolutely ballistic over a girlfriend. She tells us often enough that she wants to live long enough to meet our wives. We couldn't be further from that reality right now, but damn if I don't want to be a little closer.

I rub my forehead and type in a few replies. Nothing feels right. Lying to my mom doesn't feel right. But as I read through some of the messages I've missed, I land on one from her.

Mom: She's beautiful, Lincoln. I don't even need to meet her to know you picked a good one.
Mom: But also, please bring her this weekend or no leftovers for you.

There's no logical reason why I respond the way I do other than the fact I'd rather lie to my mom than disappoint her and take away any semblance of happiness she has over my very fake girlfriend. *Damn you, Jake.* I can almost understand why he did this.

Me: I'll bring her to the house this weekend. Let me know what we can bring.

I'm going to pay for this.

Chapter Nine

Lincoln

Stomping my boots to get the snow chunks off, I can't stop thinking about the text I sent. I have to somehow ask Myra, a woman I know nothing about, to come with me to my parent's house. I don't even know what she does for work. She could be a lion tamer or a professional street magician. Not that either of those would be a deal breaker. They'd actually be pretty cool. But the fact is that I don't know enough about her to invite her to game night with my overbearing family. They will swallow her whole and never let her leave. Mom will suggest getting matching tattoos, and Dad will offer her a green tea face mask.

And on top of all that, I have to figure out what to bring. Chocolate chip cookies or wine? Beer or grilled crostini with roasted cherries, basil, and goat cheese? I'm already sweating from the pressure of it all. I'll spend the next few days perusing recipes, reading blogs about what to bring to introduce your parents to the fake girlfriend you barely know, and frequenting my local grocery store to stress-shop for five different options. Pam in produce will think I've gone mad when I tell her. Normally, I'd just bring myself, but adding a fake girlfriend means impressing her in front of my parents.

Tonight. I'll deal with all of this later tonight. I need to put it out of my mind and focus on getting to know her more. And then ask her to be my girlfriend.

No big deal. I'll just add stress-eating to that list, too.

The lodge is small enough to be cozy but still big enough not to feel like every word you speak is heard by a neighboring table. There's a food counter along the back wall and windows matching the main lodge wrapping all the way around the front, offering a three-sixty view that the Bridger mountains always deliver on.

Myra hasn't gotten further than finding a table in a corner by the large windows. She's already shedding gear when I approach, removing my helmet and gloves. "I'll buy us some drinks. Do you prefer beer or wine?" I ask, unzipping my red coat, which has already become stifling.

"Beer," she says, doing the same. "Anything on the light side. If they only have dark stuff, I won't drink it."

Beer drinker, I add to the mental list titled *All About Myra*.

"Alright, I'll be back." I like that I don't have to guess with her. So far, she's been nothing but straightforward about pretty much everything from snow angels to beer. I hate when I have to guess what someone likes. The pressure of it feels unreal, stressing me out by all the potential options.

Weaving my way through tables to get to the bar is a route I'm familiar with. New settings are sometimes riddled with anxiety for me for the same reasons noise is. It's overwhelming. But not here, in an environment I know well. Sometimes I take

Otto up here just to have a quiet moment during our breaks. I'll get a coffee for me, water for him, and sometimes we'll share a burger. The kitchen knows to add an extra patty on the side for him. But Otto isn't here today; Myra is. The woman I told my ailing mother with breast cancer I'd bring to game night in a few days.

Was that a bad idea? It was a bad idea. *Shit.* It was a horrible idea.

Based on the last conversation with Myra yesterday, she seems like the kind of girl I could be into. Beautiful, funny, blunt, and…more beautiful. I just need to feel her out to see if there's more than attraction there. Maybe a date before game night would help? Something more official than ski lessons but a step down from matching tattoos.

Ordering two lagers from one of my favorite local breweries, I bob and weave my way back to our table. She's staring out the window, her jacket discarded on the back of the chair. Her braid hangs over one exposed shoulder thanks to her thick tan sweater with a wide neckline. I only know about her cream lace bra because the strap is visible against her olive skin.

One shoulder is enough to make me curious. Two might be lethal. I'm not sure if that makes me more nervous to screw this up or more excited for Mom to see her up close and not in a picture.

She smiles when she sees me approach, and I hand her the beer. "This color is perfect," she says.

I clink my glass with hers. "Is that how you choose a beer? By color?"

She licks the foam off her top lip, which I try not to stare at like a deprived man, and sets her glass down. "Yup. Dark beers are a definite no. Orange, or amber—whatever the hell they call it—is a borderline maybe. I have to be in the mood. Light beer is perfection. And this one," she points at the lager, "is exactly what I like."

I add another bullet point to my list: *only drinks light beer*. "I'm glad you like it."

She clenches and unclenches her hand on the table. "Sorry about…jumping on you like a wild monkey outside. It was the first time during this trip that I haven't wanted to break my skis on a tree or throw my poles like a spear."

I laugh behind the rim of my beer. "Are you saying I changed your mind about skiing?"

"Today you did." She offers me a sly smirk before taking another sip.

"I'm relieved I saved you from paying for broken skis and lost poles." This isn't a cheap hobby.

"You should be." She lightly kicks my shin beneath the table. "Oh, and I almost forgot."

She reaches into the pocket of her coat hanging on the back of her chair, pulls out a small bag of dog treats shaped like little bones, and slides them across the table.

I pick them up and weigh them in my hands. "Thanks. I might let Otto have one of them."

She laughs, making my heart swell with pride that I did that. I can make her laugh. This is a good sign. We're flirting, and I'm not retreating inside the neckline of my henley like a turtle.

Her dark lashes fan the tops of her mostly still red cheeks, and a light coating of makeup catches the light and shimmers on her eyelids. I set my glass down a little too hard and try to return to neutral territory of discovering more about her. "So, what do you do for work?"

She sips her beer. "I'm a high school science teacher."

I raise my brows.

"It's not as bad as it sounds," she defends. "They're hilarious."

I keep my brows lifted. "I was a high school boy once."

"Okay, fair. It's not always laughter and rainbows. Sometimes it's farts and pranks, but I like what I do. I know I'm genuinely making a difference when conversations move from the scientific method to their future goals and aspirations."

"I wish I could say I had those at eighteen."

She rests her cheek on her propped fist. "Did you always want to be a ski patroller?"

I shake my head and snicker. "Not exactly. It was something I fell into more than chose, even though I've been skiing my whole life. Jake wanted it more than I did. I wanted to travel and needed money to do it, so after working here each winter as a lifty, I decided to get my needed certifications when I turned eighteen and became a ski patroller. There's not much money in seasonal work, so I filled the gaps by working at a sporting goods store during the off-season."

"So, you grew up knowing how to ski like some of those toddlers with the little backpack leashes and clips on the front of their skis?" she asks, repressing a smile.

"Pretty much." I laugh at the visual. "My parents were big skiers, and it became a family thing we did every winter." Getting my job back a year ago when I moved home wasn't hard. Jake had already been here long enough to put in a good word with the new boss, and the fact I came recommended from Canada with an avy dog made it an easy process to get re-certified in the states.

It's not that I don't like what I do. After traveling for a while, I eventually made my way back to the mountains. This time, it was to Whistler. It's where I got Otto and the place that brought me back to my roots before returning to my actual roots in Montana. But without that time in Canada, I'm not sure I would have been able to appreciate my hometown like I do now.

There's pride in working in a place where I see so many people I know every day.

"What about you?" I ask, turning the conversation back to her. "Have you been in Arizona a while?"

"My whole life," she says with a nod. "I'm the youngest in my family with an older brother who would probably put chains on my ankles if I tried to move."

"You're close?"

She nods again.

"And he didn't want to learn to ski?"

She barks out a laugh. "Frankie? *Hell no.* He hates the cold even more than I do. But not as much as my ex."

I swallow my sip. It's the first time she's mentioned an ex. My mental pen is ready to jot down important details. "Did you just break up with him?"

She pulls her foot onto the chair, hugs her bent leg, and smiles sweetly. "I love how you assume I'm the one who'd break up with him."

"Well…I…no…" I stutter. "I just figured that he wouldn't want to break it off if he were dating you." I know I wouldn't. Mostly because I'm as loyal as they come, but also because Myra is magnetic. I'm instantly curious about what caused the breakup but aware of how rude it would be to come right out and ask.

Her lips part as she studies me. "We were married, actually."

Not what I expected, though it doesn't bother me. *Separated/ divorced* goes on the list. "For how long?"

"Long enough." She scoffs. "And no, I didn't break it off. That was all him. Decided he didn't want to be married, I guess. He had a lot of other things he loved more than me, but I didn't notice until he brought up the separation. Or maybe I didn't want to. But by that point, I should have known things wouldn't change. I'm just a stubborn ass who made vows and meant them.

I wasn't going to give up. He'd have to be the one to leave. And he was."

She breaks eye contact and regards her beer, biting her cheek like she doesn't want to show emotion. I want to lift her chin with my finger and tell her how strong she is. Being married to someone and finding out you want different things would shock the system, among other feelings. The need to reassure her runs thick in my veins—how this ex of hers isn't worthy to see the joy she had on her face before hugging me outside.

But instead of reaching across the table for her chin, I go to squeeze the arm hugging her leg. She stares at my hand and then my eyes. I should tell her that he didn't ruin her. At the very least, I should say that whatever her reasons for wanting to learn to ski, she can do it. I'll help teach her for as long as it takes. We'll practice early in the mornings before I start work and take the time to ski a few runs during my lunch break. I'd do that because a woman like Myra shouldn't be boxed up. She should be free and feel that every single day.

Her lips part, eyes wide and unblinking. She's surprised I'm touching her. I'm surprised I'm touching her. But the sadness that swallowed up our table in the span of a few sentences is staggering. Maybe no words are needed. Maybe just touching her is saying enough.

So, I don't pull away.

Chapter Ten

Myra

I'm two beers, one salad, and a basket of fries deep into this non-date that feels a lot like a date.

We've talked about everything from the avy dog certification test to my life in Phoenix to the perfect crisp-and-salt ratio of the fries. There really is a science to it. With little space between our words and even fewer between our sentences, I haven't had a conversation like this with someone else in a while. Not even with Frankie. Most of my friends were Wade's friends, and the others disappeared when they found out we weren't together anymore. Nothing clears a room faster than saying, *I'm divorced.* I might as well have said, *I'm going to steal your husband and suck his blood.*

Lincoln leans back in his chair, resting his ankle over his knee. "Favorite sport?"

We've been here for an hour, but for the past fifteen minutes, we've been going back and forth, asking each other random questions. I asked what vegetable he would choose to be for the rest of his life. He picked an asparagus, making me laugh and almost spit out my beer. He asked me what my favorite color was, and I was able to answer that question immediately—Hawaii ocean blue, no question. And while I don't exactly have many hobbies, I know most sports are not my thing.

I grab another fry and shrug. "None of them."

"Really? None?" he asks in disbelief. "I'm not just talking about the most popular sports like football or basketball. What about volleyball, dodgeball, golf…pickleball?"

He doesn't understand that balls and I do not get along. Well, the ones used in sports, at least. "I tried playing pickleball at my gym and had an imprint of the small holes on my forehead for three days. Not to mention, I was the youngest one there." I bite into my fry. "Volleyball looks way too intense…" I'd likely die on the court, refusing to admit defeat. "And dodgeball…" I shake my head. "I don't even want to know how many bruises I'd give people."

He laughs, but I add, "And if I have to sit through another round of golf, I will bury my head in the little sand pit they have like an ostrich."

He lifts his brows. "Fair enough. So, is that the real reason you want to learn to ski? No balls?"

I twist my lips up and cross my arms. "That's two questions."

"It's generally in the same vein," he says with a grin and a laugh that raises the hair on my arms.

I let it slide because I *really* like his smile. "Yes…and no."

"Okay. That's a bit mysterious."

"Wine made me do it."

He nods and studies me through a squint as if I'm bluffing.

But admitting I'm here because of wine isn't a complete lie. Spending my first Christmas as a divorced woman, sleeping in my old twin bed at my parent's house, wasn't how I saw my life going. A couple of glasses the size of my face later and…I'm sitting with Lincoln in this lodge.

But once I got here, I realized that skiing is basically my Everest.

"The divorce was hard." That's an understatement, but no need to spew my guts here. "I realized how much I'd lost in the aftermath and wanted to get myself back. So, skiing seemed like a good challenge, and I'm not one to turn down an opportunity to compete."

He keeps nodding. "And who are you competing against?"

"Myself." I draw my brows together like this should be obvious.

There's no way I could last another day inside my apartment alone without digging my way out with nail clippers like a full-on prison break scenario. No one locked me in my apartment. It was all me. But based on how I was living, you'd think they had. "Skiing is going to help me be happy again. Maybe I'll even ski the Alps one day."

His expression softens, and he leans closer. "For what it's worth…I think you can."

My lips part, and damn it if my legs don't feel a little weak even though I'm sitting.

Lincoln is the kind of guy who says things like this. It's what people need to hear most. His words are like a thick coating of oil that gets on everything. It stains your clothes, sheets, and couch, but you remember…every. Fucking. Word. You feel seen and heard, like all of your reasons for doubting yourself seem silly now that you're sitting with him and his words. You feel as if this trip is worth more than the flight miles and tears you shed to get here.

So, maybe it's just me.

"My turn." I clear my throat and quickly ask the first thing that pops into my head, which is a recycled question from one he asked me. "Favorite color."

"Red," he says quickly.

I lean back and cross my arms, chin jutting up in question. "Why?"

"That's two questions." He smirks.

I drink my beer and set it back on the small table. "Damn right it is. Now, answer."

He laughs, drops his foot to the ground, and scoots closer to the table as if sharing a secret with me. I love secrets, especially when they aren't mine. "When I was in Mexico a year ago, an elderly woman was dancing in the streets with two younger girls, maybe her granddaughters. Multiple people had gathered, and a few men played instruments for them. The way she danced looked like she'd done this her whole life. She was comfortable in her skin with the flow of the music. And to me, it seemed she was completely content like dancing was her reason for breathing." His gaze floats somewhere past my shoulder. "She was wearing a red skirt."

My mouth runs dry as the picture in my mind develops. "Wow. That's...so beautiful."

"She was," he says, meeting my eyes and staring at the table. "I got food poisoning that night, so the event was well documented in my memories."

This makes me laugh. The kind that starts in your belly, and you feel it vibrate up through your throat before it comes out.

His gaze drops to my lips and then back to the table, a small smile lighting his face, too.

I steady my breathing. That smile of his is so innocent, yet more deadly than I think he knows what to do with. The laughter that fills my whole body is replaced by a warmth that courses through my veins. I'm hoping the two beers will be enough explanation for my flush.

Regardless of how good it feels to be here, laughing with him, a part of me still feels like I'm cheating on Wade. He'd always get jealous whenever any man paid me attention, and they did. I wasn't trying to attract them, but I was loud and fun and enjoyed living. That woman feels miles away. But tonight…I don't know. Maybe I see pieces of her.

"So, are we skiing tomorrow?" I ask because I really want to see him again. I'll sleep better if I know I will. I'd forgotten what it felt like to look forward to something.

"I think we should. If you're going to be skiing the Alps by next winter, you'll have to practice."

I bark a laugh. "Like I'll be ready for that. I can't go to the Alps by myself. Who's going to make sure I don't get buried in the snow?"

"I will."

A promise, an idea…what?

I will.

I'm so focused on trying to read between the sounds he just made with his mouth, I don't notice the tiny human who materialized out of nowhere.

Her brown braid brings me straight back to yesterday. "Hi," she says, voice already grating on my every nerve.

I give her my best pinched smile. "Hello."

"Hey, Sadie." Lincoln gives her a small wave. "Are you with your family?"

She shakes her head and juts out a hip. "My ski instructor."

Lincoln peers around us, hunting for said instructor. "Who's with you today?"

"I forget." She shrugs and pulls off her gloves. "I left them after the chair lift."

Why does this not surprise me at all?

Lincoln tries to hide a laugh. "Sadie, you can't just ditch your instructor."

"Well, I did."

I inhale through my nose and bite my lips.

"So, are you guys boyfriend and girlfriend, or what?" she blurts out.

Sadie's question catches me off guard, so my hurried, "No!" comes out just as abruptly as her question.

"You're always together now," she says without disguising her sassy tone.

How would she know this? Has she been spying on us or something? I guess this goes with that small-town ski resort vibe Lincoln told me about. I'm not used to running into the same people, especially those who aren't even five feet tall yet.

If Lincoln's surprised by this conversation, he doesn't let on. "I'm just helping Myra with some ski lessons. You know, the thing you should be out doing," he says in an even voice.

"I already know how to ski," she spits back. I don't think she bought our responses, but she doesn't press. Instead, she wanders toward the food area without so much as a *see ya later*.

Lincoln shakes his head and pulls out his phone. "I can guarantee I know who her instructor is today."

"How do you know?"

"This isn't the first time she's ditched him." He types out a message and then puts his phone face down on the table.

I laugh to myself at the thought. As much as it pains me to admit this, I see a lot of myself in Sadie. Ditching ski instructors for her was like ditching Frankie for me. He was always hovering, and I wanted some freedom, even if I just went to the back of the grocery store by myself.

"I can't believe she thought we were together," I say, my internal thoughts now being spoken out loud.

He cocks his head. "Oh yeah? Why's that?"

I go mute. Apparently, he doesn't think it's so inconceivable. "I don't know. Because we barely know each other. I'm just some random woman who ran into you, and now you're forced to teach me how to ski since I'm a full-blown liability."

"You're not a liability." He pauses to think about that. "Well, more so to yourself than others. But I'll help you get more confident on skis, and then you'll tear up the Alps."

I lower my gaze and study him. If he's bullshitting me, I can't tell. The sincerity that's laced every other word he's ever said is his alibi, so I let it go.

His eyes land on a spot above my head. "Shoot. I need to go get Otto and check in with the other patrollers."

I straighten in my chair, placing two flat hands on the table. "Right, of course. Just because I'm on vacation doesn't mean everyone is."

He stacks our empty cups and trash while gathering our gear. There's a quiet tension pulsing just below the surface. Maybe it's the conversation we just had. He has to think the two of us dating would be at least a little crazy. We're strangers—two people who didn't know each other days ago. And I'm *divorced*—a new label I'm still getting used to.

He clears his throat and hands me my gloves. "Maybe you'd want to hang out tonight?"

Strangers or not, he doesn't seem swayed by it one bit. I can't tell if he's asking me out on a date or asking me to chill as a friend.

"You could come to my place tonight and go in the hot tub? It's great after a day of skiing. I live with some other guys, but they'll be gone tonight. Plus, we don't live far from here. I'll feed you, too." It sounds like he's rambling.

Today might not have been a date, but what he's proposing might just be the definition. Dinner, hot tub, privacy…there's really no other way to interpret what he's asking now. There's only one way to find this out.

"You're asking me out on a date," I say plainly.

His Adam's apple bobs in his throat. "Yes?"

I had dinner planned with Liv, but rescheduling would be easy enough. Then again…I'm here for *me*, not to throw all my plans out the window for another man. "I can't tonight."

"Tomorrow night?"

He isn't backing down. *Interesting.* I shrug and say, "Book club."

Liv never invited me to book club, but I like seeing the determined set of his shoulders and the light blush on his cheeks.

He nods and taps his fingers on the table. "How about Thursday?"

I almost shake my head, dragging this out even more. But then I stop myself. I *want* to hang out with him. I want to talk more and discover how he turned out to be such a teddy bear while his brother is some version of Hugh Hefner. Aren't I trying to get better at listening to what I want?

"Let me confirm my plans tonight, and I'll text you," I find myself saying. It's not like Liv wouldn't understand.

"Great, okay," he says, surprised, then sends me a text with his address.

We start to head back outside. I've gotten better at clicking into my skis without falling over—*progress*—and Lincoln brackets my skis with his to finish the run back to the main lodge.

On the way down with Lincoln's body curled around me and feeling the wind kiss my cheeks again, I notice something I haven't in a while.

There are a lot more colors in this world than I remember.

Chapter Eleven

Myra

If I thought picking an outfit to wear skiing was hard, deciding to bring the two-piece bikini I bought on a whim was harder. Along with my thirties came an extra layer of fluff around my edges. And by edges, I mean my boobs and my hips. They're softer than they used to be. Softer than before I married Wade and even softer since our divorce. I blame Frankie for making me buy this post-divorce swimsuit that says I am young, single, and ready to mingle.

I am *none* of those things.

Young passed me by when I officially hit my mid-thirties, and even though I'm technically single, I still don't feel it. Maybe I'll always twirl the phantom ring on my finger.

But after a freak-out text to Frankie and another to Liv asking to cancel, I forced the black bikini into my purse, threw a dark blue sweater and yoga pants over it—because *balance*—and drove to the address Lincoln sent me. It was only a fifteen-minute drive from Liv's in the direction of the ski resort, but every mile had me questioning whether I should turn back.

I'm mingling.

That's what's happening here. And I don't know if I'm ready for that either. I just signed divorce papers two weeks ago. Mingling should happen a year from now, when I'm happier and less likely to spam Wade's email with fake offers for pubic hair trimming.

Lincoln will soon figure out I'm a ticking time bomb ready to explode. I'm not all that great of a human, either. I don't like eating leftovers, talking about my feelings, or watching anything other than Gilmore Girls. And if it weren't for Frankie, I'd never buy myself new clothes. I also suck at parking. The last one is only relevant because I've pulled in and out of Lincoln's driveway twice already, trying to even out my car. *I need the damn lines!*

Considering it good enough, I get out and tug at the hem of my sweater. "Here we go." I release a breath I won't be able to later when I'm stripped down to my bikini and step out of my car. I immediately gaze up. Lincoln's place is like a log cabin on stilts. *Oh my God!* His house is made of Lincoln Logs. I have to text Frankie about that later.

The ground level has two covered garage ports, and the second level has a wrap-around porch with large windows in the front. I shut my car door and walk carefully toward the stairs leading to the front door. I'm huffing and puffing and ready to blow this house down by the time I reach the landing outside, but I didn't slip despite the wet steps that were recently shoveled. My boots are also new, making traction on the slippery wood a non-issue—a major win.

Between the stair climber I took up here and my nerves, I have to place a steadying hand over my heart to get it to relax.

Showing up to his house says *things*. There's tension between us, and it's not exactly screaming *I want to be your friend.* Instead, it's saying something along the lines of, *I need to see what's under all of your clothes.*

Mingling is the least of my worries.

"You don't have to do anything you don't want to," I tell myself.

I repeated this multiple times on the way over and hold firmly to it still. My bestie, Flo, dried up and left me completely alone to face the…possibilities of tonight. After five days of cramps and self-loathing, I miss her. If I have to, I'll bring her back as my crutch. I don't like doing much when periods are involved. It's truly like a third person to worry about in the bedroom.

I haven't been in this position in a long time. Standing outside a man's door, carrying a bikini in my purse, which is nestled between my antacids and pepper spray, ready to eat whatever dinner he made for the two of us. Wade never even made me dinner, claiming takeout was far easier and worth the few extra bucks. Lincoln might as well be offering me a lifetime commitment along with dinner.

The warm glow of lights from inside filters through the four small glass panels in the door, inviting me to knock and get out of the chill. All I have to do is knock.

Here I go.

Right now.

Do it.

I hover my closed fist over the deep navy blue of the door but can't seem to let it touch. It's like my body is keenly aware of how big a deal it is to be here. I might just walk into this house and leave a different person. Lincoln isn't Wade. Lincoln has a dog, which makes him ten times more likable. That's just *dog math.*

Before I can hypothesize the junk out of this situation, the door opens, and I drop my hand while still hanging onto my breath. I blink several times before realizing what I'm looking at on the other side—I didn't expect him to be in an ape costume or eating a banana. I'm face to face with a man that isn't Lincoln. "Um, hi."

"I'm Ted," he says, biting into his banana. "You're Myra."

The scrape of nails on wood is loud as it gets closer. I wasn't prepared for *three* dogs to come skirting around the corner and pushing around Ted's legs to get outside, but here we are. My knees bend on instinct, ready to be licked, loved, and welcomed unconditionally by the only animal on the planet with this ability. Fight me on this.

I may have underestimated the power of three eager dogs. I'm on my ass in two seconds flat, being given more puppy kisses than I know what to do with. And I'm pretty sure I just fell in love.

"Otto, Bernie, Milo!" Ted whistles, and all three dogs rush back inside and sit, tongues hanging out the sides of their mouths and panting hard. Otto's bushy tail thumps against the ground, but he stays put while the black lab's tongue hangs out and the golden goddess with shinier hair than me stares at me with steady eye contact. I'm so impressed, I almost forget we're not alone.

Ted offers me a hand, but I wave him off and right myself both feet again, pushing flyaway hairs off my forehead and wiping slobber from my cheeks. "I'm Myra." He already knows this, but I confirm anyway. I lift the hand that wouldn't knock on the door minutes ago. "I'm here to see—"

"Lincoln," Ted says with a nod. "He told us."

Ted is likely one of Lincoln's roommates he talks to about an assortment of things, but my stomach can't help fluttering at the thought I was one of those things.

"Ted, invite the woman in." Jake approaches and shoves Ted with his shoulder. He pets each dog and turns his attention to me, waving me in. "Sorry about him. He's more of a wild animal than the dogs, as you can tell. It's good to see you again, Myra."

I'm not prepared for what I just walked into.

I don't remember Lincoln saying his brother was his roommate. The way they're both staring at me makes me think this is serious. Like *meet the friends* serious.

"Hi again, Jake." I can't do anything about it now, so I step inside on the rug and see a bunch of large man-shoes lined up at my feet. I slide my boots off, too. Mine are like little elf shoes comparatively.

Jake shuts the front door, snatches the banana out of Ted's hand, and then gives me his most saccharine grin. "Good ski day?"

Ted scowls at Jake.

All three dogs are still just sitting there. Their energy from our first hello has waned, and they're calmly watching me. I'm tempted to ignore Jake's question and play with the dogs instead. "Yeah. Lincoln knows his stuff."

Maybe I should get three dogs instead of one…

"You're here for Lincoln, huh?" Jake asks as if, by chance, I might be here for him. He rests his bent arm on Ted's furry shoulder in a confident stance. From the front, I can't tell he has a mullet. But whenever he turns his head, the side view is all nineties. He's a wannabe Slater from *Saved by the Bell,* and I cannot unsee this.

"I am." I tuck a piece of hair behind my ear. "You're both his roommates then."

"Roommates, friends, coworkers…" Jake points at his chest, "Brothers…all of the above."

Ted keeps staring at me but puts his hand out in front of Jake. "Can I have my banana back?"

"Later." Jake clears his throat. "So, Myra, Linc told us you were from Phoenix. Are you planning to be here long?"

I'm pretty sure I blink a thousand times before saying, "I'll be here for another week. I got here a few days ago."

Lincoln must have told them a lot. Enough that they seem to know me better than I know them at this point. Arguably more than I know myself.

"What are you guys doing out here?"

I peer over my shoulder at Lincoln, walking into the increasingly small space to join the conversation—three men, three dogs, and one woman who isn't sure what the hell she's doing here. But then I do a double take and turn my body to take in the work of art that is Lincoln. His dark hair, usually hidden beneath his beanie, is thick with waves tonight and perfectly mussed up. His face is clean-shaven, but the width and height of his smile causes my breath to hitch. It's so welcoming like he's been waiting all afternoon for this. I know I have.

He walks closer, and I'm positive I'm now pregnant. I don't understand this. "Hey, Myra."

He smells of oregano, basil, and garlic, immediately triggering me to take a deep inhale and steal all the air in the room. Coming to my senses, and realizing all of the eyeballs are on me, I finally say, "Hi."

My gaze tracks down to the long, linear column of his neck where a few buttons of his long-sleeve shirt are open. *Great. His neck is perfect.* I tell myself the few extra seconds I spend there are not that noticeable as I continue my journey down, landing on the apron tied around his slim waist. My mouth is suddenly full of saliva, and I have to swallow. *Hard.*

Lincoln is like a sexy chef, complete with an apron and a dash of salt and seduction. He's wearing a basic pair of jeans that hug his ass to perfection—I don't even need a three-sixty view to know this—and a t-shirt half-tucked into the apron with marinara smeared across his low abs. My ovaries are screaming at me right now. I didn't know men cooking me dinner could be so hot. New kink unlocked. Now I know and want nothing more than to be the one to take that apron off him.

I'm very hot now, sweltering in this sweater, *v single*, and ready to do more than mingle.

Down girl.

Chapter Twelve

Lincoln

"Ted, what the hell are you wearing?" My gaze is glued to his gorilla onesie.

I pat the side of my leg and snap my fingers to call Otto over. He's had to wait for long enough and wastes no time sniffing Myra like she's a turkey leg he'd like to devour.

I get it.

We all stare at Ted's outfit, even Ted.

Jake pipes up, "He lost a bet."

Bernie and Milo follow Otto's lead, tails thwacking against our legs.

Ted shrugs. "It's comfortable. I'm kind of glad I lost."

The number of bets these two make is too many to keep up with. I don't even ask when I see one of them doing something ridiculous like chugging a cup of apple cider vinegar, wearing a tutu down the mountain, or apparently, wearing an ape costume on a random weekday night. Somehow, I've avoided getting involved in them until recently with this fake girlfriend nonsense.

My gut churns at the thought. I don't want to let anyone down, especially Mom. I shove the feeling aside and focus on the beautiful woman in front of me before she disappears.

Otto circles Myra's legs, wagging his tail and making his entire back half move with the motion. Myra's face is bright with joy as she pets him. Thankfully, she seems to be a dog person, or this would have ended before it started. Even fake dating someone who didn't love dogs would be impossible since Otto and I are a package deal.

Just not tonight.

"Cool, well, Myra and I are going to eat and use the hot tub," I explain, again but hope it sounds more casual than the mirror rehearsals I did earlier. "You guys were just about to leave?" It's a command couched as a question. I clarified earlier they needed to get lost multiple times in the two hours I'd been home. And to take the dogs. I don't invite women over. Ever. I'm not going to mess this up or share.

Jake nods. "Right, yeah. We were just leaving." He claps Ted on the shoulder, and it makes a muffled sound due to the thick layer of fur coating his body. "We're going over to Gemma's house tonight. Won't be back until real late."

"Gemma's?" Ted asks, brows drawing in. "I thought you didn't like her?"

Jake shakes his head. "I don't, dude. Not like that. Come on, let's just go."

Ted nods slowly, red hair flipped up and bouncing with the motion.

I slip around Myra and open the door for them. "See ya."

Jake gives me a wink as he slides his white Crocs on.

Ted searches for shoes, but each one is too small to wear over those gorilla feet. So, he shrugs and walks outside without any. He whistles for the dogs to follow, and they rush outside with the promise of adventure. There's really no adventure quite like riding on the icy roads in Jake's minivan he inherited from Mom at sixteen. Seven years ago.

"Have fun, Linc!" Jake calls back, but I'm already shutting the door behind them.

Turning to Myra, I try to keep calm and not act as weird as my roommates. "Are you hungry?"

She hums. "Very."

I wave a hand toward the kitchen. "Follow me."

Her eyes have barely left my apron, so with her trailing behind me, I look down to make sure there's nothing on it to draw her attention. From what I can tell, it's fine. No wrinkles or any food caked on it. I found it at a thrift store like most of my things. It's cheaper and more sustainable.

I've spent all afternoon concocting ways to casually ask Myra to come to my parent's house this weekend for games. I could just ask her on a date like I did tonight. But there's no way all the questions my parents would ask wouldn't indicate we were a full-fledged dating couple, not just on a date. They'd want to know when we met, how, why, and some obscure tidbit only I would know about her. There's no way a date would fly when they've already read the word *girlfriend*.

I don't know why I'm thinking about going through with this and asking her to come. Okay, maybe I do. This would be a gift to Mom, and though lying would probably kill me, it wouldn't kill her. Breast cancer has forced her to appreciate the passing moments with more weight, but that doesn't mean there are moments I catch her without a smile. I hate that. I hate how she's fighting so hard to be here with us while worrying about not being here one day. Knowing I could put a smile on her face with the news of a girlfriend is a big deal to me.

This will put a smile on her face for all eternity.

The excited messages I've received from them have topped all other life events. I didn't get nearly as many confetti emojis when I told my family I was moving back to Montana.

We walk into the kitchen, and I head straight for the oven. I don't want to stress about this tonight. It's an actual date, and I want to enjoy it. Not wondering, *What Would Jake Do*, or thinking of Mom. Just a good 'ol romantic evening to see if we're soulmates.

Yeah, there's no way I haven't put pressure on tonight. *Shit.* I always do this. I sink too far and expect too much when this is just a date. This isn't marriage or a long-term, close-proximity, high-commitment relationship. Mom always says I lead with my heart, but I need to remember to keep it in check here. I need to let other body parts lead.

"It smells good, like you might know what you're doing," Myra says. "What did you make?"

"Lasagna, salad, bread, and wine," I say, hearing a small humming sound come from the back of her throat behind me. Desire stretches out like a cat in my gut. Thankfully, I'm wearing an apron. That's definitely in the top five things I thought I'd never say. "This is one of my favorite meals to make. You know, secret Italian family recipe and all that."

She leans back against the counter as I move around the space, slicing bread and pulling down two green-colored glasses I found at a thrift store. My hands shake slightly, but I'm hoping I'm the only one who notices. Her hum is still echoing in my ears.

She crosses her ankles, looking even more relaxed. Is she relaxed? I hope so. "Have you been to Italy?" she asks after clearing her throat.

I nod, locating the bottle of wine and pouring each of us a glass while calling on my Jedi mind tricks to keep my hand steady. My answer kicks into autopilot when I say, "I visited

Rome right out of high school and then Naples. I didn't make it down to Sicily, which I regret. I hope to go back one day." There isn't a bottle of wine I open to this day without thinking of the places I visited there, mostly because I drank more wine than water.

She swirls her wine. "What kind is this?"

"Malbec."

"Thank God."

My brows dip together. "Is that okay?"

"It's perfect." I spent no less than thirty minutes researching it before buying, so it better be good. She continues, "Let me guess, Italy was your favorite."

I've gotten this question before, but I never have an answer. "Every place I've been is my favorite for different reasons. India for the colors and warm spices, Italy for its wine and slow-paced lifestyle, and Australia for its accents and surfing. I can't choose one place."

She clinks her colored glass with mine and says, "I've traveled some," she starts to say wistfully. "But nothing as extensive as your time abroad, it seems."

She stares off. If I knew her better, I might say she looks almost remorseful. Does she wish she would have traveled more, taken more vacations? Most people do. I guess I got the itch from my parents. Their mug collection from around the world always inspired me.

She sips her wine and says, "My favorite part of traveling is the airport. Something about passing through a place with thousands of other people headed in different directions screams adventure to me. Oh, and getting a blueberry scone. Don't ask me why, but it's critically important."

As the bite of the wine glides over my tongue, I smile at her. I can't help it. One, because she just named my favorite part of traveling, and two, she's beautiful. Even in our kitchen's harsh, outdated, canned lights, her makeup-free face, hair in a high bun, and plump, wine-stained lips make me glad I asked her out. I never do stuff like that. Admitting this was a date when she asked made me second-guess myself.

But she said yes. And now I'm under whatever spell she cast that makes it impossible to look at anything but her.

"What made you come to Montana instead of, I don't know, the Alps? Or somewhere warmer?" I swap the glass in my hand for a plate to start dishing us up.

Her laugh is low, the sound light and airy as it escapes her mouth. "I told you, I needed a challenge. I wanted to go somewhere completely different. And the Alps aren't exactly teacher budget friendly."

I hand her a plate and then work on mine. "You'd be surprised what a few more lessons will do for you." I point us toward the dining room, which is really just two barstools pushed against our kitchen counter.

She's already hovering the plate under her mouth and taking a bite as I pull out the stools for us to sit. We're close enough together that we bump knees. I like touching her, but up until now, it's been unintentional or helpful. Like when I helped her after sliding through my legs or teaching her to ski. Very few times have I been able to bridge the gap between her space and mine.

Raising my glass again, I make a toast. "To one day skiing the Swiss Alps."

Her lips peel into a broad smile. "To the Alps."

We each take a sip, and I grab my fork that I'd tucked under the lasagna so it wouldn't fall off the plate. I'm not as rusty as I thought when preparing for tonight. It could be because Myra seems like the kind of girl I *want* to do these things for, a thought I've wrestled with all day. She doesn't live here and is only passing through. Whatever this is, it has an expiration date of seven more days. But if my parents have taught me anything, it's to keep my heart open and willing.

Myra's next bite is met with a low moan and has me shifting in my seat. "This is *so* good. It tastes like I'm actually in Italy right now."

Pride sits like a king on a throne in my chest. "You think so?"

"I do." She covers her mouth with her hand as she finishes another bite. "I'm gonna go ahead and guess you have a lot of secret family recipes. So, go ahead, 'fess up. Who taught you how to cook like this?"

I take a bite of lasagna. The question makes me feel weightless and even more sentimental than a scrapbook. "My mom. She worked on the kitchen staff in one of those fancy restaurants on a few different cruise ships a long time ago. After meals were served, she'd use the leftovers to experiment with new recipes for the other staff members. Found she really enjoyed it. But this sauce," I point at my plate and meet her gaze, "is a recipe I taught her. I wasn't kidding about rivaling what you can find in Italy, but that's also because I learned the basics there and added my flair later."

"Don't tell me…" She holds up a finger. "You learned how to cook from an old Italian family who owns a restaurant and, after helping them serve food during the lunch rush, offered to teach you how to cook and gave you their secret recipe?"

I throw my head back with a laugh, raking my fingers through my hair. "You're not that far off," I finally say. "But it was a little less made-for-TV. I took a cooking class at a local restaurant there."

"Oh my gosh." She leans her elbow on the counter, her wine glass hovering near her lips as she stares at me. "I know what happened next. This family also had a daughter your age, who was back in town for the holidays…" She pauses to think, then holds up a finger. "No! The daughter came home to help her long-lost father, who wanted her to take over the restaurant. After you fell in love, you both decided to fulfill his dying wish and save the family restaurant by getting married."

"So, the father is dying now?" I ask.

She talks around another mouthful. "Well, yeah. We need to up the stakes somehow."

"It's almost like you've watched enough of those movies to know their formula." I reach for the Malbec to refill her glass. "But yes, they did have a daughter. She was much older than me with two kids, a husband, and a drill sergeant attitude, though."

She levels me with a glare, a forkful of lasagna filling her mouth while she mumbles, "You're joking."

"I'm not."

"Damn. Bummer for you." She swallows. "So, when did you start traveling?"

"After a couple years of college. I flew to Europe, picked up a few odd jobs until I could afford to travel somewhere else, and repeated the process from one country to the next."

"Good for you," she says, taking a bite of the salad and closing her eyes. Lashes fan across her cheeks, and for a second, I imagine we aren't at the kitchen counter.

I stab at my greens, but I can't seem to keep my eyes off her. The way her jaw works, her neck moves, and her lips press together have me distracted. Tonight is going better than I expected. Being around her is better than being in my head. It doesn't feel like a chore, leaving me drained. My chest is lighter, and the usual ringing in my ears is quiet.

We continue eating, me sharing more stories from my travels and her sharing about her job as a teacher. I learned that high school boys are just as immature as Jake and how rewarding it would be *not* to find questionable sketches on the whiteboard. I tell her about the day I picked up Otto and how I couldn't bring him anywhere without getting stopped by women of all ages.

I've enjoyed our conversation more than I thought I would. I want to ask her about everything from her family history to the last book she read. There's an ease I have talking to her that isn't typically there for me. I don't have swagger like Jake or a clear direction and goals like Ted. I'm just a guy with a dog who likes talking to this girl. So much that I don't want the night to end.

An hour or so after dinner, I ask, "Did you bring your swimsuit for the hot tub?"

She slowly points to the front door with a sober expression despite the two glasses I poured. "It's in my bag."

"I bet your muscles are sore. You ready for that soak?" The way I hold my breath after saying this can't be good. I half expect her to say no only because it's going so well.

She wipes her lips with her napkin, eating up all the seconds faster than she ate her dinner. "Sure."

"The bathroom's down the hall to the left." I point in that direction. "There's a white robe hanging on the back of the door you can use to walk outside. It's cold, but it's not snowing. I'll clean up our plates."

"I'll be right back." She clenches and unclenches her fists before disappearing down the hall, and I hurriedly rush to clear and stack our plates, fill our wine glasses, and change into my board shorts. I plug in the outside Edison bulb lights hanging off the gutters around the roofline's edge and open the hot tub lid. Small snowflakes start to drift down, making the steam rising off the hot water even more inviting.

Rubbing my arms to brace against the cold on my skin, I head back inside the sliding glass door to wait in the living room for Myra. She's been in there a while, but I tell myself it's because I'm used to living with a bunch of guys.

I lean against the back of the couch and kick out my legs, crossing them at the ankles. And…I'm smiling. Like a genuine smile. The kind I'd have telling Mom what made me smile that day. One that isn't forced to make Mom feel better after getting hard news from her doctor or reassuring guests at the resort. The smile on my face tonight is genuine. And it's all because of Myra. I told myself I wouldn't ask her about coming to game night on Friday as my girlfriend, but after a great night, I want to.

I hope she's having a good time because I'm sold on the idea of seeing more of her.

Maybe *all* of her.

Chapter Thirteen

Myra

I can't go back out there. Not in this tiny bikini. No. Nope. I can't do it. It shrank in the wash, or I accidentally purchased the wrong size since my ass is filling out the bottoms so well, it's moved straight to *spilling* out.

Turning to the side, I suck in, then let all the air out of my lungs. Facing the mirror, I perform another push and tuck with my breasts. This isn't a swimsuit top—it's pasties. The severe lack of coverage and the intense lighting in this bathroom make me want to attempt a window exit. It doesn't matter that I'm on the second floor. I will tie the shower curtain and towels together to lower myself down and escape if I have to.

I exhale and slump forward. I'm normally not this self-conscious. I've always been proud of what my body looks like and what it's capable of. Except for lately, which has mostly just involved planking on different surfaces in my apartment.

But if I walk out there in this, Lincoln will think I'm trying to seduce him. I can't argue that it wouldn't make me feel better. The gentle touches on my knee or leg during dinner were enough to light my entire body up like a Christmas tree on the Fourth of July. It makes no sense, but it does. I missed contact like this…and the conversation. I'd forgotten what it felt like to feel interesting. Like what I had to say was important. Maybe sleeping with him would help. I'd forget about Wade and get lost in Montana with Lincoln.

I run a hand up my stomach, between my breasts, and up my throat. It's been so long since I've felt wanted by someone else, touched by someone other than me. Having Lincoln's hands on me might feel good. For him to touch his lips to my neck and run his fingers through my hair then grab a handful in his fist. Maybe then the doubts in my head would quiet down. These last six months would be forgotten, even if just for a night. And it could all start with a swimsuit. I know Lincoln's attracted to me and not because I'm a vain woman. He stares at me. *A lot.* And the way he leans closer like he can't help himself is enough to know he's definitely interested.

I trail my hand back down my body. I know what I like. I've explored myself enough to know, which is why not once this last year did I think that I needed anyone else. I didn't need Wade to please me. And I don't need a random man I'd likely meet at a bed and breakfast after my car broke down where I was stranded in his small town to help me. That never happened, but in case it did, I don't need *that* guy either.

But maybe I *want* Lincoln. And maybe that's okay.

I examine my body in the mirror again. There are areas I'm not crazy about, parts I'd alter or change altogether. Hours in the gym didn't stand a chance against chocolate. But not once in the last year did my body give up on me. I might have been down a heart, but I had a body that carried me through.

I roll my shoulders down and back, standing taller. I don't bother sucking my stomach in. This stomach took in and sorted nutrients to help me survive when all I gave it to work with were carbs and sugar. My knees and legs kept me standing when I wanted to crumble. My arms wrapped around me in a hug when no one else was there.

I'm still here, still standing. I got through the hardest time of my life, and I'll get through this, too. I will.

Snagging the bathrobe off the back of the door, I wrap it around my shoulders and shove my arms through but don't bother tying it. I leave it open because I want Lincoln to see how proud I am of this body. It isn't tainted by another man's hands. It's ready to start over.

I shove my other clothes in my purse and exit the bathroom, stopping briefly to hang it back in the entryway. Then, I stride confidently to where Lincoln leans against the couch.

"Ready."

I look at him, but he's too busy looking at me. Down my body and raking back up again, I feel him absorb every part visible beneath my robe like the wine we drank earlier. *He's one hundred percent checking me out.* I'm pretty sure the air around us is on fire, but I can't seem to pull my eyes away from him to confirm this or ask for an extinguisher. It's fine. I'll just burn alive.

His eyes meet mine, and I don't think he realizes how long he was looking down. It was long enough to make my hands tingle and the breath in my lungs to take a leisurely stroll out of my body. To make me want just a little more.

He swings an arm out, grabs the door handle, and slides it open. "This way."

The biting cold air hits the exposed parts of my skin without much warning, and a chill skates across my body, causing the few remaining hairs to stand. I can feel my nipples hardening as I take a step toward the door.

Being cold is one of my top five least favorite things in the world. Skiing and spending ten days in Montana, where they measure the snow in feet and not inches, was a stretch for me, but I was desperate. Being cold is nothing compared to being alone.

Trailing Lincoln, I step outside onto the deck, my bare toes immediately sinking into a foot of snow. The shock of the cold hits me, and I pull my foot back. Lincoln is already shirking off his robe, stepping up and into the hot water. "It helps if you do it fast," he says, pointing toward the steps.

I don't respond, too busy gawking at the body I assumed was under his clothes. But the reality is even better than imagined. Lean, toned muscles become the star of the show right before he lowers himself into the water.

So, this is the body I'll be sharing a hot tub with.

Lovely.

I stretch my legs wide, stepping in each of the depressions he made, and quickly make my way across the expanse of snow to the steps leading into the hot water I'm craving. My nipples are still taut and hurting as I pull off my robe and drape it over the railing alongside Lincoln's.

I scramble to get in and sink below the surface. Sharp tingles that feel like small pinpricks stab at my feet and ankles, but I'm warm, and that's all that matters. Sighing with relief, I close my eyes and lean back. This was so worth the short hike through Antarctica.

I open my eyes and untuck my feet from under me, stretching them out in the middle where Lincoln's feet already take up space. Our ankles knock against each other, but he doesn't move, so I keep mine there, too.

The steam wafts off the water and floats up to disappear into the black of night. It's dark out here. So dark, the stars are visible in the sky. I let my head fall back to study them, though I'm not entirely sure what I'm looking for. I marvel at those people who can easily spot the Big Dipper or Orion's belt. They all look like Disney characters to me.

The bubbles from the jets pick up, drowning out his voice slightly. "What made you smile today?"

My gaze hones in on the man across from me in this square tub. The question is not what I was expecting. I'm pretty sure my mouth is gaping.

"It can be anything," he clarifies. "No stipulations."

I close my mouth and stare off. It doesn't take long to figure it out. "The lodge."

"Eating my fries?" he asks with a lowered gaze.

I nod. The fries at the lodge are some of the best damn ones I've ever had, but the time there made me smile because it was easy talking to him. He wasn't putting on a show to impress me, and I wasn't concerned about impressing him. We just...were. And I'll always have the lines around my mouth to remember it.

He grins at me, and I like it. The way his lips stay pressed together, and the corners of his eyes crinkle. His angular jaw is free of any stubble today, and the faint lights hanging above us only highlight the edges and shadows, making it seem sharper. It might be worth cutting my mouth on it.

I clear my throat and shift just as Lincoln hooks his foot around the back of my calf. All words have escaped me. He's touching me, but not in a we-can-play-this-off-as-an-accident kind of touching. This is an I'm-definitely-touching-you-right-now-and-I'm-not-sorry-about-it kind of touch based on the grin turned smirk on his face.

He uses his foot to lift my leg and leans forward to grab it, cradling my heel in his palms. "Do you like foot massages?"

I can only stare and maybe nod because, yes, I absolutely love foot massages. I'm not a monk. My bikini line clearly states that. And also, yes, because he's the one offering. I don't know him that well, but I was the one expecting to make the first move. I always do.

He works his thumbs into the bottom of my foot, dragging up and down firmly. I sink further into the jets pounding at my back as the water bubbles around my shoulders and neck.

His gaze stays on my face, but the extreme relaxation has my lids fluttering closed. There are no words passing between us, but his fingers rub circles higher up my calf and behind my knee. It's the most forward he's been. He hasn't been hiding his feelings, but he's a lot more reserved than the men I'm used to. Pensive and thoughtful, like he's solving problems of world peace in his mind.

He has to scoot forward to sit on the edge of the deep seat to reach the back of my thigh. This foot massage has quickly turned into something more. I'm completely still, allowing, waiting, wanting, but also worrying. I've had sex with one man for seven years, and then…crickets. I could probably use a crash course in sex-ed just to brush up on things. I'm so glad he can't hear my thoughts. I'm being ridiculous. One foot turned thigh massage doesn't mean anything more is going to happen, even if I want it to.

He leans closer until his knees bracket mine, his shorts brushing against my skin as his hand slides slightly further up the back of my thigh.

"This okay?" he asks in a gravelly tone, or maybe I just imagine it.

I give him the green light, which in this case is a mumbled *hell yeah.*

Chapter Fourteen

Myra

His thumb happens upon the inside of my thigh, and my eyes open wider, jerking at his touch.

Red light.

My skin is hypersensitive to his touch. Whether from all the bruises and sore muscles I've gained these last few days or because Lincoln's hands really feel that good. I need to just relax. I want this to happen. I want to forget. But the hard part about being here now and also having to hold it together means trusting others isn't always easy. He redirects his path, dragging long strokes on my outer thigh with his other hand. I rest my head back again and ease into the massage. It feels fantastic. He's so damn attentive.

Green light.

But I can still feel where his thumb was on my inner thigh and recall the quick pulse between my legs. I want him to do it again, if only to conduct an experiment. I want to know if it feels as good a second time. Maybe a third.

My knee bumps his chest as he leans even closer with the next twirl and drag of his thumb. If he keeps doing this, I will surely combust in a way that says, *I haven't been with anyone for a really long time.* I need to slow this down.

Yellow light.

Sitting up further, I try to put some distance between us by making it harder for him to rub my thigh. *Back to the calf for you, buddy.* Like an overly cheerful worker bee, he starts rubbing my foot again as the sound of the bubbles cresting the top of the water drowns out my disappointment. It's my own damn fault. Waffling between wanting him to touch me and feeling like I just can't do this is killing me. I'm not like this. I'm not this indecisive person.

That confident bitch who used to have men salivating is in here somewhere. I just need to find her. I need her to help me out and decide what she wants, or Lincoln's hands will.

"What are you thinking about?" Lincoln asks as he starts to pull his hands and body away.

I latch onto his forearms like a hungry piranha and hold him in place. I search his face for any protest. There is none. Instead, he licks his lips and makes them look so good, I want to try them, too, just to see for the sake of the experiment.

I must have been contorting my face again. Frankie says it looks like I'm lifting weights too big for me whenever I'm in my head and overthinking. It isn't far from how it feels, either. I'm a feeler who goes with the flow and doesn't worry too much about what I should say or how I should act. At least, I used to be. But that all changed six months ago. I'm more in my head than ever, and I don't want that. I want to *feel* again.

"I was thinking about us," I clarify.

"Us?"

I loosen my grip on his arms but don't let go. "This. You, me, tonight. What we're doing...or not doing." I'm making zero sense, but my mouth just keeps moving. I'm not one to beat around the bush. I prefer to just set it on fire and see what's left. "It's been a while since I've been with anyone...in bed, or hot tub. Like since before the divorce." And separation. And before that. God, there are probably cobwebs up in there.

The lines between his perfect eyebrows relax. "Nothing needs to happen that you aren't ready for. We've had a great night, which wouldn't change, whether we sleep together or not."

I nod in agreement. He's so damn considerate. I love it, but I also want him to rip my bikini off with his teeth.

I want more, even if I'm rusty. I'll get better. There will be no rest until it's exceptional. The first time back in the saddle is bound to be a little clunky. But I'll have to get over these annoying insecurities eventually if I ever want to let someone else in. A one-night stand with Lincoln would be the best cure.

I pull him closer until his face is inches from mine. Sliding my hands up to his neck, I cradle his head and then, without much warning, slam my mouth to his. It isn't gentle. More like abrupt and crushing. I think our front teeth even knocked together. But then our lips are frantic as they search for more friction, more heat, more flavor. I open my mouth for him, and he plunges his tongue inside, tasting the flavor of Malbec still in my mouth.

This isn't so bad.

Green light.

One of his hands threads around the base of my neck, holding me to him, while the other wraps wide around the top of my thigh. I tug it higher until it spans the width of my hip, reaching part way around to my ass. My body is taking over in a way I totally underestimated. *She knows what she wants.*

He moans into my mouth and lightly squeezes the handful of skin I've given him to work with. *You're welcome.* I kiss him like I haven't kissed anyone in half a year. Because I really haven't. Six months of not having fingers trail across my jawline and down my neck. Twenty-six weeks of no one outlining my hip bone with his thumb and making me bend like a balloon arch. One-hundred and eighty-two days without a deep groan escaping my parted lips as someone licks up the column of my neck.

He's actually licking me. It's like he wants to know what I taste like. As if he's been just as starved.

I'm not even sure I've ever groaned. Not like this. Not with anyone, including myself. He's doing things to my skin that feel different. Like I've never had hands on me that felt so good. This is better than *not so bad.*

He grabs behind my legs and lifts my thighs, tugging me through the water onto his lap so I'm straddling him. We slide back in his seat, sinking a few inches with the depth of it. I wrap my arms around his neck and lean my head back with the thrill of feeling his growing erection between my legs. *Yes.* All the green lights.

There's something primal in how we are together. I'm fascinated by it, intrigued that I move a certain way, and he follows. I make a noise. He moves faster. I grab. He touches. I'm growing mad with these new sensations.

He nips at my bottom lip then kisses down my neck, lower and lower. I stand on my knees, begging him to bite me somewhere. The thought has taken over all rational sense. I've never wanted to be bitten before. But apparently the Myra of yesterday is not the Myra of today. He licks my breast over my swimsuit still covering me. The pressure and heat of his hot mouth, as it takes my taut peak deeper, is making my entire body tense.

"Wow," I whisper between my panting breaths, threading rough fingers through his hair.

He kisses his way over to my other nipple, licking circles around it and teasing me. I want him to rip my top off and feel the heat of his breath on my skin.

Green light. Green light. Green light.

This escalated quickly. He was massaging my foot a second ago, now…this. His mouth on my sensitive nipples, practically crying out for him through the language of moans and gasps. His hands gripping handfuls of my ass as he pulls me closer to his body. The ache of longing at my center, wanting to feel him ease inside me in order to chase this sensation. He's totally leading me straight over the edge, and I can't do anything about it. I don't want to.

I have to feel him.

I sink back down to his lap and nip at his bottom lip, grinding my hips over him. He gives a low growl, voicing his disapproval of taking my breasts out of his mouth. Though, it doesn't last long. One of his hands leaves my ass and grabs my tit. I want to scream at how good his thumb feels, circling the peaks of my breasts, toying and kneading me like dough.

This isn't as bad as I thought it would be. In fact, it's amazing. It's better than amazing, but I can't think of another word since Lincoln bites the edge of my earlobe. I bark into the night air like a fucking hyena. I'm a freaking animal. I'm making noises like I need someone to hear me.

"You good?" he asks, breathless.

The heat of this hot tub has become unbearable. Even with the snap of cold slithering around my shoulders, I'm boiling alive in here. "I'm good. I just…scream sometimes." I don't, but tonight I do.

His eyes search my face. "I'm sorry. It's too fast. I didn't mean…I did just want to hang out tonight. We don't have to—"

I place a rough hand over his mouth to quiet him and smile, still feeling the strength of his quads bolstering my thighs. I'm trying so hard not to rotate my hips. "It's okay. Really. This feels amazing. You're amazing. This night…amazing."

It's still the only word I can come up with.

"Yeah?" he asks.

I nod and rotate my hips again. The strain of him against my core is too much. "Very much *yeah*."

"It's been a while for me, too," he says to my surprise.

I snap my eyes to his. "Really?"

He nods. "Last time was a year ago."

I slowly nod my head, lips parted in disbelief. "But I still think we should use protection…" My words trail off. I haven't had to have a conversation like this in a while, and my thoughts are a jumbled mess like scrabble tiles scattered on the floor.

"Okay," he confirms quickly, dragging his hands up the side of my hips to grip my waist. "I've got condoms inside if you want to go in?"

"Green light," I say in a rush, then correct myself. "I mean, let's do that."

He plants a soft kiss on my lips. It's so much lighter than all the others so far. Compared to the frantic pace we'd held just moments ago, this kiss is tender and languid. My lips drag over his wet ones slowly. My clit throbs as the tiger inside me growls fiercely.

He holds my face in his hand, tilting my head enough for him to devour more of me as he deepens our kiss. I can't help myself; I swivel my hips, searching for him to settle the beat pounding between my legs. He answers me by rhythmically thrusting his hips up.

He pulls his lips from mine, peppering kisses along my jaw. In one swift motion, he wraps his other arm around my waist and stands. Instinctively, I circle my legs around his waist, and with my arms around his neck, I squeal. He sets me on the shallow step inside the hot tub and stands between my legs. His eyes lock with mine as his hand slides between us, and his thumb finds my clit through my bikini bottoms. The motion is slow to start, but it's enough to make me loll my head back and exhale all the air in my lungs.

Except, there's no air left.

It's all gone.

He holds the power to destroy me with that one finger.

"Look at me," he says roughly.

So, I do. Lifting my head, I look at him with lowered eyes and an open mouth just as his thumb finds the more than two thousand nerve endings at my core. The urge to throw my head back and melt further is too strong. "I can't…this is…oh my…" My thoughts are all lost. All I feel is the mounting pressure building, higher and higher. "Linc."

"Say my name again," he commands.

It's brusque and demanding, not a hint of apology in that tone. Just how I like it, and so not how I thought he'd be.

I'd do anything right now as long as he doesn't stop. "Linc."

"Again." He rubs a little harder, a little faster.

"Lincoln!"

I'm glad the stars are his only neighbors.

Before I'm about to shatter, he stops.

I could kill him. "Why'd you stop? Don't," I demand. "Keep…going."

"Keep looking at me," he says through ragged breaths.

I glare at him, then loop both arms around the back of his neck so I stop slipping and buckle in for this ride. Then, he shoves my swim bottoms to the side and slips his finger inside of me. He pulls me higher and dips his head to kiss my neck. With one finger still inside me, mouth on my collarbone, I stare at the top of his head. The dark brown strands of hair move as his mouth does. I could go just like this. Right here at the sight of his mouth on me and the feel of his fist between my legs.

And I do.

He pulls his thumb out and slides it back up to my clit, expertly applying the right amount of pressure and the right amount of movement to take me to the other side of my orgasm. The pressure is so intense, so mind-scattering, so delicious; I rest my forehead on his and breathe heavily. The waves of pleasure are ricocheting through me at a speed I can't wrap my head around. I can't organize the sensations or make sense of why they feel *so damn good*. They just do.

I start slipping again, and as he pulls his thumb away to grip my waist, I collapse over his shoulder with a heavy sigh.

Whatever he just did felt like something I haven't experienced before. I'm thirty-five. Orgasms are orgasms. Nope. Not this one. Not even I have been able to make it feel this good, and I've had years of practice.

I want to ask him and to dissect everything he just did to me like this is lab class, but his rough voice fills the space. "I can't believe watching you orgasm didn't make me come."

"You're serious?" I mutter.

"Yeah, I am. See…" He grabs one of my limp hands and drags it across the front of his board shorts. The firm length pressing into my hand is enough to cause my clit to pulse all over again like it didn't just shatter into millions of fragments.

He sighs as I run my hand up to his waistband. "Wait." He grabs my wrist. "Let's go inside."

Green light.

Chapter Fifteen

Lincoln

Myra adjusts her swimsuit, the one my mouth and hands took a liking to, and stands from the water. The soft curves of her breasts are like two perfect ski hills with the right amount of slope to pick up speed and enough steepness to cause you to crash and burn.

I'm ignoring the hazard signs.

The hourglass continues down to her hips. The smooth plains of her body make my blood warm and my dick twitch. I swallow hard and force my eyes back to hers.

I rub her thigh to keep from pulling her back to me. "Ready?"

Her lips part, but she nods.

Half of our bodies have been in the cold snap of air for the last however many minutes it took for her to say my name over and over, then collapse like an avalanche. I didn't even know it could feel so good just having her repeat the consonants and vowels in my name with her soft voice, but it did. It felt so fucking good. And for once, I wasn't shy in telling her.

I stand, too, and trail her out of the hot tub, wrapping her robe around her shoulders, then grabbing mine to hurriedly get inside. I want to untie the strings holding her bikini on—the top, and then the bottom. I want to bury myself inside her. I want any position she'll have me in. Then, I want to buy her flowers, leave her love notes in her purse, and make her eggs the way she likes them tomorrow morning.

The sliding glass door is open a crack, and I shove it farther back to follow her in. I told my roommates they better not show up unannounced for any reason. Jake owes me after I once vacated our place for ten daytime hours while he was on a date. Not to mention the fake relationship he signed me up for.

Myra's teeth chatter as she moves inside and clutches the robe tightly around her. I turn to face her after locking the door, moving closer to grab her hand. "Let's get you warm."

I lead her through the living room, past the kitchen, and down the hall to my room. Since I pay slightly more in rent for the largest bedroom, I have my own attached bathroom with a soaker tub and tiled shower. I tug her inside my room, shut and lock the door, and lead her to the on-suite, driving by my nightstand for a condom.

I kiss her cheek, then drop her hand, walking straight for the shower to turn on both shower heads while also keeping my boner in check. I toss the condom on the tiled shelf and shirk off the robe, holding out my hand to take Myra's, too. She hands it to me, and I hang both of them on the hooks outside the shower, then take a minute to light a few candles. Or all five.

Nodding toward the shower, I say, "Go ahead, you can get in. Should be warm now."

She doesn't move closer or farther away. Her feet stay where she's been standing, just inside the bathroom, which is already fogging, thanks to the steam. The perfect curves of her backside are disappearing in the mirror as it clouds over.

Then, as if time stops, Myra reaches behind her neck to blindly search for the ends of her bikini. She keeps her eyes on mine as she locates and pulls slowly. I'm aware of every second that passes, every beat of my heart in my ears, and every sound the wet fabric makes as it slides against itself and finally releases.

Her top falls, still hugging the middle of her torso until she reaches around to untie that one, too. I take a step closer, breathing hard as I take her in. Her nipples are firm and pink from the chill of her suit and the stark contrast of temperature, but everything else about her is soft in ways that make me harder.

She reaches for the ties on my shorts to undo them, sliding the waistband down my hips. I close my eyes briefly as she takes my cock in her hand. She's so confident in the way she strokes me. The pressure and speed are perfect.

I can't keep my hands off her. I lean down and take her mouth, forcing me out of her hands. But her lips are better. My hands circle her entire waist, and I hold her to my chest, lifting her heels off the ground as I plunge my tongue into her mouth. I want to consume all of her at once, but my mouth can only cover so much ground in so much time. I'm not even thinking about before or after, only what's right in front of me—in my hands and inside my mouth. I've always appreciated the moment I'm in. The beauty of a sunset, the joy of hard work, and the connections I've made. But nothing compares to this. I want to lock us in it like a snow globe and never leave.

She pulls back, catching her breath as she rolls her forehead over mine. "Tell me what you like."

I crane my neck down to kiss the slight dip at the base of where her neck and shoulder meet. "Only if you tell me."

"Everything you've been doing. Keep doing that."

I stare at her. Cupping her shoulders, I rub them to keep her warm. "Everything?"

"Yes," she answers immediately. "You're really good at this. I wasn't joking. Didn't you hear me say the word *amazing* like twenty-seven times?"

I trail my hands down her arms. "If there's something you like or don't like… tell me. I want this to be good for you." As I say this, I replace her arms with her hips and draw small circles with my thumbs.

"It is." Her lips hover over mine. "Now tell me."

So bossy.

I show her instead because what feels good is her in my hands and my mouth. I bend to kiss her shoulder. Her skin tastes of honey and vanilla, and I get lost in the silkiness of it, kissing up her neck, over her collarbone, and down to where I'm holding her breast in my hand.

She answers by sucking air through her teeth.

She's silent but pliable in my arms as I stand straighter. Her eyes are closed, and her head is tipped to the side like it's too heavy for her to hold on her own. I reach my hand up and cradle the side of her face in my palm.

She opens her eyes and blinks rapidly. "I'm going to bite you the next time you stop."

I gnaw on the side of my tongue and smirk before grabbing her ass with both hands and lifting her. She squeals again but wraps her legs around me. The way her thighs tighten around my midsection has me so hard. There's no doubt in my mind I want this woman. I don't know if I've made that clear enough. But she has. She likes me. She thinks I'm good at this, and maybe I am.

Carrying her into the shower, I rest her back against the opposite wall, pressing my erection into her center as she arches into me. It's so natural just to do what my body craves and see her react. I'm not letting myself hold me back for once. Not with someone like Myra. Her moan echoes off the tiles, sounding even higher pitched in my ears.

"Please," she begs but doesn't follow it up with anything else.

The water pelts my back with a steady stream as I cradle her thighs and get lost in our kiss. Her lips are warm and pliant as they mesh with mine. I want to feel more of her and explore more of her body. But I also don't want to drop her, so I gently set her back on her feet.

Still pinning her to the wall with my hips and kissing her lazily and then faster, I undo one side of her bikini bottoms and then the other until the fabric falls in a heap and Myra is completely bare in my shower. There's no way I would have believed this would happen when we first met. Spending one evening with Myra isn't going to be enough. I want more.

Always more.

Maybe that's why nothing has ever stuck because the women I've casually dated didn't want it to be anything more than a fling. I'm not cut out for that. I'll mate for life like my parents did. I don't want to get ahead of myself here, but I am. I'm in so deep. Or, at least, I will be in a few minutes.

I pull away because I need to see her.

Her eyes are hooded, chest rising and falling, as her palms lie flat against the wall behind her. I circle my cock and slowly pump as I stare at her. Her eyes track down, and she watches me. A smirk plays out on my lips as she begins to touch herself, too. Her hands trail up between her breasts and then down her body farther and farther until her hand is between her legs.

"Lincoln," she whispers.

I pump faster, rubbing the tip against her leg and the top of her belly, teasing both of us.

This man doing these things is barely recognizable. But that doesn't scare me. It makes me want to dive deeper, jump higher, and fall even faster. I have to have her.

A low growl erupts from my chest at the sight of her playing with herself. I quickly grab the condom and rip the package open hastily with my teeth, rolling the latex over my swollen dick as I step back in the shower spray. It rushes down my back while the other stream of water beats against Myra's stomach, her hand still nestled between her thighs as the other grips the wall.

Closing the distance between our mouths, I kiss her like I've discovered something new about myself—about her—that I don't want to forget. I commit everything to memory. The sounds she makes, the water droplets dripping down every inch of her skin, and the way the heat of our mouths is no match for the steam now fully surrounding us.

I cover her hand with mine, urging her to show me more— show me *everything*.

The water is at my back again, blocking the spray from getting into her eyes as she looks up at me. Her hair is still captured in a bun on top of her head, but loose pieces are plastered to her face and neck. With parted lips, she's taking in breaths just as fast as she's expelling them. Her heart is racing like mine is. The lids of her eyes are low, weighted down with her own desire.

She squeezes my hand and then grabs my dick. She isn't gentle. She glides the tip of me over her entrance, and I want so badly to dip inside, but she only repeats the motion again and again. I use my hips as leverage to add pressure with each pass. I can't keep my eyes off her. If I thought she was beautiful before, this is unmatched. I've never watched a woman take her pleasure like this. It's intoxicating.

Her mouth falls open, and her eyes close as I grab the base of my cock and move with her, flicking, stabbing, and pressing.

Her hand still holds mine, but it's loosened, and she's letting me explore her. Seeing how her body arches into mine, searching for my hand when I pull it back, and mumbling words to herself I can't hear is better than hitting my top speed on skis. The adrenaline coursing through me has to be more than rushing downhill.

She grabs one of my hands and places it on her ass; my hand instinctively squeezes as she drags my palm down and under her thigh to the back of her knee until her legs are spread perfectly for me to fit closer between them. I follow her lead, ready to do whatever the hell she wants.

She keeps her hand around my cock, pumping a couple of times and making me lose my mind before she uses the tip to swipe up and down her folds once more. My thoughts have all gone down the drain with the water. It feels so good. She feels better. Better than I remembered. Better than I've ever had before. Nothing—*no one*—compares to her.

I brace the hand not holding her leg up on the wall beside her head, and begin to rock my hips forward, seeking the tight walls of her center and the friction I want so badly.

With one final swipe of my dick against her slippery center, she lines me up. I stare down and lift her leg higher, sliding my hand further up her thigh for a stronger grip. There's no way I'll let go. This isn't going to be slow and steady. I'm ready for her. So ready that I want to make sure I last inside her. I look down between us and push while her fingers guide me in until I'm full of her, and she's full of me. We're connected with no beginning or end.

She gasps as I push deeper and further, stretching her walls to accommodate all of me. There isn't an inch I want to miss. I start moving in short thrusts, then pull nearly all the way out and drive back in.

She screams so loud, I worry I've hurt her like I thought I did outside. But then remember, she is just vocal.

"Keep going. Harder, Lincoln. Now."

The first inch of me is inside her, but hearing my name on her lips makes me crazy and has me thrusting my hips until I'm wedged so deep, her nails are like tent stakes in my shoulders. The walls of her pussy flutter and pulse against me. I pull out. Then pump back in. Out and in, in and out. My hand slips on the wall, so I drop my other to her hip and tug her closer with every drive of my hips, holding onto nothing but her. All of her.

"Keep…going," she mutters as she trails her hands down my biceps and holds tightly.

I feel my orgasm building, but hell if I'll go before her. I want to watch her shatter again.

I slow my movements, and she moans, dropping her hands to try to make them move faster manually. Pulling out enough to add some space, I drop my thumb to her clit again and apply enough pressure and speed to pull another guttural moan out of her. She rides my hand while she rides my dick.

Her eyes are open but only in slits, looking at me and then where I'm touching her.

"Tell me when you're close," I say through a low grunt. I'm holding on to every last bit of willpower so I don't burst into flames. Though, I'd rather that than orgasm first.

Her head lolls back against the wall. "Keep. Going."

I remove my hand, and she groans again, but this time, I push my dick all the way in, pumping faster and making sure the base hits the bottom of her clit with enough tension to keep our pace. Faster and harder, I shove into her, tugging her hip with one hand and keeping her legs spread and open for me with the other.

I'm there; I can't last longer.

I stare down at her. She's panting and quaking with her own orgasm. I follow her over the cliff and dive into the great unknown of this one orgasm. This one night. With one woman I don't want to forget.

My hip thrusts slow until my pulsing dick beats within her. But I don't pull out right away. I stay in the warm embrace between her legs. I move my hand up her side and over her breast, feeling her wild heartbeat under skin and bones.

She drags one of her hands to my heart, feeling the same galloping beat, and says through a laugh, "Holy shit."

The walls of her core constrict and squeeze around my still-swollen dick. I laugh too, though it's low and gravelly as I resign to slide out of her. "Holy shit is right." Rolling the condom off, I drop it on the bench seat beside us.

She stays pressed against the wall as she pushes her hair back. "Did you give me two orgasms in what..." she mentally calculates, "thirty minutes?"

My chest fills with pride as I rinse myself off, then tug her under the spray with me. "I guess so." I press a light kiss to the corner of her mouth. She still tastes so good that even my softening cock jerks slightly. "We have a lot more time tonight, too, if you want to stay?"

I ask it like a question, hoping she'll check *yes* or swipe right. The times I've had a woman stay the night could be counted on one hand. Okay, one finger. This isn't like any of the times before. I'm an adult man who just had sex with another adult woman in my shower.

New fantasy unlocked.

Water rushes over her lips, and I want to lean down and lick it off but resist, knowing her answer is on the other side of that mouth.

She turns around, ass pressing into me while reaching for my arms to circle her waist and saying over her shoulder, "I'm staying."

Chapter Sixteen

Myra

My phone starts playing *What a Girl Wants* from my nightstand. Wait, no—Lincoln's nightstand. I stayed over last night, like he asked, and he put me through what he called *ski training lessons*.

I didn't know having his face between my legs would help me get down a mountain. Apparently, I got an "A" in that class.

I reach out from under the blankets and grab my phone, Christina Aguilera still screaming loudly. Pushing the luxurious down comforter off my face, I read the name on the screen: *Frankie*. He shouldn't be calling at…nine a.m.! I never sleep this late. Having to wake up at the butt crack of dawn for school made me an early riser. Well, Lincoln's tongue made me a late sleeper.

I can't answer Frankie's call now. He will absolutely scream or, I don't know, ask me to wake Lincoln up so he can talk to him. There's no way I'm answering while in this bed.

Lincoln is still fast asleep on his back, one arm slung over his head and the other over his stomach. Thank God he isn't one of those clingy sleepers who like to curl around you like an infinity scarf. Instead, I got to have this whole half of his king-size bed to myself. It was the highlight of the entire night.

That and the lasagna.

And the hot tub, followed by the shower.

Oh, and the three…no, four orgasms.

Last night might have been the best night of my life.

I unlock my phone and go to messages. There's no way I'm getting off that easy. Before I can read all ten texts Frankie sent, and I'm just now getting, he calls again. Christina immediately picks up my new theme song.

I slide out from under my dream comforter and stand, only to realize my legs are dead. I'm walking to the bathroom like I have cloven hooves instead of feet. My calf muscles won't allow me to put my heels to the ground, so I stop trying and snag a robe from the back of the door to put on.

I consider answering the call in this bathroom, but the acoustics are fantastic. My screams from last night sounded more like echoes, which made it even more erotic. I'm glad Lincoln's roommates were gone most of last night and didn't hear us in the shower. Or his bedroom. Or the hot tub. There's no way they wouldn't have heard if they were home. It's the loudest I've ever been, but I refuse to be shy about it.

Slipping on the robe, I tip-toe back through the bedroom— like I have any other choice with muscles tighter than resistance bands—as the phone stops ringing. I haven't been in many men's bedrooms, but Lincoln's is by far the cleanest. There's a white rug under his low-rise, mid-century modern wooden bed frame, a leather reading chair in the corner near the window, and not one cup on his floating nightstands. *Weird.* And the only thing on the floor are our clothes, but even those are folded neatly at the foot of the bed. He must have little fairies who clean up after him. Or Lincoln is a neat freak. Heavy on the *neat* and more like *freaky*.

Safely outside Lincoln's Ikea showroom, I tap on Frankie's missed call and press the phone to my ear as I close the bedroom door more carefully than if my life were on the line and I were defusing a bomb.

"Myra! What gives you the right to ignore my calls?"

I lower my voice and walk on the balls of my feet. "You called at least a hundred times while I was *sleeping*," I emphasize. "I had my phone on *do not disturb*."

"And I'm not on your emergency contact list? I should be exempt from your I-do-not-want-to-talk-to-you-after-a-certain-hour list of people!"

I pull the phone away from my ear, then return it once he finishes. "I don't know how to do that."

"Oh. I'll show you when you get home," he says in a much less high-pitched tone.

I lean on the back of the couch with a wince. Looks like my ass is sore, too. "What is so critically important that you had to call me a trillion times? Did the barista finally ask you out?"

He scoffs. "You think I'd only call you twelve times for something like that? Hell, no. I'd be on the first flight to Bozeman to tell you in person. And you know how big of a deal that is."

Fair, and very on-brand for Frankie. He thinks airplanes are the spawn of Satan. "So, what is it then?"

"Didn't you see my texts last night?" he asks in a condescending tone.

I cross my arms and stare into the kitchen, noting the sink full of dirty dishes and two wine glasses set beside it. We had left them outside after rushing in to have the hottest shower sex of my life. Someone else must have grabbed them since our hands were full of each other last night. *Fairies.*

Frankie might be my brother, but I tell him everything. Like the time I put gum on Mr. Wendler's chair. The small Care Bear tattoo I got on the inside of my thigh because he got one, too. And now, why I'm in Montana, trying my damndest to prove to myself and the whole fucking world I'm not lost, or broken, or… damaged.

Playing with the ties of the robe, I say, "I was busy doing things I will not repeat—don't you dare make me—with the ski instructor."

He gasps. "*The* cute-as-pie ski instructor who asked you out? When are you going to send me his picture? I need to confirm that your retinas aren't broken like last time."

Some kind of scoff-laugh exits from the back of my throat. "Yes!" I slap a hand over my mouth so I don't wake Lincoln, but I do wake Otto. He drags himself off his dog bed in the living room and circles my feet before lying down. "And no. I'm not sending his photo so you can harass him." I change the subject immediately. "It was the best night I've had in a long time," I say in a wistful tone, the corners of my lips tugging skyward. I bend down to pet Otto and try not to let the R-rated content flash on the screen of my mind for long.

"So, you're saying you left me and flew to another state to *find yourself,* but all you really needed was a good lay?" he asks. "You couldn't just find someone here?"

"I am *finding myself,* thank you very much. I actually stayed up on my skis yesterday and traversed down the mountain." Sure, Lincoln skied behind me, but I still felt like I was flying. "I was free." My voice catches on the last word. I curl my lips inward and straighten my spine. "I felt the same thing last night, too."

He pauses, the weight of my words filling the spaces. "I'm happy for you, I really am. But we have a problem."

My heart rate starts to pick up speed, racing faster and blurring the edges of my vision. I have to place a hand on my chest to make sure it doesn't explode out of me like confetti. "Did someone…die? Did Mom and Dad—"

"God, no!" Frankie stops me. "How the hell did you get there from what I said?"

"You said *we have a problem,* and the biggest problem I can think of would be, well, death." A list of other possibilities nags at my thoughts. "Is someone terminally ill?"

"No!"

"Seasonal cold?"

"Myra."

"Oh my God! Are Mom and Dad selling the house?" That wouldn't be the worst news. There's no answer, and he doesn't try to cut in again. "Frankie?"

"Are you done yet?" he asks.

"Yes, sorry. What is it?"

He sighs. "I'll start by saying Mom and Dad are worried about you. They think you're having a mental breakdown because you want to learn to ski. Oh, and the tattoo thing."

"You told them!" I whisper yell, then turn my back to the hall where the bedrooms are. I have to bite the inside of my cheek when my hamstrings twinge with pain.

I had to fight to make sure Lincoln never saw the small tattoo. He got close a couple of times, but I told him it was just a birthmark when he started running his thumb over it. I was hoping the dimmed light in his navy and cream room from Ikea's spring nautical collection would help me out.

"Yes, Myra, I told them! I had to since they asked about mine, and it just sort of slipped out that we had matching ones."

I rub my forehead, and Otto pushes up to a sit. He cocks his head to the side like he's confused about what Frankie is saying. That makes two of us.

The matching Care Bear tattoos were a horrible idea. I thought the inside of my thigh was a safe place. I was *very* wrong. I should have had the wherewithal to know this at the time, but Wade had just moved the last of his things out, and I was drunk. Frankie, too. And apparently, being drunk isn't an excuse when making an irreversible decision that has lasting consequences.

Margaritas do not care about your choices.

Neither does Merlot.

I should really stop trusting alcohol.

"You showed them the picture."

No answer.

"Frankie!" I groan a little too loudly.

"That's why I was texting and calling you a thousand times!" he yells.

The service in the mountains has been spotty, especially at Liv's, but I've had perfect reception at Lincoln's so far. I can only blame it on the sleep mode I have my phone set to (aka hibernation mode).

I scoff. "Because of the tattoo?"

"No, because they're worried about you…" he starts.

Otto stands and walks into the kitchen, sniffing around the floor, likely for any fallen bits of food.

Then continues, "And they want to—"

"Everything alright?"

I whip around at the sound of the new voice that doesn't belong to Frankie and pull the phone away from my ear like I'm in trouble. My quads are livid with me. The quick motion and realization that not one of my body parts isn't sore means I don't hear the rest of what Frankie says. I'm too stunned seeing Ted, who isn't dressed like an ape anymore but looking like he got in a fight with one. His red hair sticks up everywhere, and one eye is open while the other stays closed.

"Morning," I say to Ted, then press the phone back to my ear. "I have to go. Call you later. Bye."

"Read your texts!" is the last thing Frankie yells before I hang up on him.

I smile awkwardly.

"Coffee?" He points toward the kitchen.

"No, I'm good."

He points at the phone in my hand. "You sounded upset. Did Lincoln do anything…"

I widen my eyes and stand straighter, which is likely still not very straight. My back hurts. "No, no, nothing like that." I hold up my phone and then slip it into the robe pocket. "I'll figure it out later."

The robe! I drop my eyes to what I'm wearing—more like what I'm not wearing underneath this—and grip the fabric at my heart.

He doesn't seem to notice and scratches his bicep beneath the hem of his t-shirt while slowly shuffling into the kitchen. Ted isn't as tall as Lincoln or Jake, he's fit and scrappy, like a wrestler who will play dirty and go for your knees.

"If you want me to mix his darks and whites to piss him off, I'll do it," he says in a groggy voice. "He hates when his laundry gets messed with."

I like learning more about the man I slept with. "You've known Lincoln for a long time?"

He pulls out the coffee carafe and rinses it out. "Oh, no. We just met less than a year ago. He just freaked out when he saw me wearing his socks one day. It was an honest mistake." He shrugs. "I barely know what my own socks look like."

I nod and grip every surface on my way to the barstool. I'm not even being dramatic about how my calves scream at me.

They clearly need oiling. "What else can you tell me about him then? Any weird habits? Secret obsessions? Rock collections?"

"No rocks I know of, but I wouldn't be surprised. He likes weird stuff like that." He fills the pot with water and pours it into the coffee maker. As he adds the grounds, he says, "He loves his dog more than most humans but hates cake. I thought the cake thing would be an automatic red flag, but he likes cookies, so there's that. Then, the whole traveling thing. That man has seen more airports than vag—" He stops and gives me a blank stare, then decides not to take that thought further.

I'm not a fan of cake either, but Ted strikes me as someone who is very passionate about his desserts, so I don't say anything about that. "How long did he travel for?"

He pushes the button to start the coffee. "Three years? After high school, I think."

My mouth starts to drop. "You mean college?"

Numbers are flying through my head. Even if it were after college, that would make Lincoln...

"Yeah, that's right. He did two years of college, then dropped out." He rubs his eyes, looking back at the coffee pot like he's willing it to brew faster. "Some bullshit about it feeding the hierarchical food chain."

Years, months, and days run through my head, raising the alarm bells. My words are rushed as I say, "But didn't he just come back to the States nine months ago?" And to Montana from Canada a year before that?

Ted grabs a mug from the cabinet and peers over at me. "Yeah, he did. Oh, and that reminds me. He doesn't have a rock collection, but he did get a hot sauce bottle from every place he visited." He opens the cabinet next to the mugs, which is completely full of a variety of unopened hot sauce bottles.

They all seem to blur as I stare at them while the coffee maker begins to sputter with its last breath. My pulse races as the timeline of Lincoln's life comes into focus. "So, he graduated high school at eighteen…" I tick off each event on my fingers, "went to college until he was twenty, traveled for three years, Canada for another year, so that means he's…"

Shit, shit, shit.

Maybe Ted has the timeline wrong. He hasn't known Lincoln very long, right? God, neither have I. This means Lincoln is only…*no.* He can't be that young. There's no way I had sex with a…"Twenty-four-year-old," I say under my breath.

"Huh?" I hear Ted say, but I'm too busy studying the counter and adding up the difference in our age another twenty times.

Eleven years.

I'm eleven years older than him.

"You doing alright? Do you need water or something?" Ted asks somewhere nearby.

I snap my gaze up. "Water?"

He nods slowly, but his face isn't in focus.

I shake my head even slower. "I'm good. No water needed. But I…" I don't even know what to say. Ted has to know I'm not Lincoln's age. The extra lines on my forehead should have been a clue. Is that why I didn't notice the lines on Lincoln's forehead? BECAUSE THEY AREN'T REALLY THERE?

Oh. I had orgasms last night at the hands of a twenty-four-year-old!

"I need to go." I stand suddenly as the stool scrapes loudly on the linoleum.

"Uh, okay. You sure you don't want some coffee before you leave?" He hooks a thumb toward the pot, but I'm already moving around the counter into the living room.

"I don't like coffee," I lie. "I'm fine. I just remembered I need to get back home before my neighbor, Liv, goes to work. Something about needing to help with her garden."

I frantically search for my purse in the living room at the slowest crawl humanly possible, but it isn't there. Not under any of the pillows—and there are a surprising amount of those for a bachelor pad—throw blankets, or the coffee table.

He follows me into the living room. "But it's winter. What's she growing?"

Shit again!

I walk like I'm wearing pointe shoes to the entryway, remembering I hung my purse there and snatching it before slipping on my boots, or trying. "I meant she wanted me to help plan her garden."

"Alright. I'll tell Lincoln you had to leave then, I guess."

You mean your fucking twenty-four-year-old roommate? This is why you don't have sex with near strangers, kids. Finding out Lincoln is so young makes a lot of sense. I mean, he was so spry in bed. I just chalked it up to how fit he was due to all the skiing. WRONG. Turns out, his frontal lobe isn't even fully developed.

What have I done?

I peer down at my robe. There's no time to change. No time to go back into Lincoln's—the twenty-four-year-old's—room and retrieve my clothes. They're gone forever. And it sucks because I really liked that sweater. "Thanks, Ted. I'll see ya later." I shake my head and correct myself. "I mean, just…thanks." I definitely won't be seeing him later.

I back out the front door and close it tightly, exhaling deeply before descending the stairs carefully to my car. The sunlight helps me see the steps, but it's also pointing a sunny ray at the glaring mistake I made: having a one-night stand as a thirty-five-year-old woman.

Chapter Seventeen

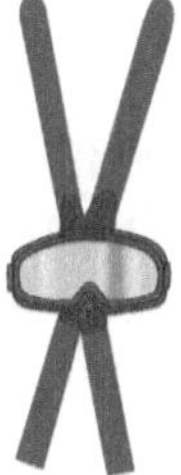

Lincoln

W hat the fuck did you say to her?" I shove an accusing finger at Ted. "Were you wearing that damn costume still?"

Ted holds up his hands while pressed back against the couch. "I didn't say anything, and I'm not wearing it anymore, am I?" he asks, leaning forward. Bold move.

I lean closer. "Why would she just take off, then?" Ted's gaze tracks to Jake quickly, but I'm right in his face and see the whole thing. I stand straighter, peering between them. "What is it? What aren't you telling me?"

After the hot and meaningful night we had, then falling asleep while talking about which foods we hate the most, I wouldn't have expected her to leave so suddenly and without any of her clothes. I'm now the very proud owner of a skimpy black bikini, some leggings, and a blue knit sweater. Oh, and I'm down a robe. She just ran off, quite literally, based on the front door camera footage, and hasn't answered any of my texts.

Otto stands from his bed in the living room and walks over to me, clearly able to sense the shift in the mood. Walking out here to find Ted pouring coffee and Myra nowhere in sight naturally raised some questions.

Ted drops his hands. "When I got up, she was out here, acting all panicked. I asked her if she was okay, and she said she was fine."

Jake starts making a disagreeing noise from behind us. I crane my neck and step back to include him in the conversation as he paces in front of the brick fireplace. "When a woman says she's *fine*, she is not *fine*. What did her body language tell you?"

Ted scoots to the edge of the couch, bumping Milo's head off his lap. "She was worried."

Jake shakes his head, then unearths a whiteboard from beside one of the chairs and props it on the fireplace. He pulls a marker from his pocket. "Give me more. What made her look worried?"

"I don't know!" Ted yells. "Her voice, I guess? Her shoulders were kinda hunched, too, and she was talking to someone on the phone. That's why I came out. I heard voices but thought it was Jake," he points at him, "since he likes to talk loudly when everyone is sleeping—"

"You're just a light sleeper," Jake cuts in while scribbling these details on the board.

Bernie lies at our feet. All three dogs are hovering close like mother hens due to our raised voices.

I hold up a hand. "So maybe it was nothing I did. Maybe something happened like a..." I snap my fingers. "An emergency."

"An ailing parent," Jake adds.

"A missed appointment?" I offer.

"Or her doctor just called to say she's pregnant with another man's baby, and she left to go get a paternity test."

Jake and I look at Ted.

"What the hell, man?" Jake says, brows drawn. He writes *not pregnant* with an "X" through it. "That's definitely not it."

I put my hands on my hips. "There's no pregnancy." She asked me to use a condom, and everyone knows you can't get pregnant while pregnant. "But something made her leave."

"And you're sure it wasn't you?" Jake levels me with a broad stare.

I shrug. "I don't think so. Maybe. It could have been." Thinking back over our night together, I can't recall anything being said or done that would have made her leave like this. Everything felt consensual. She even said the word *amazing* a lot.

Jake caps the marker and pins Ted with his stare. "And nothing else was said? She just left after you found her looking worried?"

"She said goodbye to whoever was on the phone in a rush and said something about dealing with it later," Ted says, Bernie lying across his feet. "But when she left, she told me she needed to leave to help her neighbor with her garden. That didn't seem right."

Jake draws a quick sketch of a garden with flowers and bees that is surprisingly good, and then rubs his forehead. I flop onto the couch next to Ted with a huff.

"Look," Ted starts. "She followed me into the kitchen and was asking about you. I told her you didn't have a rock collection, but you like Otto more than humans." *Fair assumption*, I think, since Otto is my best friend. I'm petting the top of his head now as he rests it in my lap. "Then, I asked if she wanted coffee. I don't know what I said that made her leave. She did turn down the coffee, though."

Jake writes *no coffee*.

I rub my chin, already feeling the makings of a beard if I wanted one. I usually don't, but Myra had me considering it when she told me she liked guys with beards last night. My thoughts have gone from beards to *what the hell did I do wrong?* "I'm at a loss."

Jake stops pacing. "If it had something to do with her family or friend and not how much you suck in bed——"

"I do not suck," I say defensively. She told me so.

"Well, Myra isn't here for us to ask now, is she?"

I sigh heavily and loll my head back on the couch.

Jake clears his throat. "As I was saying. If it had to do with her family, or she really did have to get back to help plan out a garden months in advance, then maybe you should just go over there."

"I can't just show up unannounced."

Jake chews on his lip, his tell whenever he's thinking hard. "You said she's here to ski, so what if you went up to the mountain and tried to run into her there?"

I scrub a hand down my face. "I don't know, guys. Maybe she just needs space?"

Last night was…a lot. We barreled into bed—more like the shower, then the bed—with the taste of lasagna and wine still in our mouths. I don't regret it one bit, but maybe there was a part of her that did. We barely know each other. At least mentally and emotionally. I'm positive I now know every square inch of her physically.

"Did you ask her?" Jake asks.

I meet his gaze. I know what he's not saying. "No. I wasn't going to bring up game night with Mom and Dad last night. We were on a date, and I wanted to see how it went first."

Jake nods, but Ted furrows his brow. "What are you talking about?"

I scrape rough hands through my hair and lace my fingers on the top of my head.

Jake answers for me. "Lincoln told our parents he was bringing his *girlfriend* to family game night this weekend."

Ted's brows draw in as he blinks rapidly. "You don't have a girlfriend."

"You're right, I don't." My voice gets louder. "Until Jake told them I did and now I'm forced to play along!" A fresh lick of anger climbs my spine.

Ted whistles low and slow.

Jake holds up both hands. "But you didn't have to. I thought you'd just tell them I was lying, then mess up my hair or something."

It's what I should have done but didn't. There's no way I want to disappoint Mom, but I think part of me wishes it were true. Maybe I'm not as mad at Jake as I am at myself. I've never had a real, official girlfriend. I just turned twenty-five, moved back home, and got a more consistent job. I'm finally at a place in my life where I'm ready to share it all with someone.

I drop my hands and hang my head. "I shouldn't have told them that. You're right."

The room is silent as the air absorbs my words.

"I think she'd say *yes* if you asked her. She seemed to really like you, or at least Otto," Jake says.

I laugh. "Except now I've somehow messed something up."

"Then fix it!" Ted says.

Jakes taps the board. "You're still planning to do ski lessons this week, right?"

"Yeah."

"Then, go see her and say you want to plan out your schedule. Maybe she'll see your face and remember she liked kissing you." Jake shudders as his lip curls.

I shake my head and stare at the whiteboard. Garden, no coffee, definitely not pregnant. Maybe it doesn't make sense because it has nothing to do with me.

"I'll go ask her about the ski lessons, and if it goes well and she doesn't hate me, I'm going to come clean about the game night. Maybe she'll be willing to help me out. And if not, I'll have to call Mom and Dad."

I head to my room, where everything went down last night. My covers are still thrown back, and the bathroom door is still open, filling both spaces with the smell of my soap and vanilla candles. But it isn't my soap anymore.

It's my soap on Myra's skin.

Chapter Eighteen

Myra

So, you just walked out without saying goodbye? And stole his robe?" Liv asks from the stove where she's making *morning-after* pancakes that are supposed to help with the reality I'm now a cougar, preying on young men.

He didn't act like someone in his twenties. He's got a dog he's responsible for, a roof over his head, and a job. There wasn't even an inkling he'd be younger than me.

My forehead starts to hurt, so I lift it from the counter. "I didn't steal his robe," I say, pulling the ties a little tighter so it doesn't decide to walk out on me. When I got home, I did put clothes on underneath. Though not many. "I'm borrowing it."

Indefinitely.

After leaving in a rush, I drove home to the soundtrack of me swearing at the top of my lungs while I panicked as to whether the cops could get involved. Luckily, a quick Google search when I got home confirmed what I already knew. There were no issues since we are both consenting adults.

Except, there is an issue.

I'm not okay with it.

An entire lifetime can pass within our eleven-year age gap. He was just born when I was eleven years old. I graduated high school when he was probably still picking his nose on the playground at recess. He was graduating high school when I was preparing to get married.

But the real puzzle is when he learned to use his tongue like that.

"I don't know why you're so worried about the age difference. Age is just a number," Liv says, flipping a couple of pancakes onto a plate. "It shouldn't matter that he's younger if you both like each other."

I sit taller as my mouth falls open. "Liv, he's a newborn baby-man, and I'm a decrepit old woman. How do you not see the problem with this? We are in different phases of life. I'm divorced…he's not."

She slides the plate across the kitchen island. "What's a *baby-man*?"

I lean in to inhale the scent of buttermilk pancakes perfectly tanned with a slice of butter already melting on top. Liv pushes the huckleberry syrup across, too, and I come back alive to answer her question.

I flip the top of the syrup and pour. "A baby-man is a man who just became a man. He's in his manhood infancy." Still pouring. "He hasn't been through enough life yet to have the scars and maturity of an *adult* man."

Liv reaches over and grabs my hand to steal the glass bottle so I don't continue to drown my pancakes. "You said he's done a lot of traveling, though. Maybe he's more of a man than you think. Does he act immature?"

I know some might say I'm being dramatic, but I've never slept with, let alone dated, someone younger than me. "No…yes. I don't know. I'm going back through every conversation we've had in my head, and nothing stands out. But I'm also shocked I missed this. I don't miss details like this." I blame it on my divorce-life-crisis that has basically crippled me.

"You just met each other," she points out. "It's expected you don't know everything about each other."

I pick up my fork. "Ugh. Don't remind me!"

"Age isn't always the first thing that comes up."

I take a greedy bite larger than my mouth and chew quickly, sighing at how good the dark berry syrup tastes. Montana is big on all things Huckleberry. It's in everything: milkshakes, smoothies, muffins, ice cream. I intend to sample it all. If Lincoln weren't eleven years younger, I'd eat huckleberries off him.

But he is, so I won't.

I drop my fork, and it clatters on the plate. "Oh my God. I'm a cougar."

She laughs, setting the syrup down after drizzling some on her plate. "I think it's a bigger deal to you than anyone else. Are you sure he doesn't know you're older than him? Maybe he does? Maybe he doesn't care."

Did he not notice the telltale signs of someone well into their thirties, like the cellulite climbing my thighs? Laugh lines at the corners of my mouth from the extra decade of laughing I've done? Or how about the untamed forest inside my bikini bottoms that I had to trim with eyebrow scissors before going to his place? I thought he knew what a thirty-five-year-old woman's body looked like. He didn't let on, considering he sure knew his way around.

I can still smell him on me since I used his soap in the shower, or rather, he used it on me—vetiver and orange, woodsy and citrus, like a full-on warm hug that you never want to leave.

Using the edge of my fork, I cut another bite. "I don't know for sure if he knows how old I am. If he did, then yeah, he clearly doesn't care that he bagged an old biddie. But it's never the younger man that gets the heat. It's the older woman."

My parents are both the same age, and Wade had only been two years older than me, nowhere near the *eleven years* I'm staring down with Lincoln. No one in my life has had this big of an age gap, not even Frankie, and he loves older men.

Frankie.

The text messages.

I quickly wipe my sticky hands on my bathrobe and pull out my phone. I hadn't realized how beneficial wearing a towel was while eating pancakes. The material makes a perfect napkin.

Four bars—plenty of service to get all my missed messages. Not that I even remembered checking after slamming the front door on Ted and peeling out of their driveway like a Formula One racer.

There were a few texts from Lincoln as well, but I didn't open those. I scrolled right past his name to get to Frankie's, whose message is in all caps, his version of an S.O.S. He also sent it in a series of individual messages.

MOM AND DAD

BOUGHT PLANE TICKETS

TO COME SEE YOU

IN A FEW DAYS!!!

I gasp and cover my mouth as I skim through his texts.

"What?" Liv asks.

I can't even speak past the shock welling up inside me.

Liv rounds the counter to put a hand on my shoulder. "Myra?"

"My parents…"

"Did something happen?"

I shake my head and slowly lower my hand from my mouth to my neck. "They're coming to visit. In just days." The reasons *why* are running circles in my mind until I remember what Frankie said. "They've been worried about me. I think they want to come and make sure I'm alright."

She squeezes my shoulder. "Do you want them to come?"

"No." My answer is immediate. "I'm supposed to do this on my own. And now this whole thing with Lincoln…I'm more of a mess today than when I got here a few days ago."

I know they're more than a little worried about me. I signed divorce papers and spent most of Christmas tipsy in the basement with Frankie. Then I purchased tickets to Montana and texted Liv to say I was coming. We'll just skip over the Care Bear tattoo they now know about.

I wasn't in a good headspace and was losing my ever-loving shit.

"You could tell them not to come."

I put my elbows on the counter, bracketing my plate, and drop my head into my hands. "I can't."

"Why not?" she presses, leaning on the counter in front of me.

"Because then they will freak out even more and will definitely think I've lost my marbles."

"So what?"

Liv's always been so confident in herself. She doesn't worry about what other people think and is set on making decisions that are best for her despite everyone else's opinions. I've admired it since the start of our friendship. But she doesn't know my parents. They're leeches. They don't know how to sever themselves from anyone, let alone their own flesh and blood.

I lift my head and lean a cheek to my palm. "So…my parents will send the cops to come check on me if they don't come themselves. Frankie's text said they only planned to stay a couple of days and will fly out the day I leave. I'll still have most of this trip to…" I don't finish my thought. I'm not really sure what I want to do for the rest of this trip now that Lincoln is out of the picture.

I came here to ski and give my sappy self an experience of a lifetime. I'll have a few more days to figure it out, but I'll be doing it alone again. There's no way I'll ask Lincoln to continue our lessons now. Not when I've seen that baby-man's dick.

"Everyone is going to think I'm far from okay, especially if they know I pounced on a younger man." And they're gonna know. It'll be emanating from my pores or something.

She laughs, leaning a hip into the counter. "You can talk to your parents about how you feel, just like you can talk to Lincoln."

I stare at her and then my plate. The pancakes have absorbed most of the syrup like a sponge, and my tongue tingles at just the thought of taking another bite. If my stomach wasn't so tight with knots, I might be able to eat more. But I'm too anxious for food now.

"If I talk to him about all of this, what if he *does* care that I'm older?" I'm letting my doubts show, but this is Liv.

"I don't know. Maybe he will care…" It's an honest response that doesn't put me at ease like I'd hoped. "But maybe he won't." She leans her forearms on the counter, drawing my gaze to hers. "If you aren't comfortable with the age gap, no one says you have to be with him." She pauses. "But I know you've been through a lot in the last year, especially the last month. Maybe a hot, young distraction is what you need for the next week."

There was a time when I was that hot, young distraction.

I sigh heavily and pull my phone out of my pocket. It's not like Lincoln proposed marriage or even mentioned a relationship. It was just sex—spicy, all-consuming, I-definitely-want-more sex. It doesn't have to be more or less. Maybe Liv is right, and

Lincoln is the kind of distraction I need. He's shown me just how well he could make me forget.

I glance at my phone screen, noting a recent text from him. *I've got pastries and coffee. Heading your way.*

"Ohmygod." My words run together as I drop my phone on the counter. It clatters as I leap out of the barstool chair and cover my stomach, which drops faster than on a roller coaster.

Liv stands straighter.

"He's coming over here. He…he…it's…" I point at my phone like it's possessed.

"Deep breaths, calm down." She grips my shoulders and breathes with me. I'm able to easily inhale through my nose before she continues, "Now, what did he say?"

She drops her hands away, and I feel unstable again.

"Lincoln. He's coming over here. Now. I mean, soon. But also like any second because it was fifteen minutes ago, and he doesn't live far." My eyes are officially bulging out of my head. "We had sex last night, Liv! He can't come over here. I'm going to jump him again. I'm not this strong!"

She brings her hands to her chest in a prayer position. I want to tell her this isn't time for her zen; I need to rush back to the cabin and panic-clean for as long as I can. But her presence keeps me grounded to the spot, barefoot in her kitchen with a stolen bathrobe that's making me sweat.

She has her eyes closed, then exhales long and slow. I mimic her but keep one eye open.

"There," she says. "Now, he's likely coming over here to talk, which is what you were considering just a few minutes ago. You can do this, Myra. You have been through a lot and can get through this conversation, too."

I try to lift my lips in a smile.

"What's that face for?"

"I'm smiling."

"No, you're not."

I huff. "Well, I was trying."

"Maybe practice in the mirror a bit more."

This makes me laugh. "Thank you," I say on a sigh. "You're right. I can talk to him. I'm a grown-ass woman. I will keep my clothes on."

"That's right." She nods once and grips my shoulders in another comforting squeeze. "I'm sure you'll want to clean your cabin, though. I don't think seeing your underwear on the couch is going to send the right message."

I widen my eyes again and grab her elbows. "I have to go." I'm rushing toward her back door to take the cement path Liv has faithfully shoveled after each new snow when I stop and turn back to her. "Thanks, Liv. Save me some more pancakes?"

"Always," she says with a grin and a small wave.

I close the door behind me, hopping across the smooth paving stones to get to my cabin. Remembering shoes would have been a good idea, but I forget how cold even the short walk can be. Frozen toes are nothing compared to the shock of seeing the mess in my place. Shoot. I really need to get better at cleaning.

Wasting no time, I shut the door behind me and grab a discarded shoe, skirt, pants, pajamas, pillow, and that cowboy romance Frankie slipped into my bag. He told me that going to Montana instantly heightens my chances of finding a cowboy. I told him I'd be more interested in a date with the man's horse than the cowboy.

Apparently, neither is true.

I haven't even made the bed when someone knocks on the door. But I know who that someone is since his outline is visible through the glass in the door. It's a distorted view since the glass has a foggy effect, but I can still see his hand reach up to comb through his hair. The hair I raked my fingers through more than once last night.

I need to put all of that out of my mind. I'll have to tell him we can't see each other again, at least in the naked sense. I'll tell him my age and how I didn't know he was eleven years younger. I'll tell him he doesn't have to keep teaching me to ski. I'll tell him I can figure it out on my own, watch a few videos, find another instructor…

Everything in my hands goes back into my suitcase; then I tug the covers up on my bed before walking toward the door. Steadying my erratic breathing, I put my hand on the doorknob and twist.

Lincoln's smile is wide and friendly, hopefully like mine, until the corners of his mouth begin to drop a millimeter as his eyes do. They rove over me and heat my body to an uncomfortable temperature.

It's then I realize my first mistake.

I'm still wearing *his* bathrobe.

Chapter Nineteen

Lincoln

Otto has to bark beside me to grab my attention.

I'm staring at Cinderella in a white robe.

"Hi," I say, raising a hand like a Martian.

Just beam me up now.

She grips the robe at her chest and says, "You brought Otto."

"And sustenance." I lift the paper bag and small carafe of coffee. "Ted said you didn't get any this morning, and I couldn't have that."

She gives a short, nervous-sounding laugh.

"Mind if we come in?"

Otto wags his tail.

The chill from outside is infiltrating my bones while the memories of her lips are heating my skin. I want to lean in and kiss her like I did last night. Kiss her neck, between her breasts, her stomach, and the inside of her thigh, where her birthmark is. But the way half of her body still hides behind the door stops me.

She left for a reason, and I'm here to figure out why and hopefully continue seeing her. And also ask her to pretend to be my girlfriend for family game night—*one step at a time*.

She clears her throat and shifts on her feet—bare feet that is. "Yeah, come on in."

I stomp my boots to clear the excess snow before stepping inside on the mat and take them off. Maybe it's presumptuous. She shuts the door behind us, and I bend to brush off Otto's paws. He wastes no time slinking over to Myra for a hello leg bump and tail thrashing.

"Hey, bud." She crouches to scratch below his chin.

They share a moment of unintelligible language as he sits and licks her face, and she lets him. I doubt I'd get the same treatment if I tried, which is why I will keep my feet planted here and stare at the two of them. I didn't think this would be so awkward, but I have no idea how to act.

"Nice place." I note how bright it is with the floor-to-ceiling windows in this A-frame-style cabin.

The living room has a narrow tan couch and a coffee table with a TV across from it. The rug underneath all of it is colorful with pink, blue, green, and gold. The kitchen is directly across from the living space, and her bed is straight back from the front door. The place has a small footprint, but it's cozy. And *messy*. I do my best to act like I don't see a bra strap poking out from under the coffee table.

"Thanks." She smiles up at me. "The only thing it's missing is a bathtub. I miss my weekly baths, especially after freezing my ass off in this weather."

I almost open my mouth to offer her my bathtub and then remember the hot tub and why I'm here.

"Do you want a pastry?" I hold up the bag again and reveal all thirty-two of my teeth.

I'm trying to play this cool, but I've also seen her topless. Hell, I've seen her more than topless. Or should I say just straight *less*.

She stands still, petting Otto's head. "I'm not very hungry. Liv made pancakes."

I hold my breath and ask, "So, uh, I tried calling earlier to see if you wanted to ski today. We could continue your lessons." She opens her mouth but doesn't say anything. I panic and fill the space with more words. "I just don't want you to leave without having really experienced all that Montana has to offer."

All that Montana has to offer? What am I…a brochure? A travel agent? Jake with his damn business card?

"Lincoln," she says in a low voice as she studies her hands.

Nerves nag at my gut. "Yeah?"

"We need to talk about last night."

The world shifts under my feet. We're doing this. We're having the talk I've heard women have with Jake plenty of times. Now, it's happening to me.

I shift on my socked feet, then place the coffee and pastries on the glass table beside her couch. "Okay. Let's talk."

She exhales but seems unsure of how to start. "Do you want to sit down?"

"Sure." I nod because there isn't anything else I can do. Kissing her is out of the question. Holding her hand or asking her out on another date don't feel right.

She points at the couch, and I sit. Otto comes over to curl at my feet, and I instinctively bend to pet him. He isn't trained as an emotional support animal, but he is an animal, and I'm having a hard time sorting through my emotions, so today he is.

The loveseat is likely made for lovers since it's short and cramped. Myra sits beside me, our thighs touching as we stare forward. I wish I knew how to act in situations like this. Instead, I'm floundering like a sea animal trapped on land.

Just say something.

"I'm sorry—"

"I didn't—"

We both start speaking at the same time. I put out a hand toward her. "You go first."

She exhales again, like whatever she has to say is heavy on her chest. It doesn't take a rocket scientist to understand she's about to let me down easy. Or hard. I guess my hopes of another date or a fake girlfriend are out of the picture.

"I was talking to your roommate this morning, and he told me more about you…"

So it *was* Ted.

"I started putting together the timeline and realized you're twenty-four."

So it *wasn't* Ted. "I'm actually twenty-five."

This doesn't seem to help.

She peers over at me. "Right…well, I'm not twenty-five."

We never discussed our age; honestly, it never crossed my mind. Finding someone I enjoyed conversations and spending time with was more important. I liked learning more about her, and that seemed enough for me.

She shifts slightly, and now our knees are touching. "I'm thirty-five."

I clutch my hand to my heart and sigh. "I thought you were going to say seventy."

Her mouth falls open with a gasp, shoving me in the shoulder. "You better be joking!"

"I'm kidding. I never thought you were seventy for one second."

"How old did you think I was?"

"Honestly?" I ask. "I never cared."

Her shoulders seem to relax at this.

I angle my body more, pressing my knees even further into hers. She has great knees, but I don't think this is the right moment to mention that either. "Your age doesn't bother me."

"It doesn't?"

I shake my head. "I'm guessing you thought I was older?"

She bites her bottom lip and stares at her lap. "Yeah."

"Like, how old?"

"My age."

That's fair. Jake and Ted think I'm well past my prime based on personality alone. "Does it bother you?"

Her poor lip will have the imprint of her top teeth on it.

She huffs and falls back against the couch. "I thought it did a few hours ago, but now…I don't know. I've never slept with anyone younger than me. Hell, I haven't had a one-night stand since I was in college."

I clear my throat. "Is that what you want this to be? A one-night stand?"

The question seems to catch her off guard. "Oh, I mean…I figured it was since I don't live here, and I'm leaving next week."

"So?" The word slips out before I can stop it.

"So…I didn't think we'd casually keep seeing each other for six more days. And then the age thing…I guess I just figured it was easier to end things now. Like I said, I've never slept with a twenty-five-year-old before. I don't think I should make a habit of it."

I want to keep pressing and ask *why*. Why does she think that? What is it about my age that bothers her? Does she not think I'm mature enough? I don't ask any of these questions because I remember why she's here—newly divorced and wanting to pick up the pieces of herself. Isn't that why I'm in Montana, too? Picking up the pieces of my family that shattered because of breast cancer? We're different but also the same.

"Look, I have no expectations that we continue sleeping together. If last night was it for us, I'll be okay with it." And I'll try to be. "But I also really enjoyed hanging out and talking with you."

Don't do it.

Don't say anything.

I sigh and drop my chin. The weight is too much. "I moved back nine months ago because my mom told me she was diagnosed with breast cancer. Even though I'm close to my parents and brother, we're all living this reality. Talking to you felt like I didn't have to just talk about the cancer. I could talk about favorite colors and traveling, vegetables and Otto. It felt freeing not to have to worry for once."

I didn't know I felt this way until I opened my mouth, and it all poured out. Mom's cancer has weighed heavily on my mind since she told me, and I decided to move back. We've all talked about treatment plans, dietary needs, life expectancy, doctor's visits, and more. To not feel the pressure to talk about any of it with a perfect stranger was refreshing.

"Wow, Lincoln. I'm so sorry." She puts her hand on my forearm, the warmth etching the imprint of her fingers there.

I stare at it and say quietly, "Thank you."

"I know what it's like to want to please your family. To be there for them when it's hard and assure them when there aren't any assurances to be had."

Feeling her empathy is either making this better or worse. I can't tell yet. There's no way this woman isn't my soulmate when she literally just spoke to my soul.

"Are you close to your parents?"

She pulls her hand away and shakes her head slowly, like she doesn't admit this often. "Since my divorce, my parents have been torn up about it. But they weren't supportive of the decision. They're worried about me, and I understand, but it isn't the same. I wasn't exactly in the best place before this trip. But hell if I'll admit that to them or anyone else back home." She points at me. "You better not either."

I raise my hand. "I swear."

She lowers her finger. "I learned this morning that they're making a trip out here to check on me." She pushes out a forced laugh. "And for your diary entry later, I like talking to you, too."

It's the first genuine smile I've seen on her today, making my expression do the same. The text string with my family and the lie I told come to mind. I'm a big believer that everything happens for a reason, and though I wish I never told my parents I had a girlfriend, it was worth meeting Myra.

Here it goes. "I wonder if we could help each other out."

Chapter Twenty

Lincoln

You want me to be your fake girlfriend?" Her eyes are still the size of basketballs, and she's been repeating this for a solid three minutes. "And you'd be my fake boyfriend?"

I take a sip of the now-cold coffee I brought. We've completely bored Otto to sleep at our feet. "Essentially, yes. And to be clear, I didn't tell you about my mom's cancer to sleep with you again. I'm not trying to manipulate you or anything, which I realize sounds a lot like I am." I should have never brought this up. I'm digging a deeper grave. "It's not like I *need* to have sex with you."

She raises her brows.

I can't believe I just said that. "Not because the sex wasn't great—it was fantastic, really. You're phenomenal in bed." I tip my head. "And in the shower. I just want you to know we don't have to go further. We can keep this purely a fake dating relationship with zero expectations for more."

She whispers, "Phenomenal?"

I nod. "I don't want you to think I didn't have a good time last night. It was the best night I've had in an incredibly long time. I'll never forget it. But I think if we pretended to date, we would both get something out of it."

She takes a deep breath, reviewing me from the corner of her eye to see if I'm serious. "How do you figure?"

This is good that she wants to hear me out. "You said your parents are coming next week because they're concerned about you. Well, what if you told them you came here to visit me… your boyfriend? *Fake* boyfriend, of course. But you could tell them we've been talking online and decided to finally meet. Maybe that would put them at ease to see that you've moved on."

Her eyes are trained on the ground, and she's quiet, gnawing on her thumb. I think it's a good quiet. One where she's thinking and not figuring out how to get me out of her cabin.

After a while, she scans the room and then her weighty gaze lands back at me. "That could work."

I wasn't expecting her to agree so quickly. I had speeches and references ready to deploy. Otto being one of them. "Yeah?"

"Yeah. My parents have had this weird relationship with my ex since we separated. My dad still plays golf with him, and Mom apparently invites him to dinner." She shakes her head. "Maybe if they saw I've moved on, they'd stop all that and see I'm happily adjusted. Then I could *actually* move on."

I nod enthusiastically. "And if you came to family game night with me, my Mom could see I'm still living my life and putting myself out there more. She's going to love you, by the way."

"Really?"

"Definitely. I've never really had an actual girlfriend before, or any relationship for that matter…she worries, too."

She turns her body sideways, not even bothered that her bent knee has jumped over mine to rest against the top of my thigh. "Stop lying to me right now. I don't believe you at all."

I love it when she gets bossy. I laugh and cover her bent knee with my hand. "I'm serious. I've always been the quiet nerd; not many girls were into that in high school. Then, after graduating, I started traveling. There were a couple of flings here and there, but nothing serious since I was always looking to the next destination." I stare down at my hand on her knee, and her eyes follow. I remove it quickly. "I think we could pull this off."

She pushes off the couch to stand and pace the living room floor. Her thumbnail has been held captive between her two front teeth for most of the conversation.

"What about the touching and…kissing? We'll have to show them how serious we are. I'm a touchy person, and my family knows this."

I know this.

I tear my eyes from her and scoot forward to the edge of the couch, leaning my forearms over my legs. "Side hugs, maybe a peck on your head or holding hands every once in a while. Just enough to make it believable that we have a connection." I know this won't be hard for me. There are already sparks anytime Myra touches me. "Does that work for you?" I almost don't want to hear her answer. Maybe this will be what turns this whole idea into rubbish.

She stops to face me and puts her hands on her hips. "Sure, sure. But you're not going to get weird if I grab your ass or something?"

My eyes bulge from their sockets, and I have to clear my throat before saying, "No. Nope. Fine with me." My smile is raring to split across my face, but I try to hide it. "Is there anything else?"

The neckline of her robe has opened enough for me to see black spandex. Visions of black against her cream-colored skin are enough to heat my insides. I swallow and force my eyes to her face.

"We'll need to come up with a thorough story of how we met. Online is best since we live in two different places, and most of my social interactions have included Lorelei and Rory Gilmore at times, and at others, my vibra—" She stops herself abruptly. "Never mind."

There is no way I didn't hear that. I also have no idea who those people are she just mentioned, but I go with it. "We can come up with a story while learning more about each other. I was serious earlier. I would like to keep teaching you to ski. We can continue our lessons and hang out at the lodge afterward to get to know each other more so we're ready for the prying questions?"

I pose it like a question because I already feel like I'm the one who's come up with this whole plan. There's no way I want to move forward if she isn't into it.

My worries are put at ease when her shoulders drop slightly, and her expression lightens. "I'd like that, too."

The best part of this plan is that we still get to hang out. I'll get to see her during ski lessons and spend time with her that I may not have had otherwise. Maybe sleeping together will help us make this even more believable.

She picks at her finger. "Maybe we just won't mention our ages to our parents."

"Okay. That's fair." I stand, which is Otto's cue to push himself up to sit. He yawns just as I ask, "So, we have a plan?"

I keep my eyes on hers as I do. She offers me her hand to shake. "We have a plan."

Chapter Twenty-One

Myra

I told Frankie.

Six hours into our fake dating relationship and I cracked like glass on concrete.

"So, let me get this straight." He props his phone against something on his desk so he can talk with his hands on our video call. "You and Mr. Ski Patrol Ken are consensually entering into a dating relationship for the sole purpose of convincing our parents you're fine and his parents that he can get a girlfriend?"

"Yes, exactly. But if you call him Ski Patrol Ken anywhere outside of this conversation, I will slash your beloved throw pillows—"

"How violent of you." He cuts me off and clutches his heart.

"You didn't let me finish."

He purses his lips and waves a hand for me to continue.

"I will slash your beloved throw pillows with my ski poles."

"HA!" He laughs. "They're rentals, so you have to give them back."

I scoff. "And what happens when I become a full-time skier, huh? I can already stand without falling. Sometimes. Maybe half the time. I'll be traveling to different places, shredding up the snow like a bra."

"I think it's *bro*."

"Bra."

"It's definitely *bro*." He shakes his head. "You're missing the point."

"What point?" I ask.

He shrugs and studies his cuticles. "I don't know. I just feel that's what people in my position tell people in your position."

"I should've talked to Liv about this first."

"Okay, okay. Take a chill pill and relax!" he practically shouts through a laugh across the screen.

"Who says *chill pill* anymore?"

"I do, okay!" he shouts. "Now just stay calm!"

"I'm calm."

He squints at me. "Are you though?"

"Yes, I am," I say with a laugh. "But my hand is tired." I search the ground near the bed for something to prop my phone. Spotting a stiletto, I slide down and grab it. They are the most impractical shoes I own, but Frankie insisted there is always a reason to wear high heels. "This is the part where you tell me I'm making a huge mistake and will surely regret it when it all falls apart and everyone finds out we're fakes, Franklin."

"Don't you *dare* use my full name. Someone could be listening." He jabs a finger at me. "Unlike Mom and Dad, I don't think you're losing your marbles. I think this idea is brilliant; I wish I had come up with it. Now you get the best of both worlds.

Plus, you never take my advice anyway unless it's fashion-related."

He's annoyingly correct. Unless he's telling me what colors match best with my eyes, I prefer to chart my own course.

"I need to clean and eat and sleep."

He shimmies his shoulders. "Is Ski Patrol Ken coming over?"

"No. We're *fake* dating," I say for what has to be the millionth time. "I don't think you understand what *fake* means."

"It's like friends with benefits."

I contort my face into some kind of shock. "No, it's not."

"Tell me how it's not." He lifts one finger. "You're friends until you're around anyone over the age of sixty, and then you benefit. You'll get to hold hands, smooch, and whisper sweet-nothings into each other's ears in front of everyone."

He has a point. "But we aren't going to sleep with each other again. I already told you he's too young for me. Since when have you known me to date younger men, huh?"

His brows rise. "Since divorcing Wade."

I roll my eyes and prop my chin on my hand. "I can't do it, Frankie. He's wrapped in caution tape from head to toe. I won't do it."

"But is he naked under that caution tape?"

"Now *you're* missing the point!"

He claps his hands together. "No, I'm pretty sure *you* are, even when it's pointing in your face. Or other places."

"Just to be clear, we're talking about his penis, right?"

"Yes, Myra! We are talking about your fake boyfriend's pointer!"

I rub my forehead. This conversation is making me more exhausted. Tomorrow, I'm supposed to meet Lincoln at the mountain before the resort opens. I don't even think roosters crow as early as six in the morning. I've turned into a night owl since being out of school.

"I think that's my cue to hang up on you."

Frankie doesn't let me win and taps the red X to end the call before I can. It works every time. He hates hanging up last.

I pluck my phone out of my heel and click on the social media app I rarely open anymore. Call it boredom or curiosity, but it seems like the thing to do. Scrolling through too many people living lives that are way happier than mine hasn't appealed to me in six months. But it's been a while since I checked, and I feel like I'm in a slightly better place. There isn't a pit of dread in my stomach as the app loads.

I swear everyone's faces are brighter on here. Like they've positioned themselves directly beneath the sun while it beats into their eyeballs. It's forced and almost comical how fake it all seems.

Fake.

Boyfriend.

We should post a photo on social media. It'll be like casting a wider net in case Mom and Dad decide to do some sleuthing. Mom has an account for her mini Yorkshire Terrier, Muffin, which she is very active on. Posting there would be like a soft launch of our relationship status. Though, I'm not sure anything has been described as *soft* when it comes to my family. Mom would call right away and ask all sorts of probing questions regarding net worth and family lineage. Dad would congratulate me and probably ask if he golfs. I confirmed earlier that Lincoln does *not* golf. Thank God.

They'd be up in our business in no time at all, which is exactly what I want. The more they focus on us, the less Wade is in the picture and the more stable I'll look. It's brilliant.

I mindlessly scroll down my feed, seeing baby announcements, wedding announcements, breast implant announcements, and then a different kind of announcement that stops me cold. It's a photo of David, Wade's best friend who he might as well have been married to, and a slew of other people.

Besides David, I recognize only one other person: *Wade*. He has his arm draped around a woman in a red bikini and another in a blue one wrapped around his middle. They're like the freaking American flag, seeing as Wade still can't manage a tan. All ten people in the photo are blitzed and sunburned and... *Mexico*?!

I read the location tag at the top of the photo, and my heart belly flops off the diving board into uncharted waters with sharks and gross seaweed that keeps touching my foot. We always said we'd go to Mexico on our tenth anniversary. Neither of us had been before, and since our anniversary fell in early spring, we wanted to go somewhere warm. Well, it looks sizzling there. That's for sure.

Who are all these people? Why are they just on a boat doing stupid boat things like partying and wearing bikinis? I groan, click on David's profile, and scroll down to see his recent photos. There are enough of them to see how much fun they're all having. The more I inspect the pictures, swiping from one to the next, the more my body shuts down.

Everything is tense. My shoulders, my fingers trying to keep up with all the gag-me cliche photos on David's feed, and my stomach, which is currently taking up underwater basket weaving. Hot, angry tears push at the backs of my eyes, but I lock my jaw and grind my teeth like the dentist told me not to. But I can't stop. I can't *not* be upset. This was my *husband*.

We only made it halfway to ten years before I realized Wade was married to the marriage and not me. He wanted it to survive but was willing to crush me in the process. I couldn't let him, so he broke up with me. But it wasn't just a relationship breakup, it was a life breakup. Everything about our lives had been intertwined until it wasn't.

Unlike Wade who had the means to start over, I had to leverage *everything* in order to do so. Rent, food, car payments, insurance, and furnishings for my apartment weren't cheap. I had to play the sister-card and borrow money from Frankie to get myself a bed. Wade took that, too.

I click the side of my phone to turn off the screen before rolling onto my back. Covering my mouth, I close my eyes. *Don't cry. Don't cry. Don't cry.* I bite my lips closed. I've already cried too many tears over this man. This trip is my second chance. The one where I'll figure my shit out and go home fixed. I better after the money I spent to get here. No more tears or locking myself in my apartment. No more chocolate…okay, that's not true.

I didn't come to Montana, rent the gear, purchase the lift ticket, and crash into a guy I ended up sleeping with and now refer to as my fake boyfriend for nothing. I'm here for *me*. Wade was married to someone else. I don't know that girl now. And dammit if I'll let her show up again. She's so unfamiliar; her actions, mannerisms, and life are foreign. She lost herself.

I was on the outside looking in on a life I participated in but didn't love. Hell, I didn't even like it. I just existed enough to survive. And by survive, I mean I made it through without any physical damage. But my heart…oh, my heart *hurts*.

If Otto were here, I'd hug his neck and cry into his furry shoulder. If anyone has convinced me I need a dog, it's Otto. Too bad Lincoln would notice if I stole him.

The tears fall fast down my cheeks even though I swipe them away with an angry hand like I can erase them for good. As angry as I am with Wade for being married to literally everything other than me, the *true* me, I'm more angry at myself that I lost my way. The girl who walked into that marriage isn't the same one who walked out. I should've been stronger and never let myself get so lost, but I did.

I failed.

I crawl under the covers, pull the comforter over my head, and let the tears come. The hot ones, the cold ones, the ones that thought nothing would ever change, and now the ones that won't let me give up. I cry for the wreckage and the loss. I cry because I'm not good at skiing, and damn, I just want to be good at something again. To find the confidence I had under all the shit.

There's a wet spot on my pillow, and the air around me is humid, thanks to my breaths. A soft light filters through the white comforter, lighting my small cave just enough.

I wipe my eyes and pick my phone back up, navigating to my messages with Lincoln. The last text he sent was hours ago when he got back home. *Made it*, he said. It's not even super significant, but the fact that he's playing a role in whatever life I'm trying to build makes me smile, even if it's small. I never responded, and despite wanting to text him and tell him to come back and help me forget about Mexico, I say something else that still feels a little crazy to type out but also cathartic. I never thought I'd be here, sending a message like this to a person like Lincoln.

Me: See you tomorrow, boyfriend.

I hit send without second-guessing myself, and that small act makes me feel like I won the day, even with tears streaking down my cheeks.

Chapter Twenty-Two

Lincoln

When we get to the top, point the tips of your skis toward the sky," I explain again. Chair lifts haven't exactly been good to her. "It helps for a smoother and more controlled exit. Oh, and scoot to the edge of the seat when I say, and lean forward. Don't lean back. Ever."

She exhales, her lips vibrating with the action. "I better not fall this time."

Instead of staying home to do chores as I should have, I took the rest of the week off to dedicate the extra time to Myra. I mean—her ski lessons. I left Otto with Ted today so we can practice without distraction.

I lower my goggles over my eyes and pull my poles out from under my thigh. "Well, I can't guarantee you won't fall." She's one with the ground at this point. "But if you remember what I said, you'll be safer."

"Don't lean back." She pushes air through pursed lips, grabs her poles, and lowers her goggles, too. "Okay. Let's do this."

It's cold this morning, but we're up here before the resort opens. Other ski patrollers will be riding up the lifts, too, and moving rope lines for the snow cats, tracked vehicles used to move the snow, all before nine a.m. But there are no other guests here, and being alone together takes on an entirely new meaning. Extra layers, gloves, and hats are a necessity at this hour since the sun is still working on climbing its way into the sky.

The top of the lift is in sight, and I move to the edge of the seat, holding my poles in one hand. Myra follows my cue. "Push off the bench seat with the hand not holding your poles. And remember, tips up."

"Tits up," she repeats, her breath visible. She sits up straighter, drawing her shoulders back and down.

The bright yellow of her coat shines like a sunbeam to the eyeballs as I do a double take. "What did you just say?"

The sloped ground connects with our heels, flattening our skis before she can respond. I push myself to stand, and Myra does the same. I ski down the small hill, trusting Myra's right behind me. She is, but she's also going faster than my current stopped position. She loses control and rams straight into my side, knocking me to the ground.

"Lincoln!"

My skis didn't pop off and neither did hers, so we're tangled up in a mess we'll have to get out of. I groan and tighten my hold on Myra's waist as she teeters on my hip. "I'm good. You?"

She shakily lifts her goggles, risking her balance. I roll to my back, keeping us chest to chest as her breath tickles my face. "Now I can say I've truly knocked you over."

Her laugh rumbles against my stomach, and I lift my goggles, too. "Was that a goal of yours?"

She chews the inside of her cheek. "Maybe."

"Did you say *tits up* while we were still on the chair lift?" I push my goggles up as my laugh dies down. My gaze drops to her lips.

Hers drops to mine. "Uh, yeah. That's what you said."

"No, it's not."

Her cheeks bloom with color. "Then what did you say?"

"Tips," I clarify. "Like the front tips of your skis."

Her breathing is still labored as she says quietly, "Oh."

The moment stretches before her lips turn up and then her belly starts shaking with her laughter. I laugh, too. I can't believe she thought I'd been saying *tits* this whole time.

Pieces of hair fall in her face, so I brush them away with my gloved hand like it's nothing because touching her feels like it just might be everything. But her laughter plummets until it's nonexistent. She's searching my face for something, but I don't know what. It's fleeting since she pushes herself off me with a renewed purpose. Our skis are tangled together, making it an impossible task.

I hold her hips steady so she'll listen. "Hand me your poles." She does, and I set those off to the side. "Now, slide off me to your left, keeping your feet parallel to the ground."

She starts moving and grunts. "I got it. I can do this."

Her weight is off of me, and I miss it. But I push up on the side of my hip and click the back of her bindings to release her boots. Since we're on mostly flat ground, I'm able to push up from my side to a standing position while staying attached to my skis.

"I think the first thing we'll practice today is stopping." I hide the obvious delight in my words as I brush snow off me.

"Don't act like you didn't enjoy that." She smirks, waiting for me to set her skis down before holding my shoulder to balance and step into them again.

I absolutely did. It's not that I'm complaining. Having Myra on top of me at any time or place is not my issue. But for her safety, others, and the trees, stopping is important.

"Didn't you feel how much I liked it?"

Her mouth gapes, but I lower her goggles over her eyes next so I can make it through explaining how to stop without getting distracted. Brown with caramel flecks is my new favorite color. "There are a couple of options. First, I'm going to teach you how to pizza."

She shakes her head. "It sounded like you just said *pizza*."

"I did." I grin and point down at my skis as I reposition them to show her. "Tips—not tits—together, but not touching, and heels out wide create the shape of a slice of pizza. See?"

"This makes a lot of sense why a random stranger was yelling this at me the other day," she says.

"Someone was yelling *pizza* at you?"

She stakes her poles on the ground beside her. "Yeah. I was going too fast down the hill again and couldn't stop. I guess that was their way of helping me. It wasn't helpful."

"I can see how that would be confusing." I nod once. "Anyway, you have to promise me something, though."

"I'm not just going to blindly promise you something. I need context."

I point at her skis. "This is your context. What did you think I was going to ask you to promise me?"

She shrugs one shoulder and waves her hands. "I don't know. To extend my trip and help you save your small town by selling candy canes and fire-roasted chestnuts. All while teaching the local kids at the community center a dance to instill Christmas cheer in the hearts of the townsfolk."

I gape at her, then laugh. "Are you speaking from a previous experience?"

She whacks my leg with her pole. "I'm not good with promises. Just teach me how to stop."

I lean closer, not afraid of her poles or the fierce look I know she has behind those goggles. Behind all that is a slight prickle of fear; I want to smooth it out like lotion on skin. "Promise me you won't rely on this method of stopping forever." I offer her my gloved hand to shake on it. She takes it to my surprise. "There will be no power pizza down this mountain. Okay?"

Her laugh carries on the light breeze. "Power pizza? You just made that up."

I shake my head and bring our joined hands closer to me. "It's where you do the pizza stop all the way down the mountain. Most kids learn this so they don't hit a speed where they feel out of control. Once we get you comfortable with speed, we'll practice the french fry method."

She juts out a hip and tilts her head to the side. "Liar. You just know I like french fries."

"I do, but these are actual terms, I swear. So, do you promise?"

She twists her lips to the side and squeezes my hand tighter. "Promise."

"Good." I squeeze her hand once, drop it, and push myself forward. I twist around on my skis to face her and ski backward.

"Wait!" she yells after me. "I'm not ready!"

"I'm not going far." I ski backward a little further to where the ground pitches downward. "Okay, push forward, then pizza your skis when you start going faster."

She peers down at her skis, gripping her poles tighter in each hand, then back up at me. "You just casually ski backward like it's no big deal."

It's not. "I've been doing this a little longer, remember? You'll learn how to ski backward soon enough."

"Don't threaten me with a good time."

"I will," I yell back.

She doesn't respond, and she doesn't move either. The sun is just high enough above the mountain to light our way, but I can see the fog created by her breath more than her lips from this distance.

Her skis aren't moving, and it's like she's deciding whether to trust me or herself.

"Use your poles to help guide you forward, sliding each foot on the ground like you're on an exercise machine," I call up to her.

She nods and does as I say. Her skis start to move, but her balance wavers with the movement.

"Keep your knees slightly bent, and lean your shins forward into your boots."

Her stance changes as she makes these slight adjustments. She already has better form. The grade of the slope changes, and her skis start to carry her further and faster toward me without needing to push off. Her balance is still shaky, but she isn't leaning back, a marked improvement.

"Pizza!" I say as she gets closer.

She works hard to get her tips pointed together and is able to do it at first. But as her laugh gets louder and she gets closer, she pushes her toes in too much, and her skis start to cross. She stops laughing and starts screaming instead. She barrels into my arms, but I catch her so we don't fall over again.

"I pizza'd too hard," she says into my shoulder.

I lift her until she gets her skis under her. "Is there such a thing?"

She pushes her goggles up to rest on her helmet and glowers at me.

"You're going to get this," I say, making a promise of my own.

Her eyes drop to the ground, and she shakes her head.

I don't know what motivates me to do it, but I need her to know she can. I lift her chin and look between each of her eyes. One says she can't do this and will keep failing. The other says she wants to figure this out for the life of her.

"When was the last time you felt confident in yourself?"

Her lips part, and she blinks rapidly. "Lincoln, it's fine. You don't have to give me a pep talk. I'll do it again. Let's just keep skiing."

She goes to pull away, but I still have her chin in my grasp.

"I'm serious." I lower my voice. "When was the last time?"

Her eyes track over my shoulder, somewhere other than me. She bites her top lip. "I don't want to say."

I rub the tip of her chin with my thumb. "You can tell me, Myra."

She sighs but isn't committed to eye contact and bounces her gaze again. "Before we went in the hot tub."

I let the memory from the other night play in my mind.

"When I was getting dressed or…undressed into my swimsuit," she says quietly. "I felt good about myself. How I looked, how I felt, what I wanted…"

I remember it well. The set of her shoulders, the way she left the robe open, the lift of her chin as she walked out. The way my heart pounded inside my chest, and how I couldn't keep my eyes off her. She walked out wearing less, but I could feel the *more* around her. The air had changed. She *knew* she was hot. She knew that *I knew* she was hot.

"I remember," I say quietly.

She drops her head but flicks her eyes up to meet mine. Her face is close enough that I can feel her breath on mine. The memory is emblazoned in my mind, filed at the top of my *All About Myra* list.

If I'm going to avoid kissing her right now and respect the boundaries she set, I need to stop while I'm ahead. I clear my throat and drop my hand. "You were confident then, and you can be confident now. And if you don't get it the next time, tell yourself you will." I lick my lips and let myself stare at hers briefly. "I know you can do this, so show me."

Just like at my house, the woman in front of me transforms with a sure nod. She tries again. And again. And again. Until she skis down to me, pointing her skis without crossing them. She still doesn't' cut her speed enough and rams into me but wraps her arms around my neck and laughs while I make sure we're on solid ground.

I bury my face in her neck. "I'm proud of you."

She pulls her head back. "We have to take a picture."

I laugh. "Right now?"

"Right now. I don't want to forget this."

She removes her glove, unzips her coat, and pulls out her phone to position it in front of us. Her arm tightens around my neck as she pulls my cheek flush with hers. It's warm and inviting, and I never want to leave.

Our smiles are big and bright as she snaps a photo of us. "Aren't you going to ask me?"

I try to look at her, but she keeps my head straight and snaps more pictures. "Ask you what?"

"What made me smile today."

I laugh, and my breath goes up in smoke and then disappears. "It's still morning."

She positions her phone at a different angle. "So? Ask me."

I lick my lips. "Myra, what made you smile today?"

Her smile grows, and I wish I weren't just seeing it on her phone screen. "This."

On the last one, she pulls away, and I think she's satisfied with the shots. But she still has a vice grip on my neck and decides to plant a kiss on my cheek while snapping another picture. My expression is stunned at first, but then it softens because Myra's lips on my skin will never make me feel any other way.

"That's the one."

She shows me the photo of us, and it's a good one. No, a *great* one. I'm happy, and I'd wager she is, too. My mind is in knots over this woman. "Send it to me?"

She lets go of my neck, and her thumb glides across the screen. "I'm going to post this online, too. Nothing says *official fake dating relationship* like posting this kind of photo."

"Are you sure?" I'm not sure where the hesitation sprouts up from since this was my idea to start.

"Of course. I bet I'll have a text from my mom by the time we reach the lodge."

Chapter Twenty-Three

Myra

Hi, Mom."

Her voice is high-pitched as she asks, "Myra, who is that strange man you're kissing?"

I knew it would work. By the time we racked our skis and walked inside, I had three missed calls and a long string of texts from Mom *and* Dad. The news had reached Phoenix.

Lincoln shakes his head from the other side of the table with a wide smile. After finishing the run, he ordered us a basket of fries and two cocoas—my reward for successfully getting down without falling. It turns out that learning to stop is incredibly helpful.

I wink across the table at my co-conspirator. "He's my boyfriend, Mom."

"You don't have a boyfriend."

I grab a fry for protection. "I do now."

"Since when?" Her pitch gets higher at the end of every question.

Since yesterday, I think to myself, but I don't get the chance to come up with something since she continues. "A couple of months? What about the divorce? You just officially signed a couple of weeks ago!"

I'm well aware. "Yeah, but we've been separated for a long time. That's why I waited until afterward to visit him. It's uh… celebration."

Lincoln twirls his finger in the air to show how lit this party is.

She gasps, and I imagine her clutching her pearls. Except she wouldn't have pearls, she'd have diamonds. "And where did you find this *boyfriend* of yours?"

"He's not a puppy, Mom." I laugh while flipping my fry around while I talk. "We met online."

"Online?"

I sigh. "Are you just going to repeat everything I say?"

"Myra!"

"What?" I ask, but I know exactly *what*.

Mom might have a social media account devoted to Muffin the Yorkie, but she's also spent a good deal of time reminding Frankie and me about the dangers of the World Wide Web these days. She still sends us true crime videos about internet stalkers and profilers.

"You can't meet a boy online and travel to another state to meet him *by yourself* for the first time! What if he's a psycho?"

"Mom," I chide. "He's not a psycho. I did my due diligence to make sure before I flew out here. He's sitting with me right now and just bought us both cocoa. He's also teaching me how to ski."

"Let me see."

"What?" I say again in so many minutes.

"Do the FaceTime thing on your phone, and let me see him."

I drop my fry and stare at Lincoln. His rumpled hair sticks up in different directions since taking off his helmet, and the devilish smirk he has on his face is enough to melt my insides; he looks so incredibly sexy without even trying. He's nothing like Wade, which for some reason makes me feel protective of Lincoln. It doesn't make any sense. We aren't dating, and the fact he's younger would only raise her hackles. I don't want to know what she thinks.

Or maybe I care too much.

I bite my lip and try to think this through. Ever since Frankie told me my parents were coming to visit, I've ignored their calls and texts. I figured if I didn't talk to them, it wouldn't happen. But now that Lincoln and I are a fake couple, they'll see just how *fine* I am. Let them see him.

"Myra?"

"I'm here." I nudge Lincoln's leg and point at the phone.

"Well, we want to see him," she says.

"Hi, buttercup. It's Dad."

Like I wouldn't know his voice anywhere.

"Hi, Dad." I hadn't planned that they would meet Lincoln yet. Just see that we were internet official.

"I hear we're going to meet your friend," Dad says.

"Boyfriend, Dad."

"Boyfriend? Since when?"

"Since…" I start, then pull the phone away from my ear, pressing the mute button, and lean closer to ask Lincoln, "How long have we been dating? They need specifics."

He draws his brows together while eating a fry. "Two months?

Two months. Long enough to want to meet one another in person, short enough that we're still new. I unmute them and tell my parents. They go quiet for a minute.

Then Mom says, "So, let's meet him! If he's right there with you, what better time?"

I gulp. "Alright. Hang on." I put them on mute again, knowing they won't know the difference whether I'm starting the video or not. "They want to meet you...on FaceTime. What do we do?"

He brushes the salt from his hands and pushes the basket of fries back, waving me over to his side of the table. "Come here."

I stand, pushing my chair back with a scrape. I plan on pulling the third chair at our table closer to him, but Lincoln grabs my waist and settles me on his leg, my knees touching the inside of his other thigh before I can do anything, including breathe.

"Okay, ready," he says. "Go ahead and call them."

My mind is everywhere but on calling my parents to video chat. I'm thinking of hot tubs and showers, maybe a bed. "We don't have to do this."

"FaceTime them? Yeah, that's what we wanted. It might be easier to meet them like this first."

"No, I meant *this*." I aggressively point at our bottom halves, which are superglued together by gravity. "Talking to them while I'm sitting on your lap."

His expression is so pure; it's like he doesn't understand what's wrong with this. But I do. This is not good, mostly because the thin leggings I'm wearing and his athletic joggers aren't enough to hide the shape of him beneath my ass. Only second to that is how intimate this is. I know we're fake dating, but this is showing my parents a whole new level of *closeness.*

His hand finds my waist, and my stomach flutters. "I'm okay with this if you are?"

His eyes roam my face, searching for where I put my distaste for sitting on his lap. He won't find it because there is none. I like this. So much that I'm afraid of just how much.

I wave off my earlier hesitations like a pesky fly and nothing more. "I'm good with it. Let's just call them."

I hit the video button on my phone and unmute my parents. My phone screen fills with our faces, me a little higher than Lincoln but him smiling like this is the best day of his life. My smile could haunt little children.

The ringing stops, connecting us so the eager faces of my parents, who are sitting beside each other on the living room couch, fill the whole screen. Mom's holding Muffin, the infamous Yorkie, high on her chest, nuzzling his face with hers and appearing just like the elitist woman she is. Dad is all smiles, wearing his signature suit jacket he wore before the millions.

"Mom, pull the phone away from your face a little." I can see up her nose.

She ignores me. "Hi," Mom coos, bouncing Muffin. "You must be Lincoln." She says this as if I've told her about him, and we talk about him all the time.

Lincoln squeezes my waist, which surprisingly calms my nerves and helps me relax a little. "Hi, Ken and Beth."

I breathe a sigh of relief at the fact we went over names and a brief explanation of our family members on the chair lift this morning. I'm just glad he remembered and didn't need flashcards.

"It's nice to…meet you," Mom says, her forehead completely stationary and void of much expression thanks to Botox. "I hear you're dating my daughter."

I feel seventeen again.

"I am. After talking every day for several months, I invited her out to ski."

"Well, that certainly explains a lot," Dad says with raised brows as if wanting to learn to ski was so inconceivable that I needed a boyfriend to do it.

I force my eyes not to roll. "See…" I grab Lincoln's chin. "Not a psycho. Just a hot guy I really like."

I let go of his chin, wishing I hadn't just said something so close to the actual truth. He isn't just a *hot guy*. He's freaking catnip. But what I said doesn't seem to bother him since he doubles down by kissing the top of my shoulder. I'm speechless, melted wax beneath the wick of a candle. He's *good* at this. It makes me want to be better.

He grabs the phone from my hand to hold it. "We're having a great time. Myra has made a lot of progress on the slopes, too. And she'll be meeting my family tomorrow."

Mom smiles wide and rests a hand on Muffin's head, vigorously petting him until his eyes pop out. Dad doesn't stop nodding; he's eating this up. *He loves him.* But Dad is the easier of the two to please.

I grab the phone back and nestle further into Lincoln's chest, getting as close as close can be without burrowing inside his clothes. Before we say goodbye, I have to clear something up. "Frankie said you guys were planning to come for a visit?"

Please, please change your mind.

"Oh." Dad steals glances at Mom, words passing through raised brows and slight shakes of their heads. They both face the phone again, and Mom says, "Yes, we already bought tickets."

"You should save your money." I laugh nervously. "Go to the Bahamas, or I don't know…"

"The Alps," Lincoln chimes in.

"Yes! The Alps." My neck hurts from all this nodding and trying to convince them the Alps are better than visiting their daughter in Montana.

Mom shrugs and peers once more at my dad. "I guess we could call and get them refunded. You seem to be—"

"Having the time of my life with my *boyfriend*?" I curl an arm around his neck and wonder if kissing him would be too much. *What the hell?* There is never *too* much when it comes to my parents, so I turn and kiss his temple, lingering long enough to make this seem as believable as it feels.

Lincoln's hand tightens on my waist as his expression morphs from peaked brows to a lazy grin on the phone screen. I finish catching them up on how Liv is doing and then tell them we have to get ready for our date later that night. It seems to put them at ease since they gracefully end the conversation, and we say goodbye.

"I think...I think they believed us." I stare down at my screen, half believing it was that easy. They were smiling, nodding—a lot—and seemed genuinely *elated* for me.

"I don't know them as well, but I feel like they never stopped smiling the whole time," Lincoln says.

I shift on his lap. "Right? Frankie will be pleased they won't be coming here for a checkup. I'm sure they were planning to drag him along. He's always been my buffer."

I think I dodged the visit from them. They have nothing to stress about and no reason to fly to Montana now that they know why I'm here. Mom hates the snow, and Dad is a total pool bum. Suggesting the Alps was an aggressive choice, but they didn't seem to balk.

Lincoln leans further back in the chair. Neither of us has moved despite the call being over. I don't want to go back over to my seat. Not when it's probably cold. "Did you tell your brother about us?" he asks in a low voice.

I go completely still. "Yeah. I'd planned on telling you but hadn't gotten the chance yet. Frankie won't say anything. He's definitely on our side."

"Our side," he says wistfully. "I guess since Jake and Ted already know, it makes sense."

"So, tomorrow, we'll do this all over again with your family. Tell me about your parents. I want to know everything: favorite foods, hobbies, brand of shampoo, all of it."

He rests a hand on my knee, and I try not to squirm. "Mom is bright, warm, and hard to look away from. She's just like the sun in a lot of ways. A lot like you."

A lightness fills my chest, loving how he described us.

His hand slides up an inch, but I'm not sure he noticed. He just…did it. "Dad loves to tinker with stuff. When I was growing up, he spent a lot of time in the garage, working on something different every time we went in there to see what he was up to."

Tinkering for my dad involves turning up the temperature in the hot tub. He may not be a builder by nature, but he does know how to use his phone to call someone who is. Our families seem like total opposites.

Lincoln continues, "You already met Jake and know what he's like. He's got way more game with women than Ted and I combined."

He laughs at this in a self-deprecating way. But he wasn't on the receiving end of Jake's pickup lines. They sounded rehearsed and overused. And the business card? *No thank you.* But Lincoln seems to admire him nonetheless.

"And you?" I ask.

"Me?"

"Yeah. If someone were to describe you in a couple sentences, what would they say?"

He surveys his hand above my knee like it has a mind of its own, stroking his thumb along the outside of my thigh. "They'd say I'm quiet. Introverted to most, but to others, just a guy who likes a smaller crowd and more one-on-one conversation."

This doesn't feel like enough for me. I want to know more. "Keep going."

He peers up at me and then back at his thumb rubbing circles into my leg. I gaze there, too. "They'd say I wasn't very good at talking to women."

"You're talking to me," I say, bumping his shoulder with mine.

"Yeah, but…" His words trail off.

"But what?"

He keeps stroking my leg but looks up at me, clearly trying to decide whether to say it. "But not just any talking. The kind of talking that makes someone like you and want to be around you all the time just to see what else you'll learn. The talking that leads to no talking. That's always been what Jake's good at…not me."

I'm quiet, and he studies me. There's no way a twenty-five-year-old brain is in this body. The more we've talked, the less I've believed there's an age gap. Not just because Lincoln is mature, but rather because he's genuine and aware. He knows who he is and what he's like, and while he wishes he were like his brother, he doesn't realize just how special he is as *him*.

His voice is muffled as he shakes his head. "I'm sorry. I shouldn't have said it that way.

"No, no. Don't be sorry. I was just thinking…" I start to say in a rush, wrapping my arm around the back of his neck again and playing with the hair at the nape of his neck. "We slept together, so obviously you have some game."

He quirks his brow. "Yeah, but that was only once, and now, we're fake dating, so I'm not sure it's working that well." Another laugh.

I don't like that he thinks this. It's not true. I'm not moving to straddle him right now because, one, we're in a public place, but two, regardless of how solid he seems, he is younger. Plus, we live too far to start something long-term. But if both weren't a reality, I'm positive things would be different.

Every time I've been around Lincoln, I'm his sole focus. And it's not just me. He pours his attention on anyone he's talking to. Hell, the woman at the lift scanning our passes this morning was blessed with consistent and steady eye contact from Lincoln as he said good morning. He's great at making others feel seen.

"Look at me," I demand. He does. "You do have game, alright? I wouldn't have let you see my tits otherwise." That earns me a real smile. "But the thing I would say when describing you is how authentic you are. How pure your heart is toward others, and how patient you can be. I mean, you're teaching someone who crashed into you how to ski." I stab a finger into his chest. "That's the kind of man you are, Lincoln."

I said all of these things to Liv and Frankie already. They've taken up space in my head, my daydreams, and my wandering thoughts. During the slices of times we haven't been together, I think back on the times we were.

Maybe this is why I agreed to be in this pretend relationship. Because being around Lincoln is as easy as it is enjoyable. I'm not thinking about what I don't have but rather what I do.

"Thanks, Myra," he whispers.

I tip his chin up like he did to me earlier. "Chin up, Linc. You're pretty fucking rad."

Chapter Twenty-Four

Lincoln

Knowing that we need to take pictures for social media opened a floodgate of photo ops.

In front of the resort sign, on the chair lift, in the lodge, outside the lodge, and her on my lap. We spent the remainder of our time together yesterday just taking pictures. I wonder if that's because photos allowed us to touch or if Myra is that active online.

I haven't used my social accounts in ages, but I still asked her to send me every single one of the photos. We look good in them. Myra is smiling from ear to ear in most of them, except for the ones she decided to lean in and kiss my cheek. Those are my favorites. Or the one we just took outside of my parents' house. That's my favorite, too.

She studies her phone. "You're getting better at smiling."

I lead her by the elbow up the front walk so she doesn't slip and face plant. "Better?"

"Yeah, your face seems more relaxed and natural."

"Step," I say, and she lifts her foot. "I've had lots of practice today." Except, it's not enough. I need more.

She raises her arm with her phone. "One more."

I wrap one arm around her waist, squeezing tighter than the black denim hugging her curves, and rest my chin on her shoulder, all while balancing the plate of deviled eggs. "See!" She shows me the photo, resting her hands over mine on her stomach so I don't let go—another great photo. I might even print that one. "I'm going to share it."

I don't make a move to unravel from her as she clicks through the app to share another picture of us. She said she's had family and friends reach out and ask who the man is. Some of them weren't even aware she'd been divorced, so after some clarification, the photos seem to be doing their job of letting everyone know we're official.

Despite her brother knowing about our fake dating situationship, she hasn't shown him any pictures of me yet. I haven't seen any of him either. Myra said it was because she didn't want Frankie running wild with that kind of information, but what about me? I've tried not to let it get to me. We aren't actually dating; she doesn't owe me a photo or family tree, even if I want them to get to know her better.

"Don't forget to send me—"

The door flings open, cutting me off, and Mom is standing on the other side with all of her teeth visible, clapping her hands and bouncing on her heels. She's wearing her signature wrapped silk scarf around her now balding head and a two-piece, silk green kimono set with pink flamingos.

"Mom."

"Linc!" She holds both hands out, wiggling her fingers to invite me into a hug. I don't hesitate and step inside to wrap my arms around her slight middle, the Saran-wrapped plate still held tightly in my grip. She feels smaller tonight under all the flamingos. She pulls away and peers around me. "And you must be Myra."

"Hi, yes, that's me." Myra steps inside and offers her hand, and I know exactly how that will go with Mom.

"Call me, Julia," she says, tugging Myra into a hug while I shut the door.

Myra accepts the crushing hug and then laces our fingers. The physical contact with her feels natural. I thought we'd have to try harder to be convincing, but she's as comfortable with physical touch as I apparently am. It'll come in handy tonight. Talking to her parents on FaceTime while she sat on my lap was one thing. A few hours with mine, and they'll want to see the full spectrum of PDA. Hands, legs, backs, cheeks, all of me reaching out for all of Myra.

"Come in, come in, both of you!" Mom says, waving for us both to enter further.

We slip our boots off while Mom takes the plate I've been juggling. Then, I ask, "Where's Dad?"

Her eyes are more sunken tonight, but her cheeks seem rosier with good color in her skin. Some days, her skin is grayish, and I worry. She tells me not to, that it's just the chemo taking a toll on her body but not her spirit. But I can't help categorizing each new detail every time I see her.

Her eyes bounce steadily between us. "He's in the garage and will be inside soon. Where's Otto?"

"Home with Ted."

She juts out her lower lip. "You know I love seeing my grand-pup! Bernie is in the kitchen with Jake and will be so disappointed."

Myra laughs from beside me. Mom is a true nurturer. She's always wanted grand-babies but ended up with two grand-puppies for now. "Next time, Mom," I promise her.

She waves me off. "Let's get you two something to drink. Water, tea, wine, or I just made some hot toddies?"

We follow Mom toward the kitchen and family room, and Myra squeezes my hand once. "I love hot toddies."

I squeeze back, and it feels like an entire conversation passes between us without saying a word. She's saying she has my back. I'm saying I want her like this every week, together at my parent's house like an actual couple. Is this what it's like to have a partner? Someone you're so in sync with words aren't necessary? I like it.

We round the corner from the entryway, and Jake's smug expression fills my line of sight. "Myra! Lincoln! Welcome home."

He winks at me, and I roll my eyes, tipping my chin at him instead.

Gemma walks in behind us with a plate of cookies. "Hi, all."

I beam at the familiar face I used to throw mud at. "Gemma!" It's my turn to wink at Jake, and he does the obligatory eye roll. I drop Myra's hand and pull Gemma in for a hug. "Hey, I didn't know you'd be here."

"Julia invited me." She glances over at Jake, who feigns nonchalance while Bernie licks her hand. Her blonde hair runs long down her back, and I know Jake isn't immune, though he'd like to be.

Grabbing Myra's hand again, I introduce them. "Myra, this is our neighbor and childhood friend, Gemma."

Jake and Gemma have always had a weird relationship if you can even call it that. Gemma is a badass, while Jake is…not. Despite pretending they don't get along, they spend almost every day together. And when they aren't together, they text.

Myra shakes her hand and compliments Gemma's sweater dress and tights. I catch Jake raking his gaze down Gemma's outfit, too, and smirk at him. He glares at me.

Mom ladles the hot toddy mixture into a few mugs and passes them out as Dad walks in from the garage. He's got a smudge on his cheek from whatever he was working on and the same sweater he wore for Christmas, with Santa bending over, a thong riding up his backside.

"Still loving the sweater, I see," I say as he hugs me.

He shrugs, and the gray and white scruff on his cheeks lifts with his smile. "It's comfortable."

A very *Dad* response.

He hugs Myra and gladly accepts a hot toddy from Mom. We all grab a small plate of food, which is mostly made up of desserts that I didn't bring. Mom loves to bake, and since her diagnosis nine months ago, she doesn't eat much and ends up giving them away. The neighbors are well-fed.

Mom and Dad sit on opposite ends of the table while Myra and I sit beside each other across from Jake and Gemma.

"Have you ever played Nertz, Myra?" Mom asks.

She shakes her head. "I haven't, but Lincoln said it was like group solitaire."

Mom's smile splits the line of her mouth. It's her favorite game. "Exactly!" She slides a deck of cards to each person. "Make a pile of thirteen cards face down with the top card facing up. Then, flip four cards face up to the side. You'll use the rest of the cards in your hand to draw from, just like solitaire."

Myra deals the cards. "I'm with you so far. What about aces?"

Mom finishes laying out her cards and points at Myra. "Great question. In Nertz, it's community aces, so anytime you get one, add it to the middle of the table, and we can all play off it. Same suits in the middle, alternating suits on the four cards in front of you. First person to get rid of their pile of thirteen yells, 'Nertz!'"

"But…" Jake interjects. "It's based on points. So, even if you yell Nertz, someone else could get more points than you based on how many of their cards are out in the middle."

Gemma leans closer to the table. "And you have to subtract however many cards you have left in your pile of thirteen from your total."

"Oh, and watch out for Lincoln. He cleans up every time," Jake says, sorting his cards.

The amount of times I've played this game is staggering. Everyone acts surprised that I'm so good when we literally play this every week. But maybe I'm the only one studying techniques online and playing virtually against the computer.

Myra bumps my shoulder with hers. "I can handle him. Let's play."

"I know how competitive you are," I say. The woman skis like she's trying to qualify for the Olympics. We're nowhere near reaching for gold, but Myra isn't the kind of woman I'd doubt.

She scoffs. "You've never seen me play Yahtzee."

"I don't need to." I forget we have a small audience until Jake clears his throat. I peer around at everyone's watchful gazes and focus on shuffling my cards as conversation picks up around the table.

Leaning closer to Myra, I whisper, "If you win, I'll let Otto come for a sleepover tonight."

I know how much she likes him, and I may want the excuse of driving him to her house and picking him up tomorrow morning. And Otto will love it. He's always choosing to sit by her when given the chance.

She snaps her gaze to meet mine. "Shake on it."
So we do.

Chapter Twenty-Five

Lincoln

First person to one hundred," Jake says after counting all the cards. "Well done, Myra."

She raises her hands above her head in celebration, Santa doing a happy dance on her chest. A couple of wins ago, Dad decided to up the ante and put his Christmas sweater on the line for the next winner. I'm sure Myra will be cozy in her sweatshirt snuggled up to Otto tonight.

I shake my head. "Yeah, yeah. I was right behind you. You don't have to gloat. "

"Oh, but I do. Especially when you thought you were going to win that last one."

"I had you," I retort, leaning closer to her. "Jake, count them again."

He laughs. "Dude, I've already counted twice. You lost. Let the lady have her win."

Myra keeps her gaze locked with mine and leans in, too. "Now who's competitive?"

I lean in more. "Not me."

She breaks and laughs so hard she almost knocks her second hot toddy off the table.

"I think you've met your match, son," Dad says from the end of the table. "Myra, where'd you learn how to play like that? I thought this was your first time?"

Her laughter dies down. "It was. But my brother, Frankie, and I played a lot of games growing up."

Mom nods, resting her forearms on the table. "What does your family think of Lincoln?"

Here we go. The questions have commenced. At least Mom started with an easy one.

Myra looks at me. "They love him."

"Of course they do." Mom laughs.

"Mom…"

She shoves my shoulder, and I act like she is stronger than she really is. "Haven't I always told you how happy you'd make a woman one day? You're as gentle as a baby bird."

I groan. "Because every guy wants to be compared to a baby bird."

Jake starts snickering while shuffling his deck of cards. Gemma smacks his shoulder. "Julia's right. Lincoln is a sweetheart, unlike you."

Jake rubs his shoulder and sticks his tongue out at Gemma.

Cue the discomfort. I hate being the center of attention. Add in a fake girlfriend I'm very much trying to impress for real, and I'm about to run to the bathroom, claiming active bowels. It would be less embarrassing.

"Speaking of birds…" Dad starts. "Linc, did you tell Myra about the Halloween costume you and Otto wore this year?"

I throw my head back and cover my face.

Myra tugs on my arm. "Tell me!"

"Ugh. Do I have to?"

She wrestles my arm down. "Yes. I have to know!"

"It wasn't a bird costume," I say to Dad, and he shrugs with a playful grin on his face. "Otto was a bee."

Jake sets his cards to the side. "And what were you, Linc?"

"Yeah…Linc," Myra says with a lilt to her voice.

I hold up a hand. "Before you all laugh, *again*, it was for a good cause. We were raising money for our avy dogs; otherwise, I would have never dressed up."

Mom giggles. "I helped with the headpiece."

Myra looks back at me with raised brows.

My sigh drags out for as long as possible. "I was a flower."

Everyone laughs, as expected, but while Myra does, she leans into my shoulder, grabbing my bicep. I'm now thinking *do not flex* on repeat. It almost makes telling her our costumes worth sharing. No one could ever say Myra wasn't authentic. It's what I appreciate most about her. She laughs when things are funny, tells you if she's pissed, and kisses you when she wants.

I seem to always want now.

Despite Mom and Dad's attempts at embarrassing me, she seems to genuinely enjoy herself tonight. They tell her about Christmas morning with Bernie and Otto and how they hid all their gifts around the house and made them find each one. Mom couldn't help showing off the family picture wall where I'm sporting braces in a good ninety-nine percent of them. Dad showed Myra the jewelry box he made for Mom for Christmas. She doesn't wear any right now since they irritate her skin, but he tells us all *someday*.

There are a lot of *somedays* when dealing with cancer. Days you might get and ones you might not. It makes me want to be reckless and try asking Myra out again. I want to kiss her like we aren't trying to convince our families we're dating, not on the cheek like I did during the game. On the mouth, where there isn't a beginning to her tongue or mine.

It didn't help when Mom pulled me aside in the kitchen after cleaning up to say how much she liked Myra, how proud she was of me, and how she couldn't wait for more get-togethers. Was it worth lying to her about our relationship? At that moment, yes. The grin on her face, the blur of tears in her eyes, and the hope she exuded made me want to kiss Jake on his smug little face.

But later, when I'm lying in bed, and Myra isn't next to me, when she flies back to Phoenix and leaves me here in the cold, when I show up to family game night next week without her, and when I have to tell Mom the truth, I don't know if I'll feel the same.

"You're quiet." Myra leans against the kitchen island next to me.

"Just thinking."

She crosses her arms to mirror my stance. "You do that a lot."

"Think?"

She nods. "I like that about you. You're thoughtful in what you say."

I stare, her words doing little to tamp down my rising feelings for her.

Mom cuts in before I can respond. "Does everyone want to play again, or should we watch a movie?"

"Movie. Definitely," Jake says, standing from the couch where he and Gemma played a few rounds of Madden. "I can't keep losing like this."

Gemma stands, too. "I should get going. I've got an early morning at the mountain."

"How are the ski lessons going, by the way?" Mom asks from the other couch.

"Great! I've got a solid group of kids this year. I love teaching them."

Myra leans against the counter behind her. "So, you teach ski lessons to kids?"

"I do. Have been since high school."

"I'm a high school teacher but have no skill on the mountain, so Lincoln's been teaching me how to pizza."

Gemma laughs. "You'll get the hang of it. Lincoln has more experience than me, so you're in pretty capable hands." She gives me a wink. "Anyway, it was great meeting you, Myra. I hope you'll come back and visit again soon."

Myra waves. "Great to meet you, too, Gemma."

Jake nods to the front door. "I'll walk you out."

Gemma smiles at him, but I don't think he notices. It's different from the smile she gives me, Mom, or Dad. It's the smile she reserves for Jake. But he's too busy *not* noticing.

They leave the kitchen while Mom and Dad turn on the TV in the living room. I face Myra and rub her arms, lowering my voice. "You sure you're up for a movie? I think you've successfully won them over." Mom's words come back to me. *I like her.*

"It was your kiss on my cheek that sealed the deal." She peers up at me with the same smirk she wore when she won.

I couldn't let her have all the fun. Her smooth cheek was begging me to kiss it. I mean, her neck begged for my mouth, too, but I was able to ignore that voice. "I think you're right. Too much?"

"No." She shakes her head, twisting to face me while keeping her hip on the counter "I've had a lot of fun tonight. Your family is…lively."

I drop my hands, tuck them into my front pockets, and laugh. "Is that another word for crazy?"

"Only on Thursdays. Today's Friday."

God, I want to kiss her right now. It doesn't have to be a long one, but with my parents already surfing through movie options, the haven of the quiet kitchen is tempting. Leaning in would be so easy.

Her eyes track to my lips, and I'm positive she's thinking the same thing. But neither of us moves—the deal we've made looms over us. On one hand, it's given us the excuse to hang out with each other, while on the other, it's keeping our relationship honest with boundaries. We touch, but not too much. Talk about everything that comes to mind, but don't talk about the end of the week when Myra leaves. We almost kiss but never mention it's what we both want.

I mirror her position, resting a hip against the island. Instead of kissing her like I want to, I whisper, "What made you smile today?"

"Flamingos."

I must be glowing when I look at Mom. Her legs are curled up beneath her, sitting next to Dad with bright pink flamingos dancing across her whole body. In moments like these, cancer can't touch what we've formed within these walls as a family. It's gone, and glimpses of normal life become so big they almost feel real.

The emotion of it all is going to choke me. I clear my throat and shake off the thoughts. "I'm glad you came."

She bites her lower lip. "Me, too."

We stare for a beat longer, letting the words we can't say speak through our bodies. I rest a hand on the counter beside me like a kickstand, grazing hers with my pinky finger. Even if I can't have Myra, being around her feels like enough. Small touches and stolen looks. I don't want tonight to end. I want tomorrow with her, too. And the day after.

"What if we took a break from lessons tomorrow and went snowmobiling?" I ask suddenly.

Now that we've broken the news to our families and participated in all obligatory activities, from video calls to card games, there isn't an expectation that we keep this ruse up. Our fake relationship duties have been fulfilled. But that doesn't mean I want to quit hanging out with her.

"What do you guys think of the *Barbie* movie? I heard it was funny," Mom says from the living room.

Without taking my eyes off Myra, I call back, "That works."

"A day off sounds nice. My calves would appreciate it."

I try to act as though her answer doesn't mean something more. Snowmobiling isn't part of the agreement. Ski lessons are. "You'll get to see more of the mountain."

She twists her mouth and peers up at me through her lashes. "Alright. Let's do it."

"Yeah?"

She nods, then grabs my arm. "Now, let's watch the movie. I really do want to see this one."

With that, we walk into the living room to sit on the other couch. Well, Myra walks.

I'm pretty sure I float.

Chapter Twenty-Six

Myra

So, I'm supposed to sit behind you and Otto?" I point at the open space on the seat behind Lincoln. "And I won't fall off?"

"I swear you won't fall off." He tightens his helmet before pinning me with a hard stare. "I'd never let that happen."

Okayyy. That is not helping my feelings for this man. I don't think there is anything sexier than knowing he'd rather lose an arm than see me tumble off the back of this thing. It's the best and worst foreplay since I won't be acting on it whatsoever. This thirty-minute out-and-back trip is going to feel like a lot longer since we'll be sandwiched together like peanut butter and jelly. He's the jelly, obviously. Huckleberry to be exact.

There's nowhere else to go. The logistics of this scenario weren't exactly what I thought about when agreeing to this. I was thinking of more time with Lincoln.

Now I get more time, and I get to attach myself to him like a koala bear.

"You'll want to hold onto my waist, especially when we ascend," he explains as he circles his arms around Otto to reach the handles.

"I just have to hang on?"

"Yup."

I flip my visor down, too, and carefully edge behind him, doing my best not to get too close and break every vow I made to myself this morning. After the movie last night, I almost kissed Lincoln when he dropped me off at Liv's with Otto—the five-hundred and fifty-seventh time that night. The car was dark and warm, NeedToBreathe was playing in the background, and the hot toddies I'd had hours before were alive and well in my system. He leaned, I leaned, and then we snapped out of it at the last second. When Otto licked the side of my face, it wasn't exactly the kind of tongue action I had in mind.

But I can't pretend like our situation has changed all that much. Sure, I got to know his family and maybe fell in love with them while I was at it. His Mom is a freaking warrior queen in all her flamingo glory. And his dad was hilarious. Jake was...Jake, but Gemma helped even him out. It wasn't hard to envision myself there every week. I liked being around his family. But there are still roadblocks. Big ones. Ones I can't just wave a hand and make disappear like a master magician with a rabbit and loads of confidence.

I snake my arms around his waist. As he turns the key, the beast I'm straddling roars to life with a growl and curse. The curse was from me, though.

He yells over his shoulder, "Hang on tight, and don't forget to have fun!"

Then, he twists the handle and guns it forward, forcing my arms to tighten around him. The gap of space I left between us is no longer practical. I scoot all the way forward until there is no air between him and my inner thighs.

Otto sits completely still behind the clear windshield blocking the dusting of snow that kicks up as we traverse the mountainside from the lodge. Lincoln said he's trained for this, learning to ride on a snowmobile to get around the resort and, more importantly, during emergencies.

I wouldn't be able to yell over the loud vibrations of this motorized vehicle, but I'm less concerned about being heard than I am about falling off the back. I'm already gripping Lincoln's waist like it's a life raft, and I'm starring in one of those treacherous North Sea videos online where the waves—or snow in this case—crests over my head.

The snowmobile glides effortlessly on the two skis in the front as Lincoln steers us in the opposite direction of the lifts. Soon, there are more trees than people. The machine propels us forward with the rotating traction grip tread underneath. He turns us, and we climb more of the mountain. Small snowflakes pelt the visor of my helmet but melt immediately. Yet, the higher we ride, the more snow falls in a thicker curtain of white.

It's coming down to the point that I'm not sure how Lincoln can see through oncoming snowflakes. There are so many. And the clouds are so low, I feel like we're driving through them. He seems to think the same thing as his speed slows, and he twists the handlebars to take us back down the way we came.

We start descending. This is the stomach-dropping adrenaline rush Lincoln mentioned. He cuts his speed in half and points to something in the distance. He says something, too, but it's still too loud to hear him, so I follow the line of his arm.

It's a cabin.

We've only been riding for about fifteen minutes in the opposite direction of the resort, but there is no one else out here. The cabin sits nestled amongst a few trees with a small outbuilding in the back. At least, I think it's an outbuilding and not the abominable snowman. The brick chimney juts up through the snow-covered roof, and no other snowmobiles, cars, or skis are nearby.

It's just us.

And this cabin in the woods.

He pulls in front, and Otto immediately hops off and bounds through the snow to the small wood porch with a hanging eave, seeking some protection. The snow is coming down faster now, making it hard to see far ahead.

Lincoln kills the engine. "My visibility sucks. I should have rechecked the weather report to see what it would do. Let's stop off here and wait it out for a bit."

"So this is the abandoned cabin in the woods where you murder me. Hm, quaint."

He swings his leg over after I get off, sinking further into the snow and flipping up his visor. "Are you serious?"

I laugh when I see how wide his eyes are. "I'm...not..." I can't stop giggling. Maybe I could keep a straight face if he wasn't turning into Frosty the Snowman.

He picks up some snow and tosses a soft-packed ball toward me that explodes against my chest. "It belongs to the resort. They're dry cabins available to rent for backcountry enthusiasts. There are no amenities like running water or electricity and no roads in. No one is staying in this one, though."

The snowball I throw at him hits its mark on his shoulder. "I bet you know that because...muuuuurder."

He hucks another snowball, which I deflect, and he points to the roof. "No smoke coming out of the chimney."

I take off my helmet, breathing deeply as if I just held my breath the entire way up here, thanks to the speed at which Lincoln likes to drive that thing. The air is also much thinner up here than I'm used to. Maybe that's it. Or maybe its just Lincoln, which is a more terrifying thought than thin air.

I follow Lincoln at a clipped pace toward the murder cabin. "I could use a stiff drink after that."

"It's a good thing I brought wine and some snacks."

That sounds wildly romantic. There's no one else up here with us to well…see us.

"Don't worry, it's a Merlot," he says, unstrapping his helmet and searching the windowsill. "Your favorite."

"Merlot is delicious, but we have officially broken up."

He finds the key and shrugs. "You might have to make an exception if it's the only way of keeping us warm tonight."

I can think of a few other ways to keep warm.

Wait.

I sober up while already being completely sober. "Tonight? We'll be staying here overnight?"

He's too focused on sinking the key into the lock to let us inside to notice the shock on my face. Swinging the door open for us, Otto bolts inside, and Lincoln waves me in. "We can stay and wait out the storm. I won't be able to get us down the mountain safely with the visibility how it is now. But yeah, if it doesn't clear up, we'll have to stay the night." He removes one of the boards covering the windows like this is not information to freak out over.

Forget *murder* or the snowstorm blustering outside; a confined space with Lincoln just became my biggest problem.

I quickly shut the door behind me and latch it. Thanks to the filtered light from the dirty window, I can see my breath. Alone in a cabin together with wine and snacks spells trouble. Not to mention the fire Lincoln is already trying to start while kneeling in front of the stove. God, this couldn't get any more romantic. There are at least ten potential movie titles running through my brain with *A Blizzard of Blessings* at the top.

The fireplace is an old iron stove with a chimney jutting up through the roof positioned in the far back corner of the one-room space. There's a small stack of wood by the stove—no couch—but there are a couple of chairs and a small bistro table near what I'm assuming is the kitchen. There isn't a fridge or oven in the kitchen area, but there are a few upper and lower cabinets with glass knobs showcasing small painted flowers on them.

Lincoln said it was a dry cabin, meaning no electricity, plumbing…modern conveniences that I'm used to. But that's not the worst part. Directly across from the front door where I'm standing is a bed.

One bed.

✳✳✳

"CAN I POUR you a drink?"

"Only a little bit." The last thing I need is to get blitzed by Merlot on the side of a mountain with a very attractive Lincoln and only *one bed*.

I can't even look at it without breaking out into a sweat. Sex in the shower with Lincoln was amazing. But the bed? With leverage and support, we were *fire*.

It's too hot in here.

I've been glistening something fierce for the past twenty minutes but haven't taken off my jacket, too afraid it'll somehow turn into a strip tease. My long-sleeve shirt and bra will be next. It's a slippery slope I haven't been willing to take.

But I'm roasting alive, so I unzip my jacket force it off me and hang it on the back of my chair as Lincoln pours me wine. Handing it to me, he pulls out a plastic container and sets it on the table between us. Salami, nuts, crackers, dried fruit, and a couple of different kinds of cheeses are nestled between the small sections.

"This is a fishing tackle box," I say, noting the plastic and snap closure.

He unlatches the sides and opens the clear bin. "It's a snackle box. Snacks in a tackle box."

My mouth falls open. I look between the *snackle* box and Lincoln. This man is like a unicorn of epic proportions. He spends his days rescuing people, or at least practicing how, has a dog as his best friend, is an amazing skier and teacher, a sexual powerhouse, and now he's feeding me again. My brain is having a hard time computing that he's only twenty-five. This isn't my-frontal-lobe-is-barely-developed shit. He's nothing like his playboy brother, which makes everything he does even more genuine. *Damn it.* He's making this harder.

If I'm going to be stuck up here with anyone, I'm glad it's him. He's clearly prepared for the apocalypse with all the gadgets and gear he's pulled from his backpack. He's thought of everything, from a small ax to cut kindling to collapsible cups I'm now drinking wine out of. That fact makes me want to climb him and sit outside and cool off so I don't do anything stupid.

I take a few cubes of cheese and dried fruit and pop them in my mouth one at a time. I hadn't realized how hungry I was. I never had lunch, just coffee before Lincoln picked me up.

"So, do you take all of the women you're fake dating to this cabin and feed them snacks and wine in a collapsible cup?"

He finishes taking a sip of wine and laughs. "There are no other fake girlfriends. No real ones either."

His Mom's words from the other night come to the forefront of my mind. She said whatever woman he would end up with would be lucky, and she's right. I wholeheartedly agree. Lincoln might not see himself as dateable or good with women because he's introverted and often stays in his head, but when he does open up, like he's started to with me, it's hard to miss the gold in this man.

Maybe it's the dim lighting, or the three sips of wine I've had that makes me say it, but the next words roll off my tongue before I can stop them. "You're good in bed for someone who hasn't dated many women. Like, *really* good. The tongue thing…"

The shock on his face has me thinking I shouldn't have said anything. Being honest isn't always the best trait. Once it seems the near attack I gave him isn't happening, he folds his hands across his stomach. "You don't have to have a girlfriend to know things. I like to think I'm a quick learner. I read books."

His response is felt in my toes. And my quivering knees. And…higher. He's so selfless in how he cares for everyone else around him; he's thoughtful and kind…he's freaking *perfect*. I knew that the first time we met, when I was staring up at him between his legs and admired his eyebrows. They are perfect brows, but the heart inside his body is a close match.

I stare into the remaining wine in my cup. I've been drinking it like water and popping cheese into my mouth at an alarming rate. Paired with the vivid reminder of Lincoln's tongue, it's not helping my current situation.

And that bed…

I shift in my chair so my back is to the bed.

"What about you?" he asks.

I stare at him, confused. "What do you mean?"

"How long were you married for?"

The mention of my marriage is a sobering thought. Here I am, in a cabin with an attractive man, and the brief acknowledgment of the fact I was married is enough to make me feel like I've moved two feet in an entire year. Maybe I need to be here, alone with Lincoln, to get over the feeling I haven't gone very far. This is my new normal. Not necessarily being in a

backwoods cabin alone with a man I've already slept with, but…
yeah.

"Five years." I stick to the facts. "We were together for seven."

"Do you still…" He pauses. "Miss him?"

I let the question simmer before answering, but not because I'm unsure of my answer. "No," I finally say. "I don't miss him, so to speak." I drink the last of my wine. "I miss the ease, the partnership, the comfort."

I'm still angry at myself for staying. Angry I didn't notice when he checked out, and I was the only one caring. It was always for the sake of the *marriage* and never him or me, us together.

People understand when you tell them your ex cheated or there was an inciting incident that made sense why you'd grow apart. But for us, *we* were the problem.

"I'm sorry," he whispers.

I shake my head. "Why?"

He leans forward over his knees. "I'm sorry he didn't see you."

The words go straight to the ache in my soul that felt invisible in my relationship. Wade didn't notice me like I noticed him. One person carrying the team doesn't work for long.

I clear my throat and find gaze out the window. "It's getting darker."

He follows my gaze. "The storm hasn't let up. We should stay and leave in the morning. It should simmer down by then."

"So, I guess that means we're sleeping here."

He nods and sets his cup on the table to stand. "I'm going to go check the outhouse and make sure it's good to go. Need anything?"

"No." I'm sure if I did, he could whip it out of that Dora the Explorer backpack of his. "I'm fine."

I've been fine on my own before, and I'll do it again.

Chapter Twenty-Seven

Myra

One of us came prepared with a lighter, extra food for humans and dogs, a knife, and a first aid kit. The other one brought a smashed granola bar, tinted chapstick, and an extra pair of underwear due to the irrational fear of needing one.

I brought the underwear.

"Which side do you want?" Lincoln asks from beside me.

After he came back inside, we pulled our chairs up to the fire, and he boiled fresh snow outside to make cocoa. Oh, that's right. He brought a small bag of cocoa powder, too, which I drank faster than the wine. Lincoln is the kind of person you want in an emergency. Noted.

I peer out of the corner of my eye at the bed. I still can't look at it directly. "Right."

Better to just be honest about it. I've slept on the right since before I was married and have no intention of changing now, regardless of our situation.

He nods. "I always sleep on the left anyway."

I know. We slept together in all the ways.

I peer down at my mug and the layers of clothes I've already removed. It was getting hot in here, so I had to take off all my clothes—or most of them. Okay, not really. But I did finally get brave enough to shirk off my puffer coat, snow pants, and fleece jacket, leaving me in a pair of thick leggings and a fitted long-sleeve thermal shirt.

He crosses his arms over his chest. "Do you want to play a game?"

We've already been playing one. The goal is to *not* touch, and whoever does has to walk home in the snow. The rules, or consequences, are very straightforward.

"Nah. I think I'll just head to bed. Feel free to stay up." Maybe get in bed after I've already fallen asleep?

"Oh, I found more blankets in a bag under the bed that we can throw on top of us to keep warmer. The fire won't burn all night."

He must have found them when I froze my ass off, hovering over the giant hole in the shack outside. I came back in with frostbite between my folds, only to find he'd made the bed. He'd even turned down the sheets and fluffed the pillows. But there's still one thing missing: a considerable lack of space in the middle.

At first, I thought the bed was a queen size. But I'm pretty sure we're working with a full, which is one step up from the twin I grew up sleeping on. It's been glaring at me for the last hour since I came inside. The bed taunted me when I took my coat off and hung it on the hook like I was going to remove the rest of my clothes, too. *Jokes on you, bed.* But it hasn't stopped whispering possibilities in my ear. It's not like there's any other place for Lincoln to sleep. There's no couch or even a rug to curl up on—only the bed.

I almost decide against getting up and going to sleep. It's been pleasant sitting here together and watching the flames dance and fill the inside of the small stove. We haven't needed a bunch of words to fill the silence. Otto does a good enough job as is with his snoring.

I turn to take in Lincoln, who is the picture of relaxed with his legs outstretched, arms crossed over his stomach, and his long-sleeve shirt pushed up to his elbows. He's acting like he does this all the time: sleeping in abandoned cabins with divorced women who haven't slept beside a man in six months. And also four days because that happened whether I try to remember it or not.

That is highly specific, but it fits.

I shift the weight to my heels and stand. "Okay, I'm going to bed."

He leans forward. "I'll stoke the fire and head to bed, too." He uses the potholder to open the stove and adds another log.

I put my hands out toward the fire, getting the last bit of heat. The sooner I go to bed, the faster this night will be over. I'm not a saint. I can't stay in these conditions for long and pretend like nothing happened between us, and nothing will happen again. Once I get in the bed, I'll be fighting off visions of Lincoln above, below, and now beside me.

"Well, good night." I take one step and arrive at the bed.

"I'm gonna take Otto out one more time." Lincoln closes the door on the stove and stands, patting the side of his leg for Otto to follow.

Otto gets up lazily from a dead sleep and drags himself to the door where Lincoln is putting on his jacket and boots. He opens the door, and they both exit for a blessed minute so I can breathe.

I look down at the bed. His side, plus my side, equals one whole bed. If we cut it in half and divide it by two, there's still one bed. If we multiply one bed by two people, we still have two people. I can't *girl math* my way out of this one.

The air in my lungs whooshes out of me. I need to just suck it up. So what if we share a bed? We're both adults who possess restraint and the ability to make good decisions. *Sometimes.*

I pull the covers back even more. Finding the bag of blankets, I pull out an extra one to add another comforter on top. Lincoln and Otto come back in, letting a gust of cold air in with them. I shiver and rub my arms, but it's gone as soon as the door shuts and the heat from the fire fills the gaps.

Lincoln folds a fleece blanket and lays it on the floor beside his side for Otto while I fluff my pillow and sit on the bed. It seems comfortable enough. Not lumpy, too soft, or as hard as Lincoln's—

Okay. This isn't working.

I leap off the bed like it's going to detonate. "Maybe I'll just sleep in the chair."

He peers up at me from across the short expanse that is this blasted bed. "You want to sleep in the rickety wooden chair with duct tape around one of the legs?"

There's a slight lean to it, though I wasn't sure if that was from the original wood floors or the chair.

I glance at the chair behind me and then back at him. It's the last thing I want to do and also the first thing I feel I must do. "Yeah, sure. Why not? You take the bed."

"Myra."

I grab and hug my pillow to my chest. "It's fine, Linc. Really."

He sighs. "I can't let you sleep on the chair. You'll get cold, and the chair is about to keel over and die, anyway. I'm going to stay on my side of the bed, I promise."

He's not the problem here.

Hi, I'm the problem. It's me.

"Look, how about we try this…" He grabs another thin blanket from the bag and lays it on the bed, rolling it like a taquito before putting it between us. "Now we have sides."

The thin blanket immediately makes me want to start plotting the destruction of this rolled-up barrier, but I gather myself and say, "That works," because I really don't want to sleep in that chair.

He nods and then goes to unbutton his pants. The sound of the zipper rips through the crackle of the fire and decimates my ability to think clearly. I spin away from him and say the first thing that comes to mind. "Do you always sleep without pants on?"

One man minus one pair of pants equals no pants on the one man.

"Yeah, usually, " he says from behind me. "We have a wall, remember?"

This isn't the Great Wall of China. This is a wall built from a rolled blanket.

I peer up at the wooden ceiling that's keeping the snow out and Lincoln's glutes in. "Makes sense."

It makes no sense.

The long-sleeve thermal I'm wearing is comfortable, but the bra beneath is not. I hate sleeping in bras. Handcuffing my boobs at night is cruel and unusual punishment. He's seen me in a swimsuit and also nothing, so removing my bra while keeping my shirt on is nothing exciting.

I close my eyes, pull my arms in, and reach around toward my back to unlatch my bra. It's proving difficult since wool is the new straight jacket. I can barely reach the clasp inside this clothing dungeon.

Lincoln clears his throat. "Need help?"

Hell no…but also yes.

"Sure. I just need to unclasp my bra."

He says nothing, but the creaks in the floorboards tell me he's walking around the bed and getting closer. I pull the hem of my shirt away from my body and close my eyes even tighter as his hands thread up the back of my shirt.

This was not a good idea. It's the worst one I've ever had. Catastrophic in terms of my resolve. His hands occupy all the space inside my shirt, working to undo my bra. They're warm with a touch of cold on his fingertips as he bends the fabric to his will, forcing it to submit to his attempts at unclasping it.

"Got it?" I ask. *Please* be done. *Now.*

"Almost." He finally wiggles the small hooks apart and pulls his hands out of the back of my shirt. "All set. Anything else?" he asks in a low, gravelly voice that vibrates in my belly.

I bite my bottom lip. God, it would be so easy to start something. Twenty-five doesn't seem so bad right now. He can vote, buy alcohol, and drive a rental car. All very adult things one can do. But even if his age weren't the issue, the fact I'm leaving in four days is.

"I'm good. Thanks."

There are no creaks in the floor like I expect there to be as he walks back to his side. The crackling fire is the only sound in the entire room. The soft glow is intimate, creating a shield around the inside of this cabin while snow blankets the outside.

I pull my hands forward and methodically pull one strap off at a time under my shirt. It's quiet as I remove my bra and set it on the chair with my other discarded layers. We both slide under the covers. Him with too much bare leg, and me with my protection of socks and leggings.

I study all the veins and knots on the wood ceiling. "I'm going to assume you made sure the bedding was bug and critter-free."

Laying on his back with his hands laced over his stomach, he looks over at me. "I shook out all the blankets and sheets before making it."

"Okay." I'm officially out of questions.

We lie side-by-side with only the tops of our shoulders grazing where the rolled blanket doesn't reach. I keep staring at the ceiling, trying so hard not to turn my head toward him that my eye starts twitching. I sigh and wiggle deeper under the blankets. If I fall asleep, I'll forget I'm in a bed with Lincoln, which is what I'm counting on.

Otto's nails scratch against the hardwood floor as he settles, but Lincoln is completely silent. He can't be breathing right now. I peer over at him to make sure. The fire highlights the side of his face, which has a layer of stubble. It's very manly and not at all like a baby-man's. My gaze tracks back up to the ceiling. I can't sleep. I'm not even tired. The quiet is screaming so loudly that I want to fill it with something. *Anything.*

"What's made you—"

"Are you hot—"

We both speak at the same time.

I glance at him, answering his question first. "Waking up to Otto next to me this morning."

He's asked me what makes me smile every day since I met him. I don't need full sentences to know just how terribly sweet he is. I started thinking of my answer before he even asked, and when Otto kicked me with one of his paws this morning, and I cracked one eye open and saw him, I smiled. I didn't wake up alone, and having a companion with four legs might just be better than the ones with two.

"You can have him for another night, ya know. It'll be only one easy payment of a certain Santa sweatshirt," he says, holding back a laugh.

The apples of my cheeks warm and lift. "No way. I earned that sweatshirt and have no intention of ever giving it away. It's in your truck back at the resort right now."

He exhales with a laugh. "So, what were you going to ask me?"

I swallow. "Are you hot?"

The fire is starting to overwhelm the small room and choke me while doing it. I know he said it won't be this warm all night, but right now, it's worse than wearing full body pleather on a hot day.

"Not really. It helps that I took off most of my layers," he says. "You could too, you know. It's not like anything's going to happen."

I can't do anything about my shirt since I'm already sans bra, so I reach down and take off my socks. But I'm still too hot. And he's right. If we're both sure nothing will happen, then I should be just fine.

Wrong.

I have already done things to him in my mind, so I'm not exactly innocent here. But I vastly underestimated the warmth of the bedding, and falling asleep, let alone waking up, drenched in sweat isn't a good feel.

Oh no.

I'm probably going to hit menopause when Linc is my age now. I'll be having hot flashes, walking around with ice packs under my armpits while he's *watching* me do this. This is why I can't do any of the other things running through my mind right now that include straddling and/or anything involving tongues.

I sit upright and swing my legs over the side of the bed. Grabbing the waistband of my leggings, I slide them over my hips, thighs, and calves until I kick them off. I'm in my underwear. The black, I-bought-these-for-myself ones that have lace flowers sewn together by fishing line, making them thin and transparent and totally impractical.

I don't wait for him to notice and slip my bare legs back beneath the covers. The taquito blanket is pressed against my leg from hip to foot again, and I'm safe.

But then Lincoln shifts to lay on his side facing me, and it's like his entire body is calling for all of mine. "Goodnight, Myra."

If sleep is possible, I'd be surprised. "Goodnight, Lincoln."

Chapter Twenty-Eight

Lincoln

So much for the taquito roll-up barrier.

Her eyes are closed, lashes fanning across the tops of her cheeks while her hands are tucked beneath her pillow. One leg is slung over the good-for-nothing blanket and draped across my thighs while the early morning sun peeks through the dingy curtains.

I'm not used to sleeping next to someone. Having roommates in the same house is nothing like having a woman sleep in the same bed next to me. I guess I thought it would be harder to get used to, but apparently, one night is all it took. By two, I'm ready to offer her a drawer in my bedroom or at least one of my hoodies.

The pattern of her breathing, the way she grabbed my bicep right after she fell asleep, and how she couldn't seem to pick a side, flipping from her left to her right before finally settling on the position that left her facing me and breathing on me is all so *her*. I didn't even care.

Otto sits up beside the bed, and I peer over at him as he licks his lips. He's ready for a bathroom break and food, but I'm not. I don't want to leave this bed until I have to. But Otto doesn't like that I'm still horizontal and starts to whine, which causes Myra to stir. She flips to her back, taking her legs with her, so I turn to my side and face Otto, whispering, "You're supposed to be my wingman."

His brows dance from me to the door. He isn't going to let me off the hook, so I slip out of bed, being as quiet as possible, and pad to the front door to let him out.

He rushes past my legs and bounds into the newly fallen powder. The storm has passed, leaving enough snow to completely cover my snowmobile. I'll have to spend time digging it out before we can leave. But the clouds don't look like they're carrying more than they can handle today.

When Otto finishes up, he traipses back onto the porch to come inside. I brush off his paws, and he goes directly for the bed. Not the one I made for him on the floor using a spare blanket. The actual bed right beside Myra, where I was lying down. He circles twice before sinking down, resting his head on the flimsy barrier. I glare and shake my head at him.

There's more of a chill this morning, and not just because the door was open. I quietly walk to the stove to add a few more logs to the coals.

"What are you doing?" Myra says in a groggy voice, her eyes open to slits.

I snap my gaze to where she's huddled on her side on the edge of the bed, facing me.

"Stoking the fire. Are you cold?" I shut the door of the stove and stand.

She squints and stares down before slowly dragging her gaze back to my face. "No."

I peer down at the briefs I'm still wearing and the morning wood beneath them. Without a word, because really what am I supposed to say, I walk to my side of the bed and push Otto to the bottom so I can climb in.

Myra stays on her side with her back to me, so I lay on mine, facing her. I wish this damn blanket weren't in my way. That I could fold her into my arms like I want to. Maybe she'd make the first move and roll over to kiss me. I doubt it, considering how dead-set she's been on keeping things platonic. I won't magically become ten years older overnight. I don't get why the age thing is such a big deal to her, but I'll respect it. After being with her already, I'm blessed—or cursed—with a brain that won't stop replaying our shower scene.

Wet, hot, and nude.

The barrier between us starts to get closer. I figure Myra's just shifting on the bed and diving deeper back into sleep, so I start thinking about showers again. But then the bare skin of her leg touches mine, and I jolt. She's doing nothing to move her leg from my side and is moving closer.

She keeps moving backward until the blanket takes on a curved line between us. Her rosemary and mint scent has only gotten stronger, but she continues to face away from me. The leg that breached the barrier is warm and smooth against my rough one—the things I would do to that leg if this were on purpose. But I've convinced myself it's an accident. She's going to move when she realizes how close she is.

I know she's awake; this is only an accident.

But then she jumps the barrier like a whale cresting the surface of the ocean. Not that there's any likeness; it's just what the surprising movement felt like. She scoots back until the end of her body is the beginning of mine. She can't be doing this on purpose. She has to be in some kind of sleep-induced haze. Any moment, she'll move away.

Maybe she's still sleeping?

I stay completely still so I don't spook her. But I also don't want her to freak out when she wakes up and realizes my boner is jabbing into her back. She wiggles her hips, and the urge to rock into her is so strong, I have to close my eyes and swallow so I don't.

"Myra," I whisper.

"Mhm?"

She sounds sleepy, like she's in between awake and asleep, as I thought.

"Myra, you're on my side."

She doesn't answer or move, which is decidedly still not helping quell the urge to hold her. Instead, I torture myself for a few more heartbeats with the feel of her ass pressed into me. I know she's not wearing pants. The flash of black lace before she laid down last night was enough to fill in the blanks.

I decide the only way to get out of this unscathed and enforce the boundaries she set, and I agreed to, is to pull back. It pains me, but I shift until my back is riding the edge of the bed.

She follows me.

I have no more bed to work with here. Her ass is back to warming my dick beneath the covers. "Myra."

"What?"

"You have to wake up. I'm running out of room. The blanket is…" No longer our security.

A pause, and then she says, "I wasn't sleeping."

This time, she wiggles her hips, and I let out a groan, dropping my forehead to her shoulder. "What are you doing?" I ask her.

"This feels good," she whispers. "Does it feel good for you?"

I'm stunned by her confession. "Yeah, but are you sure? I thought you wanted to keep things…friendly."

"I did."

As in, you don't want to now?

I swallow as she reaches behind her to search for my hand. There's no way I'd keep it all to myself, so I let her grab it, placing it on her hip where her skin and underwear meet. She swivels her hips again. It's enough to set my blood to boiling, making the thin sheet covering us feel like an inferno—that and Otto lying on my feet.

On pure, unmasked instinct, I push my hips forward, rocking into her. I can't see her face and tell if she's as awake as she sounds. I should stop this. Get out of bed while we still can without things becoming awkward.

Her voice is low but clear when she says, "It's okay."

She rotates her hips again, creating a kind of friction that has me sucking in air. I want to memorize the feel of her. Her ass, her endlessly smooth skin, and the way her body fits with mine. I press my hardening cock between her ass and roll my hips upward slowly. I know at this moment I wouldn't deny her anything.

Her small but still audible gasp is enough to undo me. She pushes, and I push back. She swivels, and I thrust. She grabs my hand and flattens it against her low abs, and I use it as leverage to arch into her harder than before. She moans softly, and my heart rate skyrockets. The feel of her lithe body in my grip and how easily we fall into rhythm together consumes my next thought. And the one after that. And—

"Lincoln." Her hand tightens on the back of mine as I start lowering it. I can't tell if my name is said as a plea or a warning, but I stop moving my hips and hand. "We…I can't," she finally says.

I'm breathing hard as I rest my forehead on her shoulder again. "Okay, yeah." I nod, pressing a light kiss on the back of her head. "You're right."

She isn't right. I think she's wrong. But I'll do what she's asking of me and put some space between us. I pull my hand out from beneath hers, sliding it across her bare skin, and roll onto my back with a sigh.

"Lincoln," she says again, still on her side, facing away from me and breathing heavily like I am.

I can barely muster a "Yeah?"

She flips slowly onto her back. "Maybe—"

She stops herself. The mattress shifts under the weight of her movement, and then she's facing me, coiled tension nearly radioactive between us.

The heat in her eyes tells me exactly how I feel. There's no denying we have chemistry. If I weren't in a bed with her, wearing only my briefs after dry humping her, I think it might be easier to give her the space she wants. But none of those things are true.

Reaching across the invisible barrier, I stroke her cheek with my thumb. It's a small gesture, one I'm hoping tells her how hard this is for me. I want her—more than I've wanted anyone in the past. It's terrifying, but I can't help but be curious. She fascinates me. I pull my hand back, and roll to my back ready to get up and dress, but I'm not fast enough.

"Wait," she says, forcing me to freeze.

We've been here before. In the hot tub, she hesitated, too. I've rarely seen that indecision in her. Myra knows what she wants, but she's also been through it. I can't forget that.

Fitting her leg between both of mine, half on top of me, she presses herself closer. Otto shifts at my feet but doesn't get down. The sight of her this close is too much. I can't keep my hands off her.

Trailing a flat palm up the side of her thigh and hip, I ask, "What are you doing?" I don't want to be asking this question. I'd rather be enjoying every square inch of her body—licking, tasting, touching all of her. But I don't want to be her regret.

"I don't know," she says but doesn't move.

She sighs, her dark hair curling around her neck and shoulders as she rests her chin on my chest. The beautiful points of her nipples are resting against me, so close I can feel them, but not close enough to devour.

Not yet.

"You don't know?" I ask, spanning the width of her hip with my hand, giving light squeezes.

"I know we're in this weird half-relationship. But maybe right now..." She shakes her head and says in a quiet voice, "Can't we just be here...together? In a secluded cabin that we somehow got stuck in, and we're waiting for the small town locksmith to come and rescue us."

"Is this another movie plot?"

"Of course it is," she retorts.

Being completely present in this moment doesn't sound hard for me. But in her mind, I'm too young to be something serious. She's been using me like I've used her in this fake relationship, and now what? We sleep together again and then leave, pretending we didn't. I don't want this to end. But I also don't want to put so much pressure on her that it drives her away.

She pulls herself up and on top of me, positioning herself right over my hardened length so we're hip to hip. The thin material of our underwear is the only thing keeping us separated. It's hard to remember what I was just thinking about. Instead, all I feel is Myra's stomach moving with her breaths, her flat palms on the pillow beside my head, bracing herself as I instinctively thrust upward.

If Myra's offering, I'm taking.

"Is this what you want?" I ask her.

She looks down at me, her brown eyes rolling backward as her hips rotate in a circle. I grab the thin sides of her underwear in my fists.

"Yes," she says through panting breaths.

Without any hesitation, thinking, or wavering, I flip her onto her back and press my cock between her legs at her center once, twice, three times before she moans my name when I make contact with her clit.

She says my name through her panting, and I prop myself up above her on my elbows, steadying myself in a kneeling plank position. I rock into her, making sure the firm pressure of my dick hits her in the spot that pulls my name from her lips. Another moan escapes her pretty mouth, and I want to swallow it. I kiss her hard, pushing my tongue into her mouth. It's sloppy and chaotic, but I don't stop. My entire body is tense and trembling, but I can't stop the momentum. I keep driving forward.

The sounds coming from the back of her throat, the way her nails dig into my sides, pulling me closer, and how she practically vibrates beneath me are familiar, yet not. I've experienced them all before, but the power she has over me has intensified. I want to make her feel good. I want her to arch her back and scream my name, not whisper it. I want to know that I'm able to make her come undone.

It's a power I've never held like this before, but I feel how close it is. It's in the palms of my hands.

Grabbing behind her knee, I hike one of her legs up further as I bend to kiss her pliant mouth again. It's lazy and full of gasping breaths as I push against her once more, this time harder and rougher.

Her eyes roll to the back of her head as she grabs the waistband of my briefs.

I groan. "Do you have a condom?"

She shakes her head, eyes rolling back.

Of course I'd forget one, too, thinking there's no way we'd go out on the snowmobile and end up here. Alone and…hot.

She drags her hands over my shoulders to circle my neck like she doesn't want to risk me pulling away. I couldn't. I won't.

This time, I don't even let a full breath of a pause come between us. I'm not going to let the lack of a condom stop us. I rock my hips over and over again, driving and dragging my length between her folds until she finally screams my name. Again. And another time after that. I'm breathing hard but manage to pull back slightly and drag a thumb over her soaked panties.

Otto barks loudly, startling both of us. I shush him as I apply more pressure, learning her body with the tips of my fingers and the pads of my hands. She rides my hand like it's my body, and it's all I can do to keep it together. Shuddering, I slow it down and press her lightly, just enough for her to know I'm still there, waiting to hear her reach her highest gear. The stiff length between my legs is begging for release, but I don't get the chance.

"Linc," she says, quieter this time.

"Hm?" I hum against her skin as I bend to kiss her breasts over her shirt, ready to devour more of her. There isn't any padding between my tongue and her skin, just a thin layer of fabric I have my heart set on removing.

"Otto."

"He's fine," I say quickly, kissing the taut peak of her nipple.

She pushes against my shoulders. "Hang on."

I hover above her with swollen lips and dick. "What is it?"

She peers behind my shoulder at Otto, and I follow her gaze. He now has two front paws on my back, tail wagging in excitement or confusion. I hadn't noticed. Now I remember why

I made Ted and Jake watch him the other night when Myra was over. He's never seen me like this. He probably has no clue what my intentions are here. Explaining I want Myra to come won't make any sense.

"Does he need to go out? Eat something?" she asks.

All of the above, I think but don't move off her to do anything about it. "He'll be alright," I say, trying to shrug him off. He only moves to our sides and stares with a high-pitched whine.

"It just feels weird that he's watching us."

Otto whines again, louder this time now that he has an audience.

Myra's breathing begins to even out, and though I'm pressed between her legs, I can feel her slipping away. "It's okay. Go feed him. We should probably get going anyway."

Leaving here, the safety of this bed in this isolated cabin, is the last thing I want to do. The fictional locksmith hasn't showed up yet. We still have time. I drop my forehead to her shoulder and plant a small kiss over her collarbone. "Alright."

But I'm not alright.

Chapter Twenty-Nine

Myra

Twenty-five isn't *that* young."

I pull the sleeves of my new favorite Santa sweatshirt over my hands. They still feel frozen despite being shoved in gloves for the last half hour it took us to get back to the resort.

Otto gives me a blank look from the driver's seat.

It's just the two of us since Lincoln is loading up the snowmobile, a process and a half, while Otto and I stay warm in the cab. Of course, my mind couldn't stop replaying what happened this morning. And what didn't.

It's starting to get to my head, and I haven't been able to think about anything else. I slip off my boots and tuck my legs under me, fending off the chill that has infiltrated my weary muscles. "Dogs don't care about age. You're like, what, four years old? So that makes you at least eighty-five in dog years."

He tilts his head.

"I don't know how the conversion works, but you seem wise beyond your years. Plus, Lincoln's your person, so what should I do here?"

All my question gets me is a tail thump on the leather seat.

It's not helping.

Somewhere between my moans and riding back down the mountain, I considered what came next. We did what we set out to do by being the most couply-couple in front of my parents and his, and we crushed it. I almost believed this wasn't pretend.

Maybe I don't want it to be.

But with only a few days left, we haven't talked about breaking up.

"I should just tell him how I feel." Which can be summed up in my near orgasm this morning. I didn't mean for it to go that far. I just thought we'd mess around, make out a bit. The next thing I know, I'm yelling his name and carving mine into his shoulder blade. Then, I'm looking straight into Otto's wide, brown eyes.

I wanted to keep touching him, feel his skin beneath my hands, the flavor of him on my tongue, but when Otto crashed the party, it snapped me out of whatever fantasy I was living in. We almost broke the one rule of our fake relationship: no sex.

But rules are meant to be broken, and I've never wanted to break this one so badly.

"I can't tell him I'm starting to catch feelings." I scrunch my nose. "That sounds like they're a disease. I didn't mean it like that," I over-explain to Otto. "I meant that somewhere in this fake relationship, it started feeling more real, or at least that I wanted it to be."

Otto lays down and rests his chin on the center console where my arm is. I stare out the windshield and pet his head. He's a fantastic listener, and it beats talking to myself.

"If he doesn't feel the same way, I'm sure he'll be nice about it. It's not like he's going to toss me out of his truck." I laugh a little, but there's no humor behind it, only horror at the thought of this happening. "I'm not gonna say anything."

Otto sighs, and I peer down at him. His eyes are doing that slow-blink thing where he's in between awake and asleep. His lashes lift and fall with the movement and are so long they could rival Lincoln's. He does another slow blink, but I swear the corner of his mouth is pulled up into a smile. We're both comfortable in this moment.

So comfortable that I hadn't noticed until now how easy it's been to fall into a routine with these two. Seeing each other every day, sharing meals, meeting families, kissing, and sitting in the front seat of Lincoln's truck while talking to Otto are just the highlights of my week here and why I'm starting to feel things for him. I didn't think that would be possible for a long time, but here we are.

Here *I* am.

With one hand, I reach for my jacket on the floor and finagle a dog treat out of my pocket, offering it to Otto. He perks up immediately and gently takes the small bone from my hand. "You're good at this dog thing, you know. If you ever want to retire from this avalanche stuff and switch careers to a therapy dog, you'd be good at it." He groans, and I hold up a hand. "I'm just saying."

Lincoln opens the driver-side door, and Otto whips his head around, already twisting in the seat to greet his person with his tail wagging. You'd never know he was close to sleep a second ago. Otto jumps into the back but doesn't go too far, putting his front paws on the console between us.

Lincoln flashes me his wide grin, baring teeth that have been blessed by the Tooth Fairy herself—and braces. "All set," he says, knocking snow off his boots on the truck running boards. "Did you get a hold of Liv to let her know you're safe? No animal encounters…murders…"

I giggle and hold up my phone. "I called her, and you'll be glad to know she did not call the cops. She guessed I was with you."

He climbs in and laughs. "I'm glad. I'm sure Jake would give me shit forever if he opened the door to a couple of cops after me."

"It's his duty as a brother."

Settling into the cab, I crank the heat up all the way on my side while Linc turns his down then pulls out of the parking lot and onto the main two-lane road outside the resort. With it being the middle of the day on a Saturday, more cars and trucks are trying to get in than out.

The trees along the road are heavy with the most recent snowfall, and piles of white are stacked on either side, indicating a plow had been through at some point already. The engine's hum and comfort from the heater blowing hot air on a low setting through wide-open vents aren't enough to get me out of my head.

I should just say something. Clear the air and hope for the best. Instead, I'm picking my cuticles and avoiding eye contact at all costs. Lincoln busies himself with the radio and offers Otto a treat he had stashed in his door. He doesn't know I just gave Otto one, but Otto makes eye contact with me as if to warn me not to say anything. It makes my heart grow ten times bigger seeing how much Lincoln cares for him. Another reason I'm convinced that I underestimated him. Maybe Liv is right, and age isn't a big deal.

"Do you have dinner plans?" he asks, interrupting the silence.

I hike one of my legs up under my other thigh. "I told Liv we'd have dinner together tonight. She said you've been hogging me." I'm curious what he'll say to that and peer over to see his reaction.

He laughs and grips the top of the steering wheel. "She's probably right."

Less than twenty-four hours in a log cabin, and I can feel the effects. Both of our barriers are lower. I can see him over the labels I've slapped on him and how relaxed he is to say and do what's on his mind more than before.

I may have started it this morning, but he would have finished it if we hadn't been interrupted.

"Do you want to come back later and watch a movie?" Not inferring we should Netflix and chill but also…"Or I could come to your place."

I stab my thumb into my opposite palm while waiting for his response.

"Yeah, a movie sounds good. Just none of those cheesy romance ones you always talk about."

"Deal," I say through a laugh and relax further into the seat. "Lincoln?"

His gaze jumps from me to the road. "Yeah?"

I told myself I wouldn't say anything, but I can't do it. That's not who I am.

"What happens next? With us…"

A pause. "The way I see it, you're here until Wednesday…" His tone is even and calm, so completely him. "It's only Saturday, which means we have a little more than three more days. If it were up to me, I'd see you every day."

Bold Lincoln is something to behold, like the awe of watching a butterfly come out of its cocoon and flutter around with newfound wings. It's incredibly attractive and only makes this feel even more possible. I can have feelings. I can learn to ski. I can do scary things.

My grin nearly reaches to my temples. "I like spending time with you, too."

He rubs his unshaven jawline, masking his equally large smile. "Tonight, then."

"Tonight."

That went better than I thought it would. I mean, we aren't swapping promise rings or making plans outside of tonight, but at least we're being honest. I'll have to give Otto another treat later to thank him for the advice he didn't give but somehow had a part in.

As we pull into the driveway, my phone starts going off, but I silence it to say goodbye to Lincoln. "Thanks for driving me back."

He puts his truck in park and helps me gather my things. Otto is blissfully asleep in the back as though he's done all the work and doesn't even move when Lincoln does, for once.

I bite my lower lip, overwhelmed by the rush of feelings coursing through me; I unbuckle slowly and push up onto my knee to lean across the console to kiss him. It's light at first, brushing my lips against his in slow motion. But he threads his fingers in the back of my hair and deepens the kiss.

His tongue finds mine, hot and slick, as our mouths slowly explore the other. It's tender and unrushed, two things I didn't know I needed in a kiss.

He pulls away just long enough to say between kisses, "I don't have to leave—" kiss— "I could just stay in the cabin—" kiss— "and you could sneak in throughout—" *kiss*— "dinner."

I hold him at arm's length, sinking back into my seat. "You'll get hungry. All I have is coffee and orange juice in my cabin."

His grin is devilish.

I swat his shoulder. "You need actual food."

It's his turn to lean across the console. He kisses me thoroughly, making me forget what I said five seconds ago. He lightly pecks my mouth and peppers my jaw with a few slow, well-placed kisses that have my stomach and toes fighting for tingles before promising, "I'll be back later."

He sits back in his seat, and I grip the door handle. Before I push it open, he grabs my arm. "Wait."

"What?"

"I almost forgot to ask you today…"

I slip my arms into my yellow jacket and zip it up, waiting for him to continue.

His green eyes are searching. "What made you smile?"

I linger on the question because I don't want this moment to end, and that's all we've had together: *moments*. "Lots of things," I start to say, "and the day isn't over yet."

I open the passenger side and hop out, slamming the heavy door shut. There's a new car in the driveway I haven't seen before, but it's probably someone Liv knows. The brick path leading to my front door is newly shoveled and slick, so I keep my head down. I only risk one look over my shoulder, and Lincoln is all smiles through the windshield before I disappear behind the house.

As I fumble around for my keys, I hear the roar of Lincoln's truck driving off by the time I reach my front door. I turn the knob and walk inside the cabin like it's any other day. I expect to toss my coat on the couch and take a shower before going to Liv's. I expect to daydream in peace about where Lincoln will lay me out in this cabin. And I expect to be alone.

But nothing is like I expected.

When I open the door, I'm met with three sets of eyes.

"Hi, Myra, dear. Welcome back!"

Chapter Thirty

Myra

"What. The. Hell." My feet are cemented to the few tiles in the entryway as I stare.

This can't be real.

I'm dreaming or blacking out. Am I drunk? No, I had a collapsible cup of wine over fifteen hours ago. Damn it. That means this is not my imagination.

"'What the hell?'" Mom asks, scrunching her nose.

Dad brackets her shoulders with his hands. "I think she's surprised to see us, dear."

Mom holds up a hand; all of her gaudy rings are in place and wrapped around each finger. "I know she is, Ken. But it sounds like she's upset, too."

He backs away slowly and slides his hands into his trouser pockets. "Maybe she is."

Frankie's sitting on one of the barstools in the kitchen with his elbows propped behind him on the counter. He's wearing his favorite Armani tweed pea coat, black denim jeans, and a pair of Calvin Klein loafers that will suffer a quick death in the snow outside. But he's also trying to hide a smile.

He sucks at it.

God, I *missed* him.

Pushing off the stool to stand, he strides over with the swagger he's owned since birth until he's standing just in front of me. "We're going to die of frostbite if you keep this door open any longer. This place is colder than bare feet on my bathroom tiles."

I roll my eyes and kick the door shut with a sly grin. "Always the dramatic one."

He folds me in his arms like he's been doing our whole lives, making me feel at home when I'm miles away. "Always."

I release him from my clutches and look back at my parents, who both wrap me in a tight hug. It's stiff and formal, not nearly as comforting as Frankie's. The scratch of Dad's beard scrapes my cheek while the slide of Mom's obnoxiously loud puffer vest smooths it out. They both step back and study me through a squint as though I will kick them to the snow-covered curb out front. I don't even know if there is one since I can't see it.

But they're right. I am surprised and also upset. They weren't supposed to show up here. I gave them what they wanted. Confirmation I'm doing just fine in the form of a very attractive man. And this is my Eat, Pray, Love journey. I can't have my parents and brother tagging along, or it will ruin everything. Mom and Dad have a way of making sure what I want is actually what they do.

What happened to getting their tickets refunded or traveling to some destination island? Preferably anywhere without cell service.

"What are you guys doing here?" I finally ask with a pensive tone.

Mom clasps her hands in front of her. "We're here to see you, of course!"

I briefly glance at Frankie long enough to see his brows lift and his eyes widen.

"Yeah, I see that…" I tuck my hair behind my ears and clear enough of the irritation out of my throat before I continue. "But why?"

Mom peers over her shoulder at Dad while Frankie crosses his arms like he's also waiting for an explanation from them. "Well, you see, dear," Dad begins. "Frankie planned on driving up here—"

I snap my gaze at him. "What? You did?"

"It was supposed to be a surprise." He glares at Dad, then shrugs and meets my eyes. "That was the plan when—"

"When he invited us to join," Mom finishes.

Frankie rubs his forehead and then speaks in a louder tone. "I did no such thing."

"You did. Remember?" Mom's eyes are twitching since she's opening them so wide.

Frankie crosses his arms and shakes his head emphatically. "Enlighten us all, please."

Mom steps forward, hands out to aid her story. "We were all at dinner the other night when Frankie mentioned he was going to drive out and see you."

Dad moves to stand beside her, cupping one hand over the outside of his mouth as if to hide what he's saying. "And you know how Frankie is with driving."

Frankie throws his hands in the air. "Oh my God, it's like I'm not even here."

Mom waves him off. "Anyway, Frankie said he was going, and as his parents, we couldn't let him drive on the roads in the condition they're in. We were planning to fly anyway, so we bought him a ticket, too."

"They smuggled me onto the plane," Frankie clarifies, clearly not loving the fact he had to fly.

"Wow." I slowly shake my head, realizing it wasn't just my parents who had planned to bombard my solo self-discovery journey. "I can't believe you got on an airplane," I say to Frankie. "Did they drug you?"

"Close." He uses his thumb and pointer finger to show just how close. "The effects of the melatonin are still wearing off. I'm barely standing right now, so if I pass out, just give me a blanket and pillow."

He clearly doesn't hear the irritation in my voice that he, too, was planning to drop in for a casual visit, like Montana is next door and not a full time zone away. I shift on my feet and rub my temples. "Let me get this straight. Frankie was going to crash my trip by driving out here, which you're right, he sucks at driving when it's sunny outside, let alone the snow…"

"Right here." Frankie points at his chest.

"And you both decided to buy him a ticket to fly out here instead because you were worried about me and needed to check how things were going? Even after I said I was fine?"

"Exactly!" Dad exclaims.

Mom slings her arm out to hit him in the chest. He grunts at the impact. "No, honey," Mom starts in. "We just wanted to make sure your brother got here and that you had plenty of food."

"There are grocery stores in Montana, Mom," I say with an exasperated sigh. I'm losing my patience. I knew fending them off was a hopeless cause, even after deploying my best effort by lying to them about Lincoln. Anger shoots through my veins. "You're checking up on me like I'm a child."

Maybe I want to stomp my foot on the ground like one, but that doesn't mean they should treat me like this. I'm a grown-ass woman with a fake boyfriend and a ski pass. They're constantly butting in and deciding to be present parents at the worst times. I don't understand why they're so overbearing.

Mom opens and closes her mouth, then exhales heavily. "No. We know you're not a child…" I should have said pet. "But you also introduced us to a boyfriend two days ago we had no clue existed. We wanted to see you…and meet him."

Of course. It was Lincoln they were here to see. They probably needed to confirm he was up to their standards. Looks like this whole fake dating idea just backfired. I thought giving them Lincoln on social media and over the phone would prevent them from showing up here. Guess not. It only encouraged them more.

"And you just decided to show up out of the blue like this without calling me?"

"Have you checked your phone recently?" Frankie points at my hand. "And while you're at it, I'd still love to see a picture of this boyfriend of yours."

I grip my purse tighter, which is slung over my shoulder. I had checked my phone while at the mountain. But since service is as finicky as a temperamental teen, I could only make or receive calls, which I had none of. Now that I'm back at the cabin, I'm sure Frankie's frantic texts will have blown up my phone.

This would have been ten times worse if I had invited Lincoln inside. We would have given them a show involving lots of tongue and hands.

"Check social media if you want to see him," I say flippantly to Frankie.

He scoffs. "You know I deleted all of my social media."

I brush him off. A picture of Lincoln is the least of my worries.

"At least he's handsome," Mom says with a nod toward Frankie, then directs her attention to me. The jewelry on her neck hangs heavy as she toys with it. "You left suddenly to learn to ski in Montana, and come to find out you're here to see a boyfriend you've never mentioned on the heels of your divorce…"

Adding Lincoln and fake dating into this mess is not helping my case. My entire family are now staring at me like I'm a zoo animal. I'm just trying to find *me* again. Why does this have to be so complicated?

I take another deep breath and slap my hands on my hips. "Well, now you've seen me, and I'm doing great. You can go home now."

Mom fiddles with the zipper on her vest. "Now that we're here…"

My finger is in the air, waving like it just doesn't care. "No. No, no, no. I don't even have any space for you guys to stay with me." They can't pretend like we aren't all standing inside a matchbox-sized cottage right now. "Where would you sleep? The floor? The kitchen? The floor in the kitchen?"

"No, silly. We got a hotel in town." Mom gives a short, nervous laugh and rubs the back of her neck. "We weren't sure if your boyfriend was staying here."

Glad to see Mom's knack for planning is still intact.

It doesn't matter. They showed up here unannounced and thought that would be alright. Well, it's not. It's not because I only have a precious few days with my fake boyfriend to ski and make out. Their overbearing leech ways are not welcome here. We aren't a family that vacations together. They're probably here because—

"We're worried about you, Myra. Wade is, too."

There it is. Wade. It's always about him.

Red. All I see is red.

"I don't give a—" I abruptly cut myself off, not wanting to get into anything regarding Wade right now. He's everywhere. Like stagnant air I can't blow away. I push my palms into my eyes. "I can't do this."

"Can't do what?" Mom asks, stepping closer. "We're just here to support you."

And update Wade on how I'm doing.

I hold out my hands, begging her not to come closer. My parents have always been on the sidelines of my life, interjecting when they want and retreating when they don't. Completely opposite from Frankie, who has *always* been there for me. At times, even in a cheerleading costume with pom-poms and a giant sign with some rah-rah quote on it. That happened when I decided to run track that one year in high school. Frankie had the time of his life. Me, not so much.

I can't seem to make eye contact with my parents and not see Wade. If they're checking up on me just to report back to Wade...I shake my head. The thought picks me up like a tornado and spits me out.

My hands fall to my sides. "You guys don't get it."

"Get what?" Dad asks, his brows furrowing in concern.

God, it guts me having to relive all of the pain and loneliness of the last year. I hated having to tell them Wade and I were getting a divorce. They were disappointed and confused, wondering why we couldn't fix things. I didn't have an answer. It's not like there was one definitive thing that made everything else crumble. And for a split second, that weight felt like too much, and I wanted to take it back. I wanted to tell them never mind, and we'd figure something out. Go to more therapy, more date nights, more...things. Whatever I could so they wouldn't look at me like that. Like *this.*

Like I'm as big of a failure as I feel.

It was Frankie who was the strong one and reiterated what I'd told them. He held my hand and squeezed until my fingertips turned white from the blood loss, and the feeling of protecting them from my divorce eventually passed. Five, ten, fifteen, one hundred days after breaking the news, and I survived.

I got through it.

"Dad, Mom," I say quietly, wanting them to get it—to get me. Tears spring to my eyes as the dark cloud of divorce shadows the entire one-room cottage. "As much as the divorce hurt you guys, it hurt me more."

I pause, gauging their stunned reactions to words I probably should've said a long time ago. Frankie moves to stand beside me. He doesn't reach for my hand, but he does stand close enough that our shoulders touch. It's everything to make me feel less alone.

I take a deep breath to try and hold back my tears. "After my divorce, I knew you were both upset—"

Mom jumps in. "We were, but—"

Frankie holds up his hand. "Let her finish."

I swallow and continue. "I knew you were sad to be losing Wade as a son-in-law. But I didn't expect you to cope with that loss by keeping him in your life—and mine. I've spent the last six months trying to move on and find out what I love again, apart from Wade. But then I call or check-in, and it's *Wade this* and *Wade that*. Now, you're here, checking on me and saying *Wade is worried*." The floor has just become the most interesting thing. "I can't escape him." My tone is pleading, as though I'm begging them to understand how badly this has gutted me. "You're my parents, not his anymore. And I'm not a child for you to check up on. I just want you to be there when I need you."

I want them to hear what I'm saying and not just nod along and pretend like they do. I want them to cut Wade out for good.

I want them to hug me and tell me they'll always be there for me, and then, I want them to leave. The desire to be here might have started because of Merlot and thinking I was somehow irrevocably broken. But now I want to see this trip through because I know I'm not.

Mom sighs. "Honey, Wade was a huge part of our lives for years. Even before you got married, our families had been friends. To undo all of those ties…well…"

"So, you're just going to keep inviting that prick into our lives even when she's telling you how she feels about it?" Frankie says in a brusque tone.

Dad gapes, searching for letters to create words to answer. Mom wrings her hands together while Frankie stares them down with his arms crossed.

But I open the front door and leave. I don't know where I'll go, but it isn't here.

Chapter Thirty-One

Myra

Someone should've told me this wasn't a good idea.

But no one did. I strapped on my boots, clicked into my bindings, and rode the lift up the Sunset run like Lincoln and I had done so many times this last week. However, the small miracle of skiing off the lift without falling has me living with the assumption that I'll be able to make it down this mountain.

It's bigger today.

Or maybe it just feels like that.

I stare down from the edge of the run. A fresh coating of powder dusts the top layer of the packed snow. I've fallen enough times to know it isn't that soft. But after the shit storm that was the conversation with my family earlier, I needed a time out before I said things I'd regret. I thought expressing how I felt about their relationship with Wade would help. Instead, I think it just made me angrier knowing they didn't care. They don't care like I do.

For now, I'll shove it all aside and glide down this mountain if only to prove to myself that I can do this on my own. By the end of my lesson with Lincoln the other day, I could ski behind him without falling. It won't be that different.

My knees knocking together like a couple of maracas, and my chin trembles, making me look cold. But I'm not. It's just the uncontrollable shaking happening in my body. I inch forward, careful not to unknowingly run into a small child going twice as fast as me and let momentum—and a prayer—take me down the hill. I close my eyes and remember Lincoln told me not to do that, so I fling them open again.

I fall on my ass after only a few feet and skid to a stop.

"Don't you dare give up," I say to myself through gritted teeth. I take a steadying breath and try to remember more of what Lincoln taught me.

Trust my skis, always bend my knees, and most importantly, pizza. Oh, and, "Lean forward, tits point down the mountain." It's not exactly what Lincoln said the last time we skied together. He said something about keeping my shoulders pointed down the hill, but my shoulders don't point. Tits do.

I angle my skis so the bottoms are facing down the mountain and use my poles to help me stand on the sides of my skis. The hill pitches down, and my legs are trembling so much I almost doubt they'll be able to hold me for long. "Relax. You can do this. You did this."

Every second, I can feel my heartbeat in my throat as my pulse races. But I don't let myself think for too long. I push forward, angling my skis to the left before turning them to face downhill. I garner some speed then curve to the right to attempt the "S" turns. My pizza point is so sharp I could poke an eye out, but I still manage not to cross my skis. The wind skims my cheeks as I lean and go in the opposite direction.

It's slow going, but I'm *doing it*.

I'm moving in the direction I'm supposed to and not falling.

I start laughing in disbelief as I curve back to the left while keeping my tits facing the lodge. I could kiss Lincoln right now. The practice is helping. I'm not falling on my face, though, I do fall on my glutes once. I think my muscles are remembering how to do this. The curve of the hill, the trees off to the side, and the position of the lodge coming closer are all familiar.

"I'm still standing!" I say, pride settling high in my chest as I straighten out and add a bit more speed before slowing down and stopping at the bottom. I push the release on my bindings with one of my poles and stab them into the snow before fist pumping the air. "I did it!" I scream. "I did it, I did it, I did it!"

I hop around and twirl in circles, then offer random strangers free high-fives. They don't seem fazed by this and give them just as freely.

I press a hand to my heart and breathe in the cold air, filling my lungs to their capacity. I just climbed Everest. God, I wish Lincoln were here to see this. I want to celebrate with someone.

The thought is sobering.

Apart from Lincoln, I don't think anyone in my family would understand just how good it feels to have made it to the bottom. They think I'm one crack away from nuts. And maybe I am, but I've never felt so sane at this moment.

Feeling like Everest isn't tall enough, I pick up my skis and march slowly to the map of all the runs. Green, blue, and black lines run in different directions, indicating their level of difficulty. I've only attempted green so far, and blacks, being the steepest, are out of the question. Blue runs are right in the middle.

Tracing my finger on the lift going back up Sunset, I could ski over to Cedar or Powder Park to take another lift up to get on the blues. I bite my bottom lip. I've never tried a blue, but Lincoln thought I could do it. They aren't that different from greens.

Right now, I feel powerful and confident in a way I haven't felt in a long time. Maybe even before the divorce. I was always short and demanding, making me feel like a dragon ready to set fire to anything in my path. Everything set me off. But noticing this would have meant I had to notice my relationship crumbling even sooner than it did.

I don't want to be a dragon anymore.

I want to be the hero.

Looking back at the sign, I set my sights on the blue run, then click into my skis and skate toward the chair lift like I'm racing a turtle. A larger group goes ahead of me, and then I'm next. Using my poles, I scoot forward to gain momentum on flat ground. I make it up the first lift and ski the short distance to the one labeled Powder Park.

There's a woman next to me as the operator waves us both forward. We shuffle and quickly glance back with barely enough time to bend our knees and prepare to be whisked away by the lift. I sit back in the leather seat and put my poles under my thigh, just like Lincoln. I grin to myself, feeling like a real skier.

"Erin," the woman says, offering me her gloved hand once we're situated.

She seems older, like she could be Liv's age, with kind eyes and curved parenthesis on either side of her mouth. Her jacket has her name stitched into it, and I can tell this isn't her first time on this run like it is for me.

I grab her padded hand with mine. "Myra."

Looking down, people maneuver their skis in the same way I've seen Lincoln ride his. I'm not one for speed, but after conquering the hill I've been on all week, I'm confident I can get down this run.

"Where are you from?" Erin asks after helping her pull down the metal bar I'm counting on to keep us safe.

"Phoenix. And you?"

"Here," she says. "What brings you to Montana?"

I bite my lower lip and think about how to explain it. At the beginning of the week, I would have blamed Merlot. Coming here was rash and unexpected, but now, I know that coming here was what I needed more than anything. The skiing, the fresh air, the hot, young distraction, and his dog were all more than what I paid for when buying my plane ticket.

"My boyfriend lives here." The answer is so sudden that it surprises even me, so I add, "And I'm visiting a friend."

"Right on," she says with a nod. "Beats fighting the crowds at Big Sky. I've been skiing this mountain since I was your age."

I let out a short laugh. "I'm thirty-five."

She tilts her chin to her chest as she says, "I started when I was thirty-four."

I beam at her as the slope below us gets steeper. The vast landscape is flocked in white. Tree limbs hold piles of snow until they can't, and drops the piles through other snow-covered limbs on the way down. Surprisingly, I can't hear my anger up here. I don't notice the frustration with my parents or irritation at Wade. Up here, it feels like it's just me and these skis.

I shiver and rub my gloved hands together. My phone is in my breast pocket, but I put it on silent the moment my booted feet hit the snow earlier. I knew my parents or Frankie would try to call or text, and I wasn't ready to deal with them. I'll make it down this run and check my messages at the bottom with a large cup of hot cocoa in my hands.

Erin asks a few more standard questions and tells me about the places she's skied before. She talks about the summers in Montana, her job as a realtor, and all of her grown kids. We talk all the way to the very top until we ski off the lift, which I manage to do without falling. Another metaphorical badge I'll gladly pin to my ski jacket.

She waves goodbye and immediately joins the run. But I notice something as she starts going down the hill—I mean *mountain*. It makes the magic carpet look like child's play. This is the most mountainous mountain I've seen yet. It's steep and long and *not* what I was expecting from a blue run.

A gulp gets lodged in my throat as I survey the terrain and watch Erin get smaller. She's fast. So fast that she disappears behind the low-hanging clouds and is just…gone.

I shake my head. All of my earlier confidence begins to fade. I'm not a skier. I can't do this. Maybe skiing isn't my Everest. Not when I'd have to actually ski down Everest. This was supposed to be an easy blue run, but it's more like plummeting to my death.

This isn't right.

I can't…

What was I…

The greater my confidence, the higher the fall.

Chapter Thirty-Two

Lincoln

She still hasn't responded to my text.

To be fair, it was only a picture of Otto on my shoulders and not a critical question I needed answered. But I know how much she likes getting dog pics, and I'm excited to see her again. It felt like there's been a shift in her. I wasn't just her fake boyfriend anymore, but a guy she liked spending time with. And somewhere in there, things changed for me, too. I'm more open and honest than I have been with any other woman. She draws it out of me.

I don't want to read too much into it, but the way she said *tonight* made it sound like there was a promise holding hands with that one word.

"Just drink your beer, man," Jake says. "You've checked your phone twenty-five times in the last two minutes."

After several runs on the mountain for fun instead of work, Ted and Jake convinced me to have a beer with them. I would have gone home and spent the next three hours staring at my phone. Instead, I'm sitting at the bar top doing that. I know we've already made plans for tonight, and I should put my phone away, but I can't stop thinking about the last few days. It's annoying that Jake's right.

I flip my phone facedown and elbow him before sipping my beer. "How's Gemma?"

He shoots me a mean side-eye glare. "I don't know. Text her yourself."

I lean back in my chair and shoot Ted a raised-brow look behind Jake's back.

"I saw that," Jake snaps at me. "I'm not wearing my nighttime goggles this time."

Ted snickers. "That was hilarious."

"You've been warned to watch your back, ape," Jake snaps.

I laugh. "Ape?"

"It's the new nickname he gave me." Ted shrugs, sipping his brew. "He's still pissed that I swapped out his goggles this morning after the powder dump we got. Couldn't see worth shit the whole way down."

I raise my brows at Ted. "God, I'm glad I'm not in the middle of your prank war."

"Yet," he says with a glint in his eye.

I'm sure Otto would let out an exasperated whine right about now. It's what I want to do. But he's in the kennels with Bernie and Milo, where he doesn't have to be subjected to our conversation.

Jake changes the subject. "How much longer are you two going to keep up this fake dating relationship anyway?"

I open my mouth to answer when a flurry of energy dressed in a black wool coat and slicked dark hair rushes up to the bar. "Excuse me?" the man calls to the bartender.

Leo stands up from his squat position where he'd been restocking glasses. "What can I get you?"

The man shakes his head. "Nothing. I'm looking for someone…she's gone…or maybe hiding somewhere, but we can't find her." His speech is jumbled as he tries to explain things.

"Would I have served her? What does she look like?" Leo asks, draping a towel over his shoulder.

I try not to stare, but the man's voice is frantic and strained, as if he were worried about the safety of the woman he's after. I can't help but listen in. Maybe I can help. It could be exactly what I need to distract me from picking up my phone and calling Myra.

The man starts waving his hand in front of his body, starting at his head. "She has long, brown hair—not the ashy color, but like rich dark chocolate. She was wearing a bright yellow jacket from Nordstrom Rack because she refused to spend a decent amount on a capsule wardrobe piece, but whatever. And she's on this self-imposed exile she calls a *journey*," he explains, using finger quotations on the last word. "I haven't heard from her in over an hour."

Yellow jacket? There's only one person I know who has a yellow puffer. I don't even need to hear her name, but the man says it anyway. "Her name's Myra."

Leo blows out a gust of air and slowly shakes his head. "I'm sorry, I—"

"I can help," I say quickly, jumping out of my chair to face the man. "She's lost?"

"Yes." The man lowers his gaze at me, then shakes his head while closing his eyes briefly. "I mean, no." He rubs his forehead. "She left her cabin this morning after a…difficult conversation, and now I can't find her. The only reason I'm here looking for her is because there is nowhere else to go. I've been in every one of these damn lodges and can't find her anywhere. She isn't a very good skier, so I don't think she'd try anything dumb like skiing, but I can't find her, so…"

His voice trails off, and I study him. He's giving city-slicker energy. He's taller by a good few inches, dressed well without a speck of lint or hair to be found, while my black pants are always covered in dog hair. It's at this point I consider who this man is to Myra. Is this a friend? Her brother? I still haven't seen any pictures of her friends or family.

Blood rushes from my face. Is this her ex? The guy who made her believe she was small when she's been the biggest thing on my mind all week.

She never described him to me either, so I have no way of knowing if this is the guy. If it is, they have a history. A history of marriage and sex, heartbreak and loss. He doesn't seem like an ass and sure cares about her enough to appear worried.

A cold realization trails down my spine. It's not like I have any official stake in Myra's life. I'm as good as a fake boyfriend—a fling—and nothing more. They had official government documents legitimizing their feelings for each other. Could he be here to win her back? Is this some big redemption arc for him where he ends up with the girl, and I end up with…no one?

Yet, how can I end up with no one if I started with no one?

I snap out of my thoughts and force myself to do what I'm trained for. Regardless of Myra's ex-husband, she's the one who needs help right now.

I reach behind me to smack Jake on the shoulder, and he coughs out a breath. I'm determined to find her. "We'll help you."

Chapter Thirty-Three

Myra

I'm clinging to the tree at the edge of the run like it will protect me from the inevitable: death.

I should have been more careful. I'm not a professional map reader, but there's no way this is a blue run. I could have gotten on the wrong lift or missed an important sign while Erin was telling me about her daughter's candle business. Vivacious Vanilla and Legendary Lavender were as good as bought in my mind, but I didn't even get the name of her candle empire!

"I don't want to die," I whisper against the tree I'm hugging.

Multiple skiers zoom past me and nosedive down the run as they've done for the past thirty minutes. I considered asking someone to help me, but the embarrassment was too much for my pride. They make it look so easy—effortless even—despite being able to hear them split the wind in half with their breakneck speeds. After they pass, it's quiet. But my mind only gets louder.

There was a five-second period I thought I could try and scoot down on my ass, and then I got closer and could see the pitch of the slope. It's as steep as a book standing on a table. There's no surviving this for me. But now I don't know what to do. I'm stuck. The whole point of this was to do it on my own, gain some confidence, and maybe earn a small battle wound I could show my grandkids one day. This is closer to a life-threatening injury.

I have zero phone service, so Lincoln and the rest of the world are inaccessible from here. When the lifty asked if I was alright, I told him *hell to the no* and continued to freak out and hug this tree. I'm never leaving. I will build a log cabin at the top of this steep-ass mountain and wave at everyone who passes by like I'm the mayor of this newly formed settlement. It might get tricky if I want to mate and have babies, and someone will have to bring up a headstone when I die. But I don't care because I'm stuck here forever.

I grit my teeth and lift my jaw. I was supposed to prove to myself that I could learn to ski without Wade. I can live by myself, pay bills by myself, and hang a fucking picture on the damn wall by myself. I whimper and hug the tree tighter. All of my pictures will just have to be crooked. It's too damn hard! I've tried all the tricks, and I still suck at it.

"I will never use Command Strips!" I yell to no one.

I peer around the tree, the bright white of the snow causing my irises to hurt, so I pull my goggles back down over my eyes. "I'm a…failure."

That word tastes like a burnt bite of casserole in my mouth.

I breathe deeply, loosening my grip on the tree. My arms hurt. But I think it's time for some reverse psychology. The self-help book I've been reading talked about the power of the mind.

The words I think are just as powerful as the ones I say. Unfortunately, both of what I'm thinking and saying right now are total shit.

"Okay, I just need to start saying different things. Think positive," I coach myself as I take another inhale. "You *can* do this. It's hard, but you've done hard things before." I'm not sure it's working, but I keep going. "You signed divorce papers; you moved out on your own; you changed the batteries in the smoke detector and cooked a sandwich without a recipe. You can get down this mountain."

I closed my eyes at some point during this speech to me, myself, and this tree. So I open them and peek around again. The mountain is still steep, and my chances of being able to ski down it without a broken limb to show for it are slim. But I'm just desperate enough to try.

Or the fact my stomach is growling at the mention of a sandwich. Either way, I need to do this. My skis sit discarded behind me on the packed snow, along with my poles. I start to see them as they are—not just tools but life-saving devices that will get me where I need to go.

"Damn it. I'm going to try this, aren't I?"

I sink to the ground, letting go of the tree, and start crawling toward my skis. I guess I answered my question. Using my poles to help me stand on shaking legs, I attempt to click into my bindings with little success. My skis are slipping from under me and threatening to go down without me if I don't get it together.

Get. It. Together.

"I bet Lincoln wouldn't be afraid. This is fun for him." My bindings are packed with snow, and I can't get my foot in, so I get back on my knees and try to clear the snow out. "Frankie would be crying hysterically. I'm not crying. Maybe that counts for something."

I stand and push my toe into the first binding, then click my heel in quickly. The familiar *click* sound brings a wave of relief—just not to my knees; they're still shaking. I repeat the action with the next ski, swallowing the bile threatening to surface when it clicks in, too.

Once I make it down, I'm going to get a sandwich and fries. And cocoa. I won't skimp on the marshmallows either this time. I'll ask for extra. Then I'll call Lincoln and tell him I need to kiss him and apologize for using the pizza move all the way down because I will have to use it. It's my only hope. Once those steps are complete, I will call my parents and tell them I no longer want to hear anything about Wade. I'll be strong and fearless and kind. I won't get angry and scream like I did before.

More skiers pass me, oblivious to the fact I'm about to launch myself down this hill with nothing more than hunger in my gut and a few positive thoughts shoved in my pockets.

It's fine.

I awkwardly shuffle toward the tree and brace my hand on it. Standing makes the angle of this hill even steeper, and I have to close my eyes. If I lean forward, I'll join the run and be wholly committed to making it down. If I turn around and go back… well, there is no back.

"Just do it. Open your eyes, and go," I say out loud in a pinched voice. My hands sweat inside my gloves as my thighs clap together, and my shoulders rise to invade the personal space of my ears. "Open your eyes."

Slowly, as if I were peeling open a wrapper, I open one eye and then the next.

Positive thoughts.

"Do this."

I look down at my skis, but they aren't moving. My legs and brain are not working together and might as well be a part of two different bodies right now. The sound of fiberglass thudding on firmly packed snow captures my attention as someone else goes off a jump beside me and hits the snow. Their hips don't move as they lean forward and barrel down the mountain at a speed that causes sweat to bead on my forehead.

I breathe in. And out. "Don't think, just…go."

Chapter Thirty-Four

Lincoln

By the time I suit up in the locker room and ensure Otto's ready to roll, I get a call on the radio.

"Hey, Lincoln, it's Mikey."

I press the button and reply. "Go for it."

"There was a woman up here on Hawk with a yellow jacket mumbling your name. She was terrified."

I pause outside the locker doors, Otto dancing around my feet in figure-eights because he's ready to go to work. Hawk is a short black run off the Powder Park lift. Why is she up there? Did she think it was Sunset?

"Was?"

He replies quickly. "I don't see her anymore, but Jake said you were looking for her."

I'm more than looking for her. I'm worried. Jake had already put out on the radio what Myra was wearing, hoping to get ahead of this. He said she had a yellow jacket and dark brown hair. But he forgot to mention how her stunning eyes and lips could make a man forget where he was. He and Ted stayed with the ex while I head up the hill. I don't even want to know what they're going to talk about while I'm gone.

I click the radio to reply. "I'm riding up with Otto now."

Mikey says goodbye, promising to let us know if he sees her. I don't delay grabbing my skis, heading outside to the Sunset lift, and then on to Powder Park. There's no way Myra would go on a black run. She made that clear enough. This makes me think maybe she meant to go left for one of the blue runs. It's an honest mistake and one I've had to help coach people down from before.

On the lift, I tap my fingers nervously on my knee while loosely holding Otto's collar beside me. He's completely still, absorbing all of my anxious energy like a vessel that can handle it. I'm committed to finding Myra no matter what, but knowing her ex is at the bottom waiting for her is less than ideal.

Why is he here? Flying to Montana after signing divorce papers seems weird. But if he still loves her and wants her back after realizing what a tool he was, then of course he'd show up. Grand gestures are textbook.

Seeing his nicely trimmed face compared to the chaos of a short beard now growing on mine with clothes that made him look like he just walked out of a men's clothing magazine, we couldn't have been more different. He seemed put together, like he isn't spending his winters working at a ski resort and summers guiding people on rafting trips. He probably makes a decent income, doesn't have a nosy family like mine, and I already know he didn't need to enter a fake dating relationship with Myra. He married her. Then divorced her, but he's here now for reasons I have a feeling I'll find out about soon enough.

I just need to find Myra first.

Putting the ex out of my mind, I focus on getting off the chair lift and skiing to the right to catch the next one. Since it isn't crowded, we ski right onto the Powder Park lift, going farther up to where Myra was spotted.

Like all the runs, I've been on this one plenty of times. So has Otto. But what I'm not prepared for is what we might find on the hillside. I'm realizing that if something happens to Myra…if she's hurt…we are her recovery team, the ones who will find her in whatever state she's in.

Minutes later, we're off the lift again, veering to the right where the black run starts. I don't stop but join the paved area with others, scanning for any signs of yellow.

"Heel," I yell to Otto, so he runs beside me, following my lead.

There are a few skiers who pass me since riding with Otto means I'm not going as fast. His mouth is open, and he's staring straight down. Visibility is clear, and we aren't straining to see very far ahead. Low-hanging clouds or fresh powder days can make it harder to see, but today is the kind of day you want in an emergency.

"Out front." Otto runs ahead of me.

Normally, I wouldn't bring him for something like this. His expertise is searching for people and items buried beneath the snow. But I trust him with my life, Myra's too, and any help I can get out here is needed. His nose is better than mine, anyway.

The terrain is steep, and I imagine Myra trying to go down this. She's still afraid of her speed, which is exactly what a black run encourages. Cardiac arrests are one of the primary calls we respond to out here, seeing upwards of three to five a season, but skier-on-skier accidents, or skier-on-tree, aren't uncommon. If Myra ran into someone because she couldn't stop…I shake my head. I need to keep focused. I may be looking for Myra, but I need to have a clear head to do my job.

I scan either side of the run, looking around trees and areas the other skiers wouldn't veer off to, but someone with less control might. There are marked trails through the trees on many of the runs, but Myra's not familiar with those. I doubt she'd meander through them.

Her ex said she was upset, though. Could she have done something outside her skill level because she was upset? Or was it an accident? I'd swear she was probably trying to go on the blue run—an honest mistake.

Maybe she'd already run into her ex at her place, and he followed her here. It wouldn't surprise me if she ran out on him after everything she's said about their relationship, which isn't exactly a ton. But it's enough to think she wouldn't want to talk to him.

But it doesn't matter what made her do it. I'm still here, still needing to find her.

We're only a portion down the mountain, Otto out in front, when I notice his ears perk up. They do this often since he's always listening and aware of everyone around him, but this looks different. His gait slows some, and his eyes lock on something. I follow his gaze, not expecting to see what I do.

Off to the left of the run, where the snow and trees meet, and my heart rate goes to die, I see yellow. I see *her*.

Chapter Thirty-Five

Myra

L incoln!" I manage to scream above Otto's barking.

I'm waving my arms above my head like I just don't care because I don't. I'm sure I look like a human flare, trying to get his attention. Never have I been more relieved to see red ski jackets.

Otto reaches me first, greeting me with his famous cheek kisses. It calms me just ruffling his fur and feeling his heart beat wildly between my gloved hands. I haven't exactly been calm. My tears have all frozen to my face, and I was just starting to develop the blueprints for the cabin I'd have to build up here.

People have skied by, but on this run, everyone has been going too fast to notice me.

"Myra!" Lincoln shouts, digging his heels out to stop short of where I'm at. His eyes are wide as he looks me over and clicks out of his bindings faster than I've ever seen. Angling his skis, he kneels in front of me, biting the tips of his gloves to remove them and cradling my face. "Where are you hurt?"

I cup his hand with mine and close my eyes. The tears start again, melting the ones frozen beneath my eyes. Heat reenters my face with the swell of emotion coursing through my body.

"What is it? Tell me where you're hurt," he pleads, resting his forehead on mine.

I just shake my head, too overcome with relief to speak. And my lips are still thawing out, making it difficult to use them. He pulls me to his chest and holds me on the side of a run I tumbled part way down. I had to crawl over here so that I wouldn't cause a ten-skier pile-up.

"Myra, please," Lincoln begs in my ear. "Tell me you're okay."

I nod against the cool of his jacket where I've burrowed my face in and plan to stay forever. "I'm okay."

He sighs in relief, then pulls back, inspecting my face one more time. "And you're sure?"

"I'm sure."

He breathes steadily through his nose, then sits beside me. "What happened?"

"I…" I can't even say it; shame is too thick in my throat.

He sits next to me and pulls me to his side. I rest my head on his shoulder while Otto sits between our thighs, one paw on mine as if he's still unconvinced I'm okay. I breathe in and out, seeing small puffs of each breath in the cold and being thankful for each one. "I'm not hurt, just…" I close my eyes and let my words drift off. *I'm safe.* "I'm just…" I open my eyes and look over at him, cataloging the worry in the lines between his brows, downturned mouth, and rigid jawline. "I'm just cold."

He responds by rubbing my arm furiously and tucking me closer to him.

I nestle further in, though the frozen snow on his coat is anything but helping. "I lost my poles."

"And your skis?"

Good question since they are no longer on my feet. "They skied down a ways. See, by that tree." I point to where they went on without me. I couldn't even scoot down there to retrieve them; I was too scared. New tears rise. Lincoln and Otto are here now, and I'm safe. "I couldn't do it."

He doesn't say anything right away; he just holds me while I cry.

And I cry. Tears wrack my body because I didn't think he'd find me. I thought my mistake would cost me. My failure would bite me in the ass again like the divorce did. I can't even stand on my own two feet.

"I couldn't do it," I repeat.

He holds me closer, the other arm wrapping me as close to his chest as possible. It doesn't matter it's borderline crushing because feeling his sturdy frame is what I need. "We have to get you inside to warm up. How long have you been out here? Why did you—" He shakes his head furiously, chin resting on the top of my head. "Never mind. Don't answer that. Let's get your skis and go back to the lodge."

My skis. The lodge. "No! I can't."

He untucks me from his embrace and stares down at me. I don't even bother wiping the tear streaks on my warm cheeks. "Why?" he asks with pinched brows. "We can't stay here."

I shake my head faster than one of those ice cream ball mixers in the hands of an eager kid. "I won't do it. I can't ski, Lincoln. This is a blue run, and I couldn't even make it very far. I fell too many times. And this run is *steep*. I can't get down on skis. Can't you bring a snowmobile up to get me?"

His mouth opens as he studies me and then wipes my face clean regardless of the new tears forming in my eyes. I'm sure I look terrified. Wide, pleading eyes, frantic and rushed words, and chapped lips that will need roughly a pound of chapstick.

He starts slipping his gloves back on. "Myra, this isn't a blue run."

If shock had not already become my best friend while stuck on the side of this hill, I would have looked more surprised. But we've already made friendship bracelets and agreed to braid each other's hair in the course of one afternoon. My eyes are propped in a permanent width while my mouth is open, catching stray snowflakes from the sky or the ones floating off Lincoln's jacket.

Of course this is a harder run. I'm clearly incapable of even getting on the right chairlift.

"What color?" I ask in a stupor.

"Black."

I square my shoulders with his. "Holy shit! I can't get down a black run! You have to get the snowmobile." My voice is beyond the verge of begging; it quakes and screeches like wet brakes on a car.

He exhales and pets Otto's head, which he accepts willingly. "We can't bring the snowmobiles up here. There are strict rules, this is too steep for them, and skiers are going too fast. We have to ski down."

I shake my head. "No, I won't do it."

"Myra," he says softly, but I keep shaking my head.

He doesn't understand how I feel since runs like this one aren't hard for him. He could probably close his eyes and ski backward. Hell, he probably loves how fast this hill forces you to go. But this is impossible for me. This is Everest times five. I'm no match for this run. I already tried.

I've never felt so small, so scared. My muscles have all locked up, and I likely won't even be able to stand, considering how much I'm shaking. *Scared* doesn't even seem to do this kind of emotion justice. It's not familiar to me, but I can't turn it off.

My heart is racing fast, and I feel a tingle in my feet every time I peer down, which is too often when I'm stuck on the side of a mountain, and all I'm doing is looking down.

"I know you're scared, but I'm going to help you." He scratches Otto's jaw. "Otto, too."

"I'm going to fall," I say in protest. I didn't exactly make it this far in an upright position.

"And I'll be here to help you get back up."

"I don't even have my poles."

He wipes my face clear again. "You can use mine."

I want to be the brave, fearless person he thinks I am, but I just can't. I'm not her.

I shake my head as my chin quivers and whisper, "I can't."

He shifts to a kneeling position in front of me again. "You can."

I drop my chin to my chest and cover my face. Maybe I could have done it years ago, but not now, not today. The confidence I wanted to find on this mountain ran off with my ex. I've been living scared for the past six months. Scared to live by myself. Scared to support myself on one income. Scared of failing at life.

And scared of being alone forever.

"Myra, look at me." His voice is strong as he says this.

My gaze lifts slowly.

He brushes my cheeks yet again with his glove. "This run is hard. But I know there's a part of you that isn't afraid of hard. There's a part of you that *can* do this. We need to find her."

"She's gone, Lincoln. Dried and shriveled up for good."

He shakes his head and plants his fists beside my thighs, hovering in front of me. "You've done this before—hard things, that is."

My brow furrows. "Not in a long time."

"You've been doing them—every day. You've been waking up, getting ready, and learning how to live. You flew here to try something new. You're breathing, Myra, and while you still have that ability, you can make it down this mountain."

The change in his voice has made me unable to look away from his unblinking expression. I don't have all the confidence I need for this, but maybe I don't have to. Maybe Lincoln could have enough for both of us. I could trust him. I could breathe through this and let him guide me. It's not like he's going to steer me into a ditch or another tree.

"Will you ski behind me?" I'm not talking feet behind me, more like inches.

His lips part, and he shakes his head. "It's too steep of a grade and wouldn't be safe. Plus, I've got Otto with me this time. You're going to have to ski on your own, but I'll give you my poles and coach you the whole way as you follow me. I'm not going to leave you."

The promise of Lincoln being with me the whole time causes a lift in my spirit. I sniffle and wipe my face of any remaining tears. I'm not ready to try this again, but maybe that's how life goes. Maybe I won't always be ready for things when I want to be.

Maybe I just have to be.

"Okay," I say with a nod.

He pushes to stand and helps me do the same, holding both of my hands while his back is to the lodge. My feet are wobbly, and no good at doing something as basic as this, but I try my best.

"You're up," he says, our chests centimeters apart.

I look into the dark green of his eyes. Lincoln is my ski coach, yes. But he's also been some kind of a life coach with great brows, helping me see what I couldn't. He sees the beauty in life, unlike many others. Maybe it's because of all his travels or because of his mom's diagnosis. Regardless, he's present in every moment he's in. And right now, I'm confident he's here with me, and I want to trust him.

"I'm up. And ready."

Chapter Thirty-Six

Myra

"Myra! What were you thinking?" Frankie circles me in an urgent hug.

It took us an hour to get back to the lodge. When I asked Lincoln how long it usually takes him to make it that far, he replied *no comment*. He said it with a grin that made my legs weak for a different reason. Amazingly, I'm still standing on them, considering all I put them through today.

Now, I'm just insanely grateful to be back on flat land and warmer, thanks to the blazing fire in the lodge hearth. Lincoln took Otto back to the kennels while I came to thaw out my fingers. And despite wanting to remove my parents from my contacts, my anger has waned since walking out on them. I guess I have a bruised tailbone and ego to thank for that.

"Would you believe me if I said it was an accident?" I mumble into Frankie's wool jacket. It smells of sugar, spice, and everything nice, so I'm not complaining.

He pulls back, holding me at arm's length. "Yes, but—"

"Myra!" Mom walks toward me with open arms.

The hug is even more intense than Frankie's since Dad decides to get in on it, too. I'm now smashed between them, looking for a pocket of air to breathe. This is what it's like to be hugged by leeches.

We're boxed in by the many other conversations happening around us, standing in the center of it all while people pass us with heavy footfalls. A swishing of fabric so loud, it grates on my ears as they walk since thigh gaps are nonexistent for everyone wearing snow pants. No one else here knows I just accomplished the hardest thing I've done in a while. It wasn't like the emotional flavor of hard I've known for months, but rather a physical one. And…I did it.

"We're so glad you're okay," Dad whispers before pulling back.

"What were you thinking?" Mom starts to say with a death grip on my shoulders. Her gaze drops to my sweatshirt, and she steps back with a startled intake of air. "What is that?"

I look down at my chest to see what she's talking about. *Ah, yes.* After coming inside, I shed my jacket since the stone fireplace makes it toasty inside the lodge. But I forgot what I was wearing…Santa in a thong.

Dad's eyes widen, and he quickly stares at the ceiling like he's seen something inappropriate. Probably because he has.

Frankie curls his lips in, then points at his chest. "You have something here."

I point at Santa's ass. "Oh, you mean here."

"To the left—"

"Myra!"

I bounce my eyes to Mom.

"What were you thinking?"

I let my exhale carry the explanation with it. "I'm okay. I didn't mean to go down the black run, but I'm alright. Otto found me, and Lincoln…" I peer around the bodies closing in on me to find Linc. He's standing a few feet away, just behind everyone, staring like it's the first time he's seeing me. "Lincoln helped me."

Mom twists in every direction to try and spot the elusive boyfriend they'd only met on our video call, who is now a bonafide hero worthy of a plaque with his name etched on it.

Dad turns and extends his hand to Lincoln. "You saved our daughter's life."

Dramatic much…

Lincoln nods and shakes his hand. Our eyes lock, and he smiles, but it looks almost sad. "I'm going to get going, give you all a chance to, uh…catch up." He regards Frankie and then drops Dad's hand.

"No!" I practically attack his arm, looping around it with even more desperation than I've shown today. I'm not ready to put the dramatics to bed quite yet. "You can't go."

I can feel my mom's gaze burning a hole in the side of my face. Everyone has their eyes on us. I'm sure seeing me with another man is different for them. They still had my wedding photo hanging in their house on Christmas.

"Yes, don't go," Frankie says, looking from me to Lincoln with an amused grin.

Lincoln peers down at me. "Are you sure you want me here? Don't you think it'll be better to talk to," he clears his throat, "*him* without me around?"

I don't think my brows could pull together any closer. "Who? My Dad?"

He shakes his head and strains his neck to point it in Frankie's direction. His voice is low when he says, "Your ex."

I don't register what he says right away. "Frankie?"

He hooks a sly thumb toward my brother. But to Lincoln, it's not my brother since he's never seen a picture of him before. He thinks he's...

I shake my head. "What?"

He shifts on his feet while everyone seems to lean closer, straining to hear. "Your ex-husband. Don't you want to talk to him?"

I want to laugh.

Or maybe cry.

There are a lot of conflicting emotions happening inside me right now.

"Oh my God," Frankie says loudly, garnering attention from others. "Is he here? Is Wade here? I will throw him out on his ass in the damn snow!" He spins in a full circle with searching eyes, ready to shoot lasers.

"Shh-shh-shh! Frankie!" I scold, so he doesn't draw even more attention. "Wade isn't here." I peel away from Lincoln's side and stand in front of him. "My ex isn't here. Frankie is my brother."

"Your brother? The one who doesn't like the cold?" Lincoln asks.

"I'm right here." I peer over my shoulder at Frankie who continues, "But yes, I hate the cold. I'm like the opposite of Elsa. I throw sunbeams out of my hands instead."

"Am I missing something?" Mom asks, bending around between Lincoln and me.

I sigh heavily and drop my chin to my chest.

Lincoln whispers, "Sorry. I could have sworn he was your ex when he started telling me about you...but I..." he pauses, "I'm sorry."

His eyes are locked on mine as his hands stay shoved in his pockets. The gratitude I have for him is overwhelming. The kindness, support, and friendship he's shown me is beyond what he had to. But he did. Over and over, he's been there.

The plains and valleys of his lips are familiar, and the way I push up to my toes and kiss him squarely on the mouth is, too. I'm overwhelmed by all of the feelings coursing through me. Tears and laughter, relief and desire all war for space inside me. The kiss is brief enough that the rest of the guests in the lodge aren't getting more than they asked for and long enough that his tongue licks the seam of my mouth, sending heat coursing through my body. I drop back to my heels and slowly blink.

He stares down at me, mouth wet, and my desire mirrored on his face.

"What's up?" a small voice chirps.

I look around for the new voice. My gaze tracks down.

"Sadie?" Lincoln steps away from me like we're in trouble with an eight-year-old. "Where are your parents?"

"Somewhere." She sighs and then points between us. "Did you just kiss her?"

I swear I can hear myself blinking. Shifting, I cross my arms. "Didn't your parents ever teach you it's rude to point? And no, I kissed him."

"Didn't your parents ever teach you not to kiss strangers?"

Pretty sure my mouth falls open. "We're not strangers."

"Well, you're not boyfriend and girlfriend, so..." Sadie crosses her arms like she dares me to disagree again.

"Who is this child?" Frankie swirls a hand in front of Sadie. "She's giving, like, Myra circa 1996 vibes, but without the butterfly hair clips and overalls." He shudders.

"Myra, do you know her?" Mom asks, using her manicured finger to point at Sadie.

"No," I answer immediately, then correct myself, "I mean, sort of."

Sadie pulls out her sweet Huckleberry syrup smile she's so freakishly good at. "I'm Sadie."

Mom beams at her like she does with her Yorkie since she's been sucked into Sadie's vortex now, too.

Lincoln opens his mouth but doesn't get a word in before we hear, "Myra!"

Chapter Thirty-Seven

Myra

"Liv?" I say in disbelief as she rushes over. We're the size of a flash mob now, and I'm embracing it now.

She hugs me, and I can feel all of the places the mountain beat me up. Pulling away, I note the prominent worry lines on her face as she hooks a thumb toward Frankie. "He said you were stuck?"

"Lost," Frankie corrects from behind her. "But stuck works, too."

"Hi, Mrs. Dabney."

Liv steps back, looking between Lincoln and me, then down. "Oh. Hi, Sadie. Where's your parents?" She frantically searches around the lodge.

Now, I'm pointing at Sadie. So much pointing. "You know her?"

Liv nods, but Sadie answers for her. "She's my principal."

My mouth falls open. This really *is* a small town.

"I get to hang out with Sadie in my office…often," Liv says in a mostly cheerful tone. "So what happened?"

"Myra got mad," Frankie starts, "and decided to throw herself down a mountain—"

"Did not," I retort, arms still crossed.

Frankie shoots me a glare. "Anyway…she's fine now. Lincoln rode his white horse up there to save her and slayed all the monsters." He winks at Lincoln. "I forgive you for thinking I was Wade, by the way."

Liv runs a hand through her gray curls. "I'm still confused."

Sadie's points at Lincoln. "They kissed."

When I peer at Lincoln, he looks like he's sweating.

"Okay." Liv drags out the word.

I sigh and tell her, "I'll explain later."

Mom, clearly over the conversation, steps forward, clasping her hands in front of her and says, "Myra, I'm sorry. I should have run after you, stopped you to tell you how I never meant to hurt you."

Back to the reason we're all gathered here today. My mind is on overdrive, trying to keep up with this conversation. Mom has never been the apologetic type, so hearing *sorry* fall from her lips feels monumental in a way, if not shocking.

"I know you've both been concerned about me after the… divorce." I've rarely used this word with them. It felt final, and seeing their reaction to *final* felt more awkward. "But I'm a divorced woman now. There is no more Wade, and I'm also not biding my time before trying to make things work with him again. That part of my life is over. And it was the hardest thing I've ever gone through."

A faint *yes* falls out of Liv's mouth, and I know she's internally clapping for me. Tears prick at the backs of my eyes, having been close to the surface all day, but I tamp them down before they overflow, needing to get the rest out, or I'll never be able to. Lincoln pulls me into his side for support, his arm looped around my waist.

"You guys have always had a close relationship with Wade. But he's my ex, and to move on with my life, I can't keep looking back. If you want to have a relationship with him, I can't be a part of it. I don't want to hear what you're doing or where you're going with him. If you invite him to family dinner, I won't be there." I take a steadying breath. "I need time to heal."

My words shake by the end of my speech, but I did it. I said what I needed to say for a long time. Maybe the magical powers of skiing did give me my confidence back. Or knowing my support system is here with me.

Frankie starts to slow clap, and because the lodge is filled with people, a few other strangers join him even if they have no idea why. His clapping gets louder as heat crawls higher up my neck. But Frankie holds my gaze, and my watery eyes are no match for the love I see in his. I mouth a *thank you,* and while he could say *you're welcome,* he doesn't. He says, *I love you.*

Mom looks around at the attention we've drawn, then back at Liv, Lincoln, and finally me. "Well, I suppose Wade's family is a little showy. His mother would never shut up about her crystal duck collection. I mean, who *really* needs that many ducks? And his dad?" She groans. "Don't even get me started on how he always drones on about his big boat. God, you'd think he was talking about something other than his actual yacht the way he describes it!"

Dad widens his eyes and tips his head toward her while shaking his head.

She adjusts her sweater and runs a hand over her perfectly styled hair. "What I'm trying to say is that maybe we don't need to spend so much time with Wade and his family. They've been friends of ours forever, but…" Dad simpers at her, and she continues, "Maybe it's time we all move on."

I nod, smiling through the blur in my eyes at hearing Mom admit this. It feels monumental inside me. Dad hands me the handkerchief he always keeps in the breast pocket of whatever jacket he's wearing, and I take it from him to dab the corners of my eyes and wipe my still partially frozen nose. Then he leans in to kiss the top of my head like he did when I was a little girl. It's enough to know he agrees with Mom.

"We're going to fly home today, Myra," Dad says, breaking the silence.

I hand Dad his handkerchief back, but he refuses it as I peer between them. "You are?"

Dad pats my shoulder. "Well, we still have to book our tickets, but we can see you are just fine. There's no crisis, and we might have been too forward in coming here in the first place."

"We just got here, Ken—" Mom starts, but Dad cuts her a sharp look, and she exhales enough that her normally perfect posture slumps. "Your father's right. We'll fly home as soon as we can."

My chin connects with my chest, and I close my eyes. I'm relieved at this small act that makes me feel like they've finally heard me. But now I feel awful for keeping this fake relationship from them after their mostly heartfelt apology. I lied to them to make it seem like I was fine. Well, I'm not fine. So *not fine* that I think I've been lying to myself, too, about how much I like my fake boyfriend.

Liking Lincoln is easy. Like rolling out of bed in the morning and stretching or falling into bed at night with a sigh. It feels right to want to be with him even when there are plenty of things that indicate it's too complicated. We don't share the same zip code, he's younger, and I'm…figuring things out. It's just weird timing overall.

"I have to tell you all something." I thread an arm around Lincoln's waist and squeeze. He pulls me into his side again, and the breath I have to take just to get my mouth to open is huge. "Lincoln and I aren't dating."

"What?" Mom squeaks.

Dad shakes his head. "But you just kissed him."

I nod once. "True."

"But they aren't dating," Sadie repeats for me.

She's still here?

"Sadie," Liv starts, "why don't we go find your parents?"

Sadie lets out an exasperated sigh. "Yes, Mrs. Dabney."

As Liv and Sadie walk off, I face at my family. "I did kiss him, and I didn't lie about spending time with him this week. We've spent nearly every day together."

"Can you blame her? He has great eyebrows," Frankie adds.

We all look at Frankie.

He shrugs and points at Lincoln's face. "Look for yourself."

We all look at Lincoln.

Lincoln eyes me briefly. "I have great eyebrows?"

My mouth curls up. "You do."

"I don't understand," Mom says. "You...you told us on the phone you were dating, and you're here because...you're dating."

I shake my head. "I lied."

"You lied to us?" Dad clarifies.

I chew on my bottom lip. Making eye contact with either of them is impossible, so I bounce my gaze to Frankie, who is giving me *what the hell are you doing?* eyes. I don't know. I just can't keep pretending. That's not me or the person I want to be.

"I did. And I'm sorry. I just hated calling home or visiting and hearing all about Wade. I thought if I had a fake boyfriend, you'd see I was moving on."

Dad points at Lincoln. "Is he a paid actor then?"

It's cute that my dad thinks I'd pay someone. "No. He's someone I met the first day I was here."

Frankie pipes up. "She slid between his legs."

"Between his legs? Myra!" Mom chastises.

I shoot him a glare. "Not helping."

She sighs heavily and rubs her forehead. "I can see our actions took a toll on you."

Dad brackets his hips with his hands and looks at Lincoln. "So, is your name Lincoln?"

"Dad, yes. That's his real name."

"Why don't we all start over." Lincoln extends his hand to Dad. "I'm Lincoln, and I'm *not* Myra's real boyfriend."

Dad shakes his hand. "I'm just Ken."

Mom lifts both of her hands. "Obviously, something is going on between you, but I need a glass of whatever they serve besides water before I try to understand all this." Without waiting on any of us, she starts walking toward the bar at the back of the lodge.

Frankie and Dad follow her, and I start to as well when Lincoln holds me back by grabbing my elbow. He peers at my family, walking away with their backs to us, then leans in and whispers, "Are you alright?"

I try not to stare at his mouth, but it's right there. All of these emotions tumbling around inside me like a dryer set on wrinkle release need a place to go. Lincoln's lips could work.

But I don't kiss him. I respond with, "I think so." The heightened emotions of the conversation start to settle, and it's like I'm looking at Lincoln with fresh eyes. "I'm glad I told them the truth."

He nods while searching my face. I expect him to run for the hills. If our families have one thing in common, it's how involved they like being. But apart from that, they are nothing alike.

But he doesn't run, and he doesn't hide himself from me. He tugs me into his chest and puts his chin on the top of my head. At first, my body is rigid. This isn't a hug you give someone who just broke up with you in front of her family after saving her from the side of a mountain.

But soon, I sag further into his embrace with every breath I take. Being held by him is like wrapping paper around a present, but even more than that, it feels like getting the perfect crease on the ends of said wrapping paper. When the corners tuck in perfectly and lie flat on either end.

I don't know what comes next or how we're supposed to say goodbye in a couple of days.

But I do know that this feels *right*.

Chapter Thirty-Eight

Lincoln

What just happened?" I say out loud for the twentieth time since stepping inside Myra's place.

She blows a piece of hair out of her face as she picks up a stray shirt off the floor. "A lot."

I bend to make sure Otto's feet are dry, before he checks the living room for any steaks Myra might have left lying around, then take off my coat and toss it on the couch. "I just can't believe it's over."

We spent an hour catching everyone up on the last few days, including the start and end of our fake dating relationship. Her parents made good on their word and bought plane tickets to leave tomorrow morning, and Frankie was adamant about getting a photo of me for his *own collection*. I was shocked to hear Myra bring our relationship up at all, but I can't say I'm not relieved that everything is out in the open now. It gave me some ideas on how I'll tell my family.

She waves me off while opening the fridge. "Me either. If it counts for anything, you were the best fake boyfriend I've ever had."

Little does she know what it's done for me. Myra has a way of pulling my thoughts out of my head while still making me feel safe. She makes me want to be outspoken and honest like she is. This can't be over. At least, I don't want it to be.

Shoving my fingers through my hair, I take three steps to follow her into the kitchen, leaning into the counter. "How's the…you know?"

Unscrewing the orange juice, she chugs some, then wipes her mouth with the back of her hand. "You can say *ass*, Lincoln. I won't be offended." She smirks.

"Okay. How's your…*ass* then?"

"Sore as hell." She stares at me from across the kitchen. "But it was worth it in the end when I finally said what I needed to." She takes another swig and then grabs her phone from her back pocket.

I lean my palms into the counter. "It was nice to meet all of them."

She sets her phone down and smirks from across the counter. "Even Frankie?"

I won't say I didn't release every clenched muscle in my body when I found out that Frankie was her brother and *not* her ex. That could have played out differently.

"Definitely Frankie."

She sets the carton on the counter, grabs a banana, and opens it to take a large bite. Otto comes to sit at her feet, and she opens a random kitchen drawer, pulling out a bag of treats I've never seen before and offers him one. I don't know when this happened, but it seems so normal for her to do this.

"Have you always had those stashed in there?"

She nods and closes the drawer while Otto chomps happily on his treat. "I have them stashed everywhere. The drawer, my ski jacket, Liv's car, your truck…"

This makes my laugh lines show. Beyond the physical attraction and fake dating, I think Myra has started to see me differently, too. But now isn't the right time to bring it up. It's the first time since the rescue I notice how tired she is. There are dark circles under her eyes, and she slumps over the counter on her forearms like she's too exhausted to stand up. The hair in her braid is falling out, and her normally rose-colored cheeks are paler.

I round the counter's edge and cup her elbows, steering her toward the bed.

"What are you doing?" she asks, stepping over Otto.

I do the same since he's still enjoying his bone. "Helping you to bed."

"Lincoln…"

"Hm?" We make it to the bedroom in two seconds flat.

She doesn't say anything more, though, and lets me take care of her as I pull back the covers of her bed. We can talk about everything we haven't said later. Right now, because I can, I lift the Santa sweatshirt over her head. I can toss the fifty-seven throw pillows off the bed. I can tuck the blankets over her shoulder and under her chin. I can turn off the light. I can take all of the cups on her nightstand to the kitchen—there are a lot of those.

And I can promise her, "I'll be here when you wake up."

She nods, closing her eyes before I've even left the side of her bed.

I walk backward, away from the undertow wanting me to lie down, and step back into her kitchen, setting all the cups beside the sink. It's brighter in here because of the windows, so I lower the shades and walk into the living room. Otto decides to jump up onto the other side of Myra's bed and curl beside her. Then she instinctively reaches out to pet him like she does this every night.

And I'm left wondering when it started to feel like I never want to say goodbye to this woman.

✳✳✳

"NOW WHAT ARE you doing?" Myra's voice is groggy, and her eyes are half open as she sits up in bed, rubbing at them. Otto stirs beside her but doesn't bother getting up.

I've been cleaning her place mostly by braille since I turned off all the lights and lowered the shades so she wouldn't wake up. I guess she still did. "I didn't mean to wake you up. I'll stop."

She peers around, the only light coming from my... "Are you wearing a headlamp?"

I stare at her directly, and she squints, rearing back like the light is attacking her. It kind of is.

"Yes." I angle the headlamp toward the ceiling so I can stare deeply into her eyes without her going blind. The light has only helped me see whatever's been directly in front of me. I side-swiped my knee on her coffee table and tripped on the edge of her rug while attempting to clean.

Her brows form a harsh crease between them. "Why?"

I'm holding a few stray pieces of clothing I found in her living room and a bottle of all-purpose spray. It's gotten me through all the purposes I've needed it for in the last two hours.

I thought about leaving after the first hour. There wasn't a reason to stay other than because I said I would. Then I started cleaning as the sun dipped below the mountains, hence the headlamp. And there was enough here to keep me busy.

"I didn't want you to wake up by turning on all the lights." I point at my head. "I found this in a drawer."

She still peers at me through a squint and then around the cabin again. "Did you clean this whole place?" Tossing the covers aside, she slides out of bed and pads into the kitchen. Otto still doesn't follow, too busy sleeping off the events of the day apparently.

My arms are full, but I shake my head. "I haven't made it to the bathroom yet, and the dishwasher still needs to be emptied once it's finished running, but the rest of the place is clean."

Her lips part as she takes in the space. All the dishes in the sink have been taken care of, the counters wiped off, and I picked up most of her clothes. I put them in her suitcase or near it so I could sweep, and the living room just needed a good straightening.

Her long-sleeve shirt is askew on her body, putting the few snaps normally in the center of her chest now over her left boob. The hair that had already been falling from her braid is now completely free since her hair tie seems to be missing, and she has a red crease on the side of her cheek from the pillow.

Her eyes are on what's in my hands as she lifts the corner of the underwear I'm holding.

"I swear I mean nothing by this. Just found it under the couch in the living room, and I was going to put it away."

She gives me a small grin and shakes her head slowly. "You didn't have to do all of this."

I swallow and shift on my feet. "I didn't want you to wake up in a messy place. Not after today." And selfishly, I wanted to stay. Leaving her after the kind of day she had didn't feel right. I needed to stay if only to make sure she had enough food and ice for her ass.

She rubs her arms vigorously, her teeth lightly chattering. "Thank you. Here, I can take those," she says, putting out her hands to take the clothes.

I shift the spray to my elbow and hand her the items. I'm not sure what I should do at this point. Stay? Leave? Talk? She's had a long day, and even with a nap, maybe she wants some time to herself.

"I'll just finish the bathroom and then leave."

"No, no," she says from near her suitcase. "I'll get to that tomorrow."

I rub the back of my neck. "Do you need anything? Are you hungry? I could make you something."

She walks closer, the glow of my headlamp still pointing upward as our only light. "I'm not hungry right now."

"Do you need ice?"

She presses a hand to her low back and arches in a stretch. "I'm good for now."

I nod and tuck my hands in my pockets. I've officially run out of reasons to stay. "I'll take off then."

She shakes her head and reaches for my forearm. "No, stay."

Two words said in the form of a statement have never sounded so good. I relax my shoulders. "Okay."

"I'm going to shower, but make yourself comfortable, and I'll be out in ten."

She heads for the bathroom, and I turn to face the living room. There's a stove in the corner with a few logs stacked beside it. I'm already walking there to get it started when I realize my headlamp is still on. I think it's safe to turn the lights on now, so I flip on the standing lamp by the couch and click off the light on my forehead.

I busy myself with starting the fire, adding a few pieces of kindling and cardboard to get it going before sitting on the couch. Otto is still strongly committed to Myra's bed, but he'll be ready to eat soon, which means I'll have to head back home before I'm ready to leave. I want to talk to her more, if only to tell her thank you. But it doesn't seem like enough. She agreed to fake dating for her own reason, but I want her to know what it meant to me. More than just giving my mom something to be excited about, Myra has done that for me. With her, I've started looking forward again and not back.

She comes out of the bathroom after twelve minutes, but it takes only one millisecond to realize she's in nothing but a towel. It's wrapped around her torso, and she's clutching it at her chest. On light feet, she tip-toes toward her suitcase. "I forgot to grab clean clothes."

I think I make a noise in the back of my throat to indicate I heard her while trying not to stare. She's making it difficult. Her slick, toned legs are glowing with a wet sheen as her hair runs long down her back. The number of times I've seen it out of its braid can be counted on one hand. She always wears her hair pulled back, but with it wet and long, it makes me more speechless than all her bare skin.

She grabs her clothes and disappears back into the bathroom, so I tear my eyes away and back to watch the now roaring fire until she exits a few minutes later and asks, "Want some coffee?"

I check my watch. "It's four-thirty."

She shrugs. "I know. You're young; you can handle it."

My lips turn upward at her from across the room. "So, we're joking about my age now?"

"Yes," she says with a nod. "I guess we are. Now, tell me if you want coffee, or I will just pour you a mug."

"I'll drink some."

She starts moving around the kitchen. Filling the pot with water, she pours it into the coffeemaker and sets the machine to start brewing. The smell immediately takes over my senses.

While I wait, I put another log on the fire and drape a throw blanket beside me for Myra. She might still be cold since the cabin temp has been set to a balmy sixty-seven. Once the pot makes its last splutter, she pours two cups, adds a splash of cream to both, and walks over to the couch. She hands me my cup and curls a leg up under her, tucking herself under the blanket.

I'm not sure when she figured out that I take a splash of cream in my cup, but this feels comfortable, like seeing her take the dog treats out of her kitchen drawer. Like we've been doing this for months and not just days.

She clinks her mug with mine and stares at the fire, the silence becoming a weightier blanket than the warmth. She curls her legs up, and her knees knock against the side of my thigh, but she keeps them there. I like that she feels she can.

"I told my parents before we left that we were actually dating. Not just faking it."

I peer over at her after she says this, barely knowing how to respond or what to do with this information. "What did they say?"

She gives a short laugh, her lips widening into my favorite shape. "That's what you're going to ask?"

I purse my lips and shake my head. With Myra, I want to be braver than I feel, so I say, "It's not what I really want to know."

"Then ask me," she says quietly, drawing me out one second at a time.

I set my coffee mug on the table and take a deep breath. "Do you like me enough to date me…for real?"

My question sounds like teenage Lincoln asked it. There is so much insecurity wrapped around every word.

"Like what?" she asks, concealing her amusement behind the rim of her mug.

"You're really going to make me say it?"

"Yeah, I am."

If there were any time to be honest about how I'm feeling, it would be now. I'm fully aware of how close she is, how much closer I wish she were. And with the soft light emanating from the fire, it's like we're sitting in a pocket together, protected and safe, hidden.

My voice is quiet as I start. "I didn't meet you when you were married or in the middle of your relationship when you felt your lowest. I met you afterward when you were doing something for yourself." I pause and search her face. She doesn't look away. "When you told me you were here to ski because you wanted to compete against yourself, I swear it was the sexiest thing I'd heard."

Her laugh is low. "You're lying."

"I'm serious," I say. "You were confident and determined—"

"Stubborn?"

"That too," I agree. "But you had your mind set on something bigger than yourself. You may think you've completely failed, but really, you've just been trying. I think that's where more of the growth is. Less in the accomplishment and more in the trying."

She takes a steadying breath through her nose.

"I like you, Myra," I finally admit. "I like you when you're trying and when you're failing." The words leave with a whoosh of air. "I like you when you're wearing that big yellow jacket," I drop my voice to a whisper and run my knuckle along her bare leg, "and when you're wearing nothing at all."

I break the invisible wall constructed between us and lift my thumb to stroke her cheek. Or maybe I've just thought there's a wall when it never existed. Touching her feels as natural as anything else I've ever done.

Her eyes glisten, and her voice comes out strained. "Lincoln." My name on her lips scrambles every other thought. "I like you so much. It's wild, right? How this could happen?

How could I like you this much even though you're a baby-man?"

"Baby-man?"

She tilts her head. "I'll explain later. But you aren't anything like that. You're mature and wiser than most people get to see."

I lick my lips and trail my thumb along her jaw and then her lips. "I like that you make me want to be more honest with what's going through my head." I shift and rest my forehead on hers. "And I like that, by you just being *you*, I feel like I can be me. You've helped me open up more than I have in a long time."

She grabs my hand stroking her cheek, and holds it in her lap. "I don't know that I did all of that."

"You did," I insist. And so much more.

The need to be closer, to touch more of her skin, is so strong I almost close the gap between us. To kiss her and tell her I want to create so many more memories with her. But I don't because she's setting her mug on the coffee table and crawling onto my lap to straddle me. My hands are on her hips before she sits back on my thighs and loops her arms around my neck.

My voice is quieter than the crackles of the fire. "What made you smile today?"

She nudges my nose with hers, then rests her forehead on mine. "When I told my parents we were dating. And maybe when I just told you."

I laugh and squeeze her hips lightly. "Do I get a say in this?"

She kisses my cheek. "Of course." Her lips press along my jaw and down my neck.

I close my eyes and savor the sensation. "I accept."

"You accept?" she murmurs as she kisses her way back to my lips.

"I accept the position as your boyfriend."

"Good." She throws her head back with a laugh. When she looks back at me, her expression changes. Her lips straighten, though not entirely, and her eyelids lower. "Why do you always ask me what makes me smile?"

"Because..." I look beyond her at the fire, casting a glowy haze around her while I weigh my words. "Smiles can remind us of things we don't want to forget. The really important moments that matter and make us *feel* enough to smile."

Her lips part as her expression is incredulous.

Then, I hover my lips over hers and whisper, "You make me want to smile, Myra."

Chapter Thirty-Nine

Myra

I'm not sure what came and took over my body. Call it a hallucination, aliens, or maybe it's just intense longing that had me straddling Lincoln's lap and kissing him like fake dating—fake *anything*—was a thing of the past.

And for all I care, it was.

The way he leans forward, arching into me and pressing a flat hand to the middle of my back to bring me closer, feels too good. His lips are just like I remember them. Soft and so warm that they heat mine. I didn't even know they were cold. The stubble lining his cheeks scrapes lightly at my hand cradling his face, and after opening his mouth for my eager tongue, his is wet and familiar in ways that scatter my thoughts.

He squeezes either side of my hips, rubbing my center along his hardening length and turning my brain to jello. Thinking is a lost cause because, at this point, all I sense—all I feel—is Lincoln.

"Myra," he whispers between the slow, languid kisses before going deeper, answering the call of my name with an answer for more. My name has never sounded so sensual. My legs are practically quaking with the desire to feel more of him.

His hands paint trails down my thighs and back up again. If he wants my leg, he can have it. He can have *both*. If he wants me on the couch, the bed, the hot tub, the doorway, he can have me.

"Myra," he says again, pushing my shoulders lightly until we separate. I'm breathing hard, and shadows highlight his lips and make me want to dive in for seconds, but he tips my chin up with his finger until we're looking at each other. "And my age…that doesn't bother you?"

It's a statement and a question all in one.

My chest heaves as my already swollen lips pulse with heat and longing. I want him. "No," I say with certainty because now I know what I think. "It's nothing like how I expected. You aren't shallow and immature. Hell, you're probably more mature than I am."

Lincoln isn't a baby-man. Far from it. He's gentle and mindful. Until he's in moments like this where our bodies take over, and he has this commanding presence about him that makes my heart flutter and the space between my legs wetter.

I go to lean in to kiss him again, but he stops me. "Now that we're officially dating, we have a lot we need to talk about…"

"And we will." I rotate my hips. "Later."

He closes his eyes briefly against my rolling hips. "What was I saying?"

"Nothing."

He strokes my face again, and I lean into his touch, still wiggling over his lap.

He spreads his hand wide on my hip. His gaze drops to my lips, and my mouth immediately starts to water. I suck in a breath as he says, "I want to lay you out on this rug and take off these shorts."

My insides go weak. "What else?"

"I want to kiss your lips, neck, stomach, and that birthmark on the inside of your left thigh."

"It's a Care Bear."

He laughs. "I don't know what that is."

"I'll explain later," I say. "What else?"

He pulls my hips flush against him. "I want you to hold me in your hand and guide me inside of you."

I bite my lip and feel a swoop low in my gut. "What else?"

He curls his long fingers around my neck and pulls me closer until his lips are near the edge of my ear, sending shivers racing over me. "I want to thrust into you deeper than I ever have." He rolls his hips upward, and I gasp. "Over…and over…and over."

The beat of my heart is audible in my ears, and I wonder if he can hear it, too, but I don't take the time to ask. Instead, I slam my mouth to his and rotate my hips, searching for the relief found only in him. The way my stomach falls and then is swept up in a tangle of want has me moving faster. "I want all of that, too," I say between breaths.

He smiles against my lips as his hands roam the skin beneath my shirt. Then, gripping beneath my thighs, he stands, and I squeal. "What are you doing?"

He pushes the coffee table over with his foot and lays me on the rug. "Step one."

I smile up at him and release his neck so I can hook my thumbs in my shorts. Tugging them down slowly, his eyes lower to watch. He sits back and helps me take them off my ankles. He swallows, the column of his neck moving with the motion as he looks down at me.

I pull him closer by the waistline of his jeans until he's on top again. His mouth is on mine, and we're frantic, biting and nipping, lips and tongue. His mouth melds against the pulse of my neck and continues lower. Teeth scrape across the top of my breast, and I dig my shoulder blades into the ground, pressing further toward the teasing warmth of his mouth.

"Step two," he mumbles.

Lower and lower, his tongue brands me until he peppers a line of kisses along the inside of my thigh. I quiver under his steady hands as he sits back on his heels. Smiling down at me, he kisses the pink bear on my inner thigh, and I bite my lip through a smile.

"Condom?" I ask just as Otto jumps down from the bed and shakes.

He reaches into his front pocket and hands it to me. Then, he reaches into the other one and pulls out a small chew bone. Throwing it on the ground toward Otto, it slides on the linoleum before the happy (and spoiled) pup grabs it in his mouth.

"You were carrying those around?"

He laughs. "You didn't feel the bone in my pocket? And it's always a good time to practice safe sex, and with Otto distracted…"

I laugh, but it turns serious as his mouth moves higher, disregarding the weird bear on my leg. I've forgotten what day it is, where I'm at, what my name is. I close my eyes and let every sensation ride on the back of the last. The way his tongue slides between my folds and flattens on my clit, how his hair feels in the circle of my palm, and the way I'm shamelessly searching for purchase to ride his face.

The swell of desire builds and builds until it crashes with a crescendo of pleasure. He grips the sides of my hips to hold me in place as I barrel over the edge of my orgasm, and my body vibrates with a low hum of pleasure. I go boneless on the rug as his tongue swirls once more over the tightly coiled nerve endings in my clit, and I shudder through the aftershocks radiating through me.

My panting breaths are ragged and uneven. Running lazy fingers through my hair, I laugh at how much Lincoln just made me feel, and the uncontrollable smile he glued on my face. In minutes, he'd undone me in ways I've never experienced. He opened his heart and welcomed me home before branding me with his mouth.

He's above me again, hovering as he places light kisses under my jaw. "Still have the condom?"

I hold it up between us with a wobbly hand. "Held it the whole time."

He smiles and places a hand on my hip bone, propping himself up. His erection is thick and needy against my leg. "Put it on for me?"

My arms are as good as two pool noodles after the way he played with my body, but I reach for the button of his jeans, making quick work of undoing them and helping him push them off. His briefs go next, and nothing prepares me for feeling the breadth of him in my hand again.

"I heard somewhere that women have a stronger orgasm within four minutes of the first," he says, staring as I roll the condom over him.

Once on, he settles himself between my legs, the firm pressure of his dick causing me to gasp at the contact. I'm so sensitive.

"How long do we have? Two minutes?" I ask.

"One," he replies through a strained breath.

I circle my hand around him and guide him inside me, taking a few seconds to tease my clit with his tip first, swirling him around until the scene becomes hazy, coated by the vibrant layers of another build. With one slow push, he slides all the way in.

His eyes are dark when he says, "Step three."

All that's left is his shirt, so I pull him closer and scrape my nails against the warm skin beneath. He pushes his hips toward mine with a slow roll like a wave crashing against the shore, except this time, it's crashing against me. He rolls them again, and the firm pressure he applies on my clit with his hand is enough to bring a rush of need back into my bones.

His kisses are more demanding now as they trail back up my neck, over my jaw, and to my lips, where he takes my mouth with his. Our hips align, our mouths meld, and we *move*.

I lock my ankles at his lower back, and he grabs my breast, squeezing hard and rolling his thumb around my nipple. I can't take it. My body is a ball of tension, begging for release at the mercy of his hands.

"You're going to scream my name," he says somewhere between licking my neck and biting my bottom lip.

"I will." It's not even a question of will I or won't I. If he keeps talking like that, I'm going to fashion him a whip out of whatever I can find in this cabin and make him use it.

Then he pulls out and thrusts inside me. Harder. Deeper. We've done this before, but tonight, I'm thanking him. I lift my hips, my walls tightening around him as I thank him for giving me directions back to myself. Gripping his shoulders, he pumps into me, and I imagine my body taking him even deeper. I relax and open myself as he hits the farthest point and back again.

"Step four."

He slows his hips, rolling in and out of me like the tide. It's slower but somehow more intense. Eyes and mouth open, his moans mingle with the whispers of my name as I shout his. My brows draw together while digging my fingers into his hip bones. He fills every one of my walls as I clench around him, feeling the wake and pulse bend and then snap.

His motions turn sloppy, all rhythm lost as he barrels closer to climax with me. The release is as hard and fast as his hips have been moving, and he fills the condom completely. My skin is slick with sweat, my heart as full as my body.

He bends over me, propped on his palms and breathing heavily. He brushes the stray hairs out of my face as his fingers linger on my jaw. His smile is contagious. "Now, can you tell me what the bear is all about?"

I start laughing uncontrollably, my ab muscles working hard. He's still inside me as my every minuscule muscle holding him tightens.

Shivering, he pulls out of me and removes the condom, laying beside me on the rug. "What?" he asks.

I shake my head and try to rein in my laughter. "Nothing."

He presses a light kiss to my mouth, and the way he tastes—maybe the way I taste—has me grabbing the back of his head and holding him to me. Our tongues twirl together in an erotic dance meant for bedrooms or...floors. He deepens the kiss, and I feel the same as when I skied down the mountain with the wind in my hair and balance in my legs. It's the same as riding on the snowmobile with snowflakes pelting my chilled face and stealing the breath from my lungs. It's a sensation I know, and yet I'm just learning.

It's him.

Epilogue

One Year Later

Lincoln

Y ou didn't have to take me to the airport," she says, though it's just a formality. We're already driving through the terminal on our way to departures.

She's leaving today. Again.

I hate when she does that. We had an entire week together to celebrate our first anniversary while Myra was out of school for winter break. We skied with Otto, shared fries in the lodge, and stayed in bed for entire days. I think I showed her all the ways being twenty-six has its benefits. She agreed by the end of the day (against the wall).

"There's no way I'd let you take an Uber." I peer at her in the passenger seat.

"Because I'm a woman?"

"No, because there aren't as many drivers around here. You basically have to have their number and text them directly."

She laughs, and I already miss the sound.

I'm not eager to say goodbye to her. Weekends here and there have worked for us, and Myra came to stay during her summer break, but I still want more. We came up with a long-distance relationship plan that I wrote in the notes app on my phone a year ago. I'm glad we'll finally be able to put that to rest.

"I'm sure your mom knows their number. I could have asked her."

I love that she and Mom have struck up a friendship. My family got more than they bargained for after Mom added Myra to the family text thread, and she started sending candid photos of me. In one of them, I was stoking the fire while bent over on my knees. In another, I was sneezing. Yeah, not my best angles.

"I would have told her not to give it to you," I say, curving around the roundabout.

"What if I took the bus?"

"I'd hire someone to pull the cord at every stop."

She glowers at me. "And if I hitchhiked?"

I shrug. "Then I'd pick you up."

"What if I asked Jake to take me?"

I think on that one. "I'd shave off his mustache in the middle of the night."

"We both know you wouldn't." She laughs again, the sound ringing as she pets Otto's head between us on the armrest. "I'm going to miss you," she says wistfully.

I glance at her and reach for her hand. "I'm going to see you soon."

She sighs and looks out her window. "Spring break is months away. It's too long. Remember the mariachi band last year?"

Oh, I remember. Myra sent a series of *gifts* a few weeks before spring break to show me how much she missed me. The mariachi band was the least shocking out of all of them.

I smile and then train my features when she looks at me. "We have FaceTime, phone calls, texting, or texting's feral cousin, *sexting*. The modern world is practically built for long-distance relationships."

"Boo."

I head straight for the arrivals parking lot since departures are closed. The Bozeman airport really is as small as it appears from up in the sky. With only a few terminals inside, drop-off and pick-up zones are mostly suggestions anyway.

I slow down to find a parking spot. "What if we didn't have to say goodbye?"

She rolls her neck against the headrest to look at me. "I told you. This isn't some movie where the guy gets the girl, and the girl has to change her entire life to accommodate the guy. I'm just starting to find my sparkle again, and upending my entire life for a man—yes, even you—isn't a good idea. No matter how much I love that thing you do with your tongue."

I smirk and rest my hand on the wheel. "You mean the thing on your thigh."

"Yes. Why are you even asking?" She drops my hand and crosses her arms.

"I just like to hear you say it."

A car pulls out, and I swoop in to take their spot. I peer out my driver-side window and search for the other vehicle that followed us here. No signs...yet. "Let me help you with the bags."

I tell Otto to stay, and he whines in protest as I shut the door and round the back of my truck, opening the tailgate. Inside is Myra's suitcase, which I pull out carefully to not bruise my shin again, and then my backpack, which she isn't expecting.

She points at my bag. "That's not mine."

It's mine because a small bag that fits on my back is all I need to start over…for now.

I slam the tailgate shut and meet her stunned expression. "I don't expect you to quit your life and start over with me in the mountains, even if I enjoy those cheesy storylines."

She scrunches her nose with a look of disgust.

"They're cute."

She crosses her arms and glares.

"Fine. No cheesy movie for us. But I'm not about to let you walk into the airport without hearing me out."

This softens her since her shoulders relax. She's still squinting against the sun that never seems to go away, even in the dead of winter.

"I want to come with you," I say with finality. I'm working on being more direct with Myra's help, but I can't help hiding my nerves by adding a small shrug.

"You're joking."

I shake my head, clenching and unclenching my fists at my sides. "I'm not."

"Otto. What about him? There's no way you'd just leave him behind," she retorts.

She's right. I'd never leave Otto, which is why I packed his favorite bone in my bag. "He's coming with." He's a service dog with more qualifications than me to get through security.

Her mouth falls open, and she points at the Bridgers behind us. "And what the hell are you and Otto going to do if not saving people's lives in the mountains?"

A solid point and one that took the most amount of work to figure out. Ultimately, my supervisor was understanding. He hated losing the two of us for the rest of the season, but I'm committed to keeping up with our training. There are ski mountains near Phoenix.

"I quit."

Her jaw drops then her voice crack as emotion rises in her throat. "Your Mom…"

"Wants me to go. She practically packed my bag for me and told me if I didn't go, then she would."

Mom has been through several rounds of chemo within the last year, and her numbers are looking good. Since I've been home, taking her to appointments, staying at their house when Dad needed the extra help, and of course, family game nights to boost her morale have all been possible. This move will change all of that.

But if Jake hadn't agreed to work less and spend more time helping Dad, along with Gemma's offer to take Mom to all her follow-up appointments, I wouldn't be considering this. Mom has a solid team of people in place.

Myra laughs through a gasp, the frown on her face only there because of the tears she's holding back. I step closer and search for each of her hands to hold. Her tears are visible on her cheeks now, and I swipe the first one away with my knuckles.

"Where are you going to live?" she asks, eyes widening.

I smile at her because she's been slipping a key to her apartment into my coat pocket, mailbox, or car cupholder for the last six months. It's a wonder how many copies she has lying around.

"With you."

She gasps and covers her mouth. "You really are joking this time."

I reach deep into my pocket and unearth a palmful of keys. "I'm moving to be with you today, tomorrow, and the day after. I don't want to miss any mornings waking up next to you. Who else will make your scrambled eggs just the way you like?"

She closes her eyes, and I catch another one of her tears. "You can't be sure you want to do this. In a month, another year from now, you'll be tired of me. You could hate Arizona. Things will change, and then…I don't know. Something will happen. Something I don't want to happen."

I drop her hand and cradle her cheek, using my thumb to swipe all of her tears. "Myra, I'm committed to you. I'm not moving so we can get engaged tomorrow and married the next. I'm moving because I *love* you. I want to be in your life and not just run alongside from another place. I know we had a plan, but I want to explore *us* even more. Picking up my life and starting over has never scared me. The possibilities of what's to come on the other side are worth it every time." I stroke her lips with my thumb. "I want to experience those possibilities with you."

She kisses my finger, then covers my hand as I wipe away her tears. "So, it's just that easy?" She sniffles. "You're just going to move to Arizona? Just like that."

"Just like that."

Her lips quiver with the restrained emotion. She barrels into my arms, hiding her face in my chest and wetting my shirt with her tears. It's fine, though. I've got a few more in my backpack.

"Are you two ready?" another voice drawls.

I peer back over my shoulder at Jake.

Myra lifts her head and wipes her face. "Jake?"

I look back at Myra. "He's here to help with the one question you didn't ask…"

Confusion stamps its way across her face.

"Ted drove him so he could pick up my truck," I explain. "I'll have to leave it at the house until I can drive it down when more snow has melted in the spring."

She squints at Jake, smiles, then starts to laugh, resting her head on my chest. I circle my arms around her and laugh, too.

"Hey, Myra," Jake says. She looks up at him. "Still got that business card?"

"Hell no."

He snaps his fingers and then reaches into his back pocket. "Don't worry. I'll get you a few more so you can pass them out to your friends. You know, if anyone needs skiing lessons."

"Like men?"

Jake slips them into the top of her purse. "Like women. Only."

She shakes her head, letting go of me so I can hug Jake. He snatches my truck keys, and I yell, "Don't you dare ruin my truck!"

He was all about this plan since he gets to retire the minivan for a few months.

"Yeah, yeah." He waves a hand over his head as he hops in.

I offer my hand to Myra, and she laces her fingers with mine. "Come on. We have a plane to catch."

Not ready for this story to end? Subscribe to my newsletter at authorchristinahill.com for a bonus epilogue from Myra's perspective!

Acknowledgments

I'm so honored you chose to pick up this book and give it a read! Regardless of whether you ski or not, I hope this book not only made you laugh but also encouraged you. I didn't grow up skiing very much (in fact, I started on a snowboard), so writing about Myra's experience learning to ski as an adult was very much my own. My husband also learned as an adult, but he, along with our kids, are all significantly better at traversing down a mountain than I am. They are bombing black runs while I am perfectly content staying on greens and blues. FOREVER.

But there is something to be said about learning a new skill or hobby as an adult. It oftentimes feels like climbing a snow-packed mountain in rigid and clunky snow boots—difficult and sweaty. Yet, like Myra, we might just surprise ourselves with our own capabilities and gain a little more insight in the process. I believe with my whole heart that you, too, can do hard things.

I had so much fun researching for this one. Thank you so much to my friendly, local ski patroller, who was kind enough to answer all of my questions and then some. Your wisdom and expertise were invaluable while writing Lincoln and Otto's characters as well as developing a day-in-the-life snapshot of what it's really like to be a ski patroller. I'm honored you and your pup are keeping my family safe every time we visit the mountains.

A huge, gigantic, over-the-top, obnoxiously loud THANK YOU to all of my fellow authors and beta readers for reading and offering your feedback. Kayla, Hannah, Haley, Paige, Marie,

Amy, Ashlyn, and Erica, you have each helped mold this book into the best possible version. Thank you for expertly finding those pesky plot holes and helping me patch them up. And Tracey, my editor and proofreader, you always catch more than I think you will, and for that I'm so grateful and forever in awe of your mad skills.

To my Mom and Dad who are always faithful to ask about what I'm working on and fully support me regardless of what's actually written on the page. And specifically to my Mom, to whom this book is dedicated and Lincoln's Mom is based. You are officially considered a breast cancer survivor now, and though the journey to finally say those words took some time, I'm so proud of you. I'm proud of us as a family, too.

To the Fab Four and my husband, Samuel, thank you all for taking the ride from the first inkling of an idea to the final product. You see and hear the most—all of my excitement and the insecurities. Thank you for cheering me on and supporting me the way you do.

Thank you to everyone else who played a role in making this book a reality. Erika, for your genius in creating this book cover and the other promo material. Adrienne, for your outfit inspo. Angela, for teaching me how to become a better skier so I can keep up with my kids. And lastly, to every reader who has picked up this book, I love you for it. Thank you for laughing out loud at my jokes, reviewing, and sharing.

If you are interested in seeing my inspiration for some of the characters, scenes, outfits, etc. discussed in this book, you can find me on Pinterest @authorchristinahill.

I also love connecting with readers on Instagram and TikTok: @authorchristinahill. If you loved the book, please consider writing a review on Amazon and Goodreads. This is such a tangible way to help authors and for this book to reach more beating hearts.

With all of my love,
Christina

About the Author

Christina is a lover of love who has been writing stories in her head since middle school. She also holds the titles of 'mom' and 'babe' and lives in Montana with her four children, husband, and cat.

When Christina isn't reading or writing, she is wrangling her kiddos, homeschooling, taking baths, baking, or raising a glass into the wee hours with her book club ladies.

For more information or to sign up for my newsletter, visit www.authorchristinahill.com.